STORM GIRL

STORM GIRL

LINDA NICKLIN

FIRST EDITION

First published by Fantastic Books Publishing 2020
Cover design by Ramon Marett
ISBN (ebook): 978-1-912053-28-5
ISBN (paperback): 978-1-912053-27-8

This book is dedicated to
Hannah and Lawrence.

ACKNOWLEDGEMENTS

Hannah, Lawrence, Sue, Lilian, Lois, Moira, Jane, Mary, Libby, Deb, Gill, Rick, Kay, Linda, Steve, Sarah and members of the SCBWI Central North group have all given me support and encouragement through the ups and downs of writing Storm Girl. Their patience on the days when I had no words left in my brain, but still needed to talk was true friendship in action. I would also like to thank Helen Gould for giving Storm Girl a sensitivity reading. Any errors are entirely my own.

CHAPTER ONE

The sack over Angel's face smelled of old vomit and her cheek was tender and sticky. Her shoulder was bruised, and her throat burned from thirst and stomach acid. The water that they had forced down her throat was doped ... just the thought of it made her retch.

She had tried to fight them, but they had just laughed and shoved her back in the locker. It fitted her like a coffin. She stretched her legs and braced her back hard against the side. Her naked feet pushed against rough wood. Her muscles ached from inactivity and unspent adrenaline, but she had to control her fear, and focus. She had to be ready.

Angel knew that she'd been stolen. Harvested. They hadn't touched her yet ... but that would come.

She calculated that they'd been on the move for three days. At first, they had travelled at night, but now she could tell from the birdsong, that it was daytime. The sense of tyres rolling and spitting over rough stones had given way to a sideways rise and fall of open water. And these were not the sounds of woodland birds. The screeching that she could hear, reminded her of the winter gulls; scavengers and bringers of disease, that moved inland from the sea when the weather turned cold.

She took a deep breath and shifted the weight on her hip. She knew what she had to do. Her stepfather had taught her well. She reckoned that she had one day left … at the most. She scanned her body. Her parts were probably already traded. She was just an incubator for her organs. Her eggs would be the prize, farmed fast and traded. No tats, no pox, no scars; they would take her skin too.

• • •

'Why would they want me?' she had asked her stepfather when he told her the story. The girl in the tower was her favourite, but this was the one about the girl who ran away.

'Why *not* you?' he had asked softly, 'You know there's no rescue, right?' She sighed at the space that he left for her reply, 'No daddy, nobody gets rescued'.

'That's right. Always be safe,' he spoke in a musical, fairy tale voice, 'Guard … Hide … Run … Kill … or Die.'

Angel concentrated hard as she uncurled a finger for each action. When he had finished, her little hand was spread out like a starfish and her daddy had kissed her sticky palm.

• • •

She breathed out … trying to calm herself with the memory of his safe fresh-air smell.

She breathed in … instantly alert.

Somebody was undoing the lock. Her heart pounded in her ears as she strained to listen. There was no chatter, no bustle, just the sound of the engine accelerating, and the padlock being unhooked. Cold air touched her skin. Angel closed her eyes against the light. Rough hands pulled at her shoulder.

'Get up!' ordered a gravelly female voice. Angel felt the plastic ties on her wrists and ankles pinch and then snap off.

'Stand up!'

They're definitely Reapers, she thought as she struggled to get out of the locker. I'm dead. The hood was ripped away. She blinked hard then turned to look at the woman. She was short and thick set, dressed in a stained boiler suit, waterproof apron and white wellington boots.

'No funny stuff! You want to die right here ... it can be arranged.' She looked Angel up and down. 'Shame not to be a breeder, though.'

'But ...'

'No buts,' she mocked, 'you should have been more careful.' The woman clicked her tongue and shoved Angel away from the locker.

'What's happening?' Her throat was raw. The woman grunted and pushed her towards the door.

'Move! The farm ship's waiting,' said the woman touching Angel's silver hair. 'Out you go.'

Angel stumbled into the glare of the afternoon sun. The air tasted of salt. She glanced around, and saw a muddy channel etched between makeshift buoys tethered to the shadows of buildings that were submerged beneath dirty, foaming water. Lamppost heads bobbed in and out of the waves. Further away, the arc of a rollercoaster swayed to and fro.

She'd heard stories of whole cities that had been lost to the final tidal surge. They said that coastal sea routes were treacherous now, punctuated by church towers at high tide and trees and rooftops at low tide.

The woman pushed her further along the cold greasy deck. On the horizon, Angel could see white specks where gulls dipped and reeled in a line of soot-black smoke.

In the pit of her stomach, Angel knew that each passing minute took her further away from land and closer to the gulls and the factory ship. She had to find a way to get off this boat.

She shuffled forwards; her legs trembled with the effort of moving. In front of her, there was a line of shivering people, wide-eyed and silent, as they rose from sedation into a nightmare reality. A man in a white coat moved along the queue, holding a gun-shaped instrument in his hand. He scanned each person's arm. They've chipped me! Angel gasped.

Behind him, a woman with a box of syringes snapped on a plastic glove. The one who had got her out of her crate, pushed roughly past and disappeared below deck. From the size of the boat, Angel guessed that there was probably room for another twenty lockers. This was a good harvest.

At the front of the queue, two men hosed down a naked and crying man.

The girl in front turned around to look at Angel. Her hair was the colour of caramel and her skin was so pale that it seemed blue. She leaned towards Angel,

'I'm meat. You look good for a cycle of eggs.'

Her eyes are blank, she's already dead, Angel thought.

'What?'

'Eyes too blue, they'll fog. You're lucky, they should let you keep them.'

Angel leaned in towards her; she could feel the girl's body heat on her shoulder.

'We have to escape. Jump. Jump now … one … two …'

'No, they shoot,' the girl hissed back 'I can't swim that far.'

'You have to!'

'I can't.'

'Try!' said Angel pushing her hard.

The girl screamed as she slipped and stumbled across the deck. She missed the railing and fell flat into the sea. The others in the queue turned, as if in a dream. The woman threw the syringes down and ran to the rail. Sensing a chance to escape, a man and two women jumped overboard. People began to scream.

Angel crouched low and crossed to the other side, ducked under the rail and slipped silently into the water. Hoping that no one had noticed, she walked with her hands around to the back of the slowing boat, where a red and white dinghy slapped in its wake. The propeller stopped, and it drifted towards her. On the far side, she could hear shouts and screams over the crack of gunfire. She edged along, glanced around the hull and caught a glimpse of a girl treading water and hiding close to the side of the boat. There was the noise of fighting and then two more people jumped into the sea over Angel's head. She had to go before she was seen.

Weightless, Angel took a breath and slipped under the water. The pulse of the idling engine thrummed against her chest. She grabbed hold of the rope and pulled hard; the dinghy resisted and then slid toward her. She looped it around the stationary propeller, then kicked hard and struck out for land.

Water was her element; she had swum in the lakes as a child. She used to listen to the water, feel the flow with her hair; lie under the surface and watch birds fly overhead. She could find the energy of the lake and let it take her.

She surfaced behind the crest of a wave, took a breath, then dived back under. Her heart pounded in her ears. She checked her stroke rhythm, searched for calm in her adrenaline-fueled brain then swam for her life.

The water fluttered between her fingers, a surge of cold pushed her forward. The tide had turned.

Nine lung-burning strokes later she rose and gasped for air, she felt a splat as a bullet hit the water close by. Shrill voices shouted in alarm. She heard a loud splash, glanced back and saw that a man had just dived into the water. A woman was directing him towards her. He kicked off in a thrashing, twisting stroke; inefficient but strong.

She took another breath, pulled herself under water and swam for the town. She needed to get away fast; the tide was bringing him towards her.

• • •

Two sets of binoculars watched from one of the ragged houses on the edge of the town.

'Impressive, wouldn't you say, Mary?'

'Depends on what you call impressive, Jim, one dead, some still in the water, one swimming our way.'

'Where? Oh, yes, the Reaper's chasing her, no style but he's got power.' Jim whispered.

'She's there! Breathing between the waves. Good girl!' Mary leaned forward to get a better view.

Jim checked the boat; black smoke lay low on the water.

'They haven't realised the propellers snagged; they're burning the motor out! Not very bright. Where is she now?'

'Heading for the old town, away from the channel. Come on!'

'I'd better get ready for what the tide brings in.' Jim stood up.

'Got your knife?'

He tapped his pocket and nodded, picked up a cloth bag, felt for his torch, and slipped the strap of his binoculars over his head. Mary watched him square his shoulders, pull his collar up, and step out into the light.

'Come back safe,' she whispered after the door had closed.

• • •

Angel had reached the edge of the town. She could feel the pull of the undertow between the buildings. Swimming in the Old Lakes at home, could be cold and dangerous, but this was a restless, deceptive sea. She could see glass-smooth water where it raced over the ridge and slopes of rooftops. But it churned and rolled in the angles of the buildings. She had to fight against being dragged into the rush between the walls.

Checking back, she saw the splash of the Reaper about fifty strokes behind. He's strong! She kicked and dived under the surface. Through a tangle of dead branches, she could see the silted rectangular shape of a garden fence. She moved closer and saw the flap of a shed roof opening and closing like an envelope in the swell.

A carefully timed kick got her through the gap and into the shed. Desperately, she searched for a weapon in a tangled pile of metal and debris. The roof opened and let in more light; she saw a board on the wall holding rusted, silt-covered tools. Angel snatched at the hammer and screwdriver; their clasps disintegrated into brown clouds around her hands.

Above she could see the dark shape of the swimmer. He was treading water, looking for her. She pushed hard against the shed roof and kicked with all of her strength. Legs pumping, she powered up through the water and drove the screwdriver into the Reaper's stomach. His flesh resisted for a second, then yielded, the blade sank deep into him. The cold water and his exhaustion dampened his reactions for a second, but then his body spasmed, just as Angel rose out of the water and brought the hammer down hard on the base of his skull. She settled his unconscious body face down in the water and then, without pausing, turned and swam away from the widening pool of blood.

• • •

'Tidy!' Mary whispered to herself. 'One to watch, that one.'

She tracked the Reaper's lifeless body, as each wave carried him closer to the broken remains of the town. Then she turned her attention back to the distant swimmer.

'Now where has she gone?'

CHAPTER TWO

Further into the town, Angel was treading water searching for somewhere safe to hide. It seemed that the seafront area had once been a row of single storey shops and cafés, but further on she found the remains of rows of tightly packed houses. She could see emerald fronds of seaweed and jewelled garlands of mussels clinging to the gaps between the buildings and tangled shreds of opaque plastic hanging from the weathervane on the top of an almost submerged church tower. The reverberation of a sunken bell, pulled into action by the waves, pulsed against her body.

A flash of light caught her eye. Turning quickly, she scanned the ragged roof line. There it was again. It flashed at her and then flicked left, to the top of a solid, square church tower further along the old sea front. She swam toward the church, stopping once to check, but the light was gone. She supposed it might have been the sun reflecting in a window in one of the houses on the hill.

The tower was still above the rising tide; but waves were already breaking over the long, leaded ridge of the body of the building. She dived under and snaked through a ragged hole in the top of a stained-glass window. Tangled lead and glass twisted and curled back on to the black and white tiled floor below. Inside, she could see overturned pews and a pulpit on its back. Books were strewn on the floor, the pages stained with sediment.

She found a pocket of air in the apex of the roof, rested for a moment, then edged along the grimacing carved heads, looking for somewhere to hide. She was beginning to wonder if she should leave when her knee hit the top of an archway. She took a lung full of air, dived through the arch, found the ladder that led up to the bell tower and swam towards the daylight. Careful not to disturb the silt or touch the bell ropes, she dragged herself out of the water and on to the tower floor.

Exhausted and gasping for air, she lay on the wooden boards and tried to catch her breath. Waves slapped against the outside. Inside, she could see that the walls were stained with damp and circled waist-high with strips of brown seaweed. She raised herself up on to her elbows and looked around. There were arches to the east and west, one looked out to sea, the other to land. The sun shimmered low over the treetops in what remained of the town. She needed to stay here until dark. A lone figure running across land would be easy for a sniper to pick out.

Angel sat up and gathered her long hair into a rope, twisted it, to squeeze the water out and flicked moisture from her arms and legs. She checked outside to see if she had been followed and saw nobody, then she turned to check the room. In the centre, she saw a line of three bells suspended over an opening in the floor. Dark water slipped over the edge, crept towards her feet, then receded. She knew that it would soon be up to her knees and if the seaweed around the walls was an indicator, it would be up to her waist by high tide. Her body was cooling, she needed to find somewhere dry to hide until nightfall.

The floorboards were spongy beneath her feet; she edged along a line of rusted nails that marked the position of the supporting rafters. The bells were salt-stained but solid and the massive beam that supported them still looked dry. It might be possible to climb up there and wait out the tide, she thought, but first she needed something to fight with. She wondered if the old hammers were still inside the bells.

Angel ran her finger around the curve of the largest one and felt a mark on the side. Taking a closer look, she found a crudely scratched star. She checked the others ... no star. She squatted down and reached inside each one, feeling for their hammers. There was nothing ... but wait ... there was something hidden inside the largest one. She stretched further and felt the end of a rope... something was attached to it... a small bag of some sort. She pulled it free, ducked back into the room and settled on her heels to have a look. Who would do such a thing? The bag looked as if it had been there some time and yet it was dry ... old and dry, made of blue sun-bleached cotton and fastened with rusted buckles.

Cold and exhaustion were beginning to take their toll. She began to shiver, and her fingers were too weak to undo the strap, so she had to use her teeth. She felt it give, swiped rust from her mouth with the back of her hand and peered inside. There was a glass jar of water, a foil emergency blanket that had been folded and re-used many times and a piece of paper inside an old plastic bag.

Angel shook the foil blanket and wrapped it around her shoulders. Then, she unscrewed the top of the water container and sniffed. Nothing. She poured a little of the water into her palm. No taint, cloudiness or scum. Her thirst was aching, but could she be sure it was safe drink? She took a small sip, swallowed it, put the container down and rested with her back to the wall, waiting to see if it made her sleepy.

She reached for the piece of paper. On one side, she could make out a mix of blurred words and signs, on the other, there was a star like the one etched on the bell and next to it was a large smiley face symbol. Angel pulled the blanket tighter around her shoulders.

She looked at the jar, desperate for a drink. She couldn't be absolutely sure it was safe, but she couldn't afford to be more dehydrated than she already was. If she was going to survive the night, she needed to be able to think clearly. So, she took a mouthful of water, rinsed her mouth and spat into the dark seawater that was now creeping across the floor towards her. There was no aftertaste.

She paused with the jar to her lips … something about the sound of the splash wasn't right. Then she heard a second splash and a third. The noise was coming from outside!

Instantly alert, she sprang to her feet to search for a weapon. Anything would do! Anything. But there was nothing. Could she climb up and get a roof slate? Was there a nail in the wall? No! It was too late! She picked up the jar of precious water and smashed it against the wall, chose the largest piece and moved back into the shadows.

She looked out of the west arch expecting to see another Reaper, but instead she caught a glimpse of a canoe, old, plastic, and covered in algae. And pedalling quietly towards the tower was an old man, counting as he maneuvered between the trees, rooftops and lampposts. When he got closer, he stopped paddling and shone a torch into the tower. Angel shrank back into the corner and held her breath.

The canoe crunched against the wall. He whispered, 'Peace … Peace … Star …' His voice was soft and reassuring. He pulled a star-shaped pendant out of his pocket and held it up. She heard a rustling sound and saw that he was holding up a piece of bread. Spelt, dense and grey with flecks of cheese baked in. He placed it down on the sill of the arch. Her stomach groaned.

'Are you there?' he asked softly. 'It was me with the light.'

Angel moved slowly out of the shadow; torn between the overwhelming need for the bread and the impulse to dive out of the arch behind her.

'I'm coming in.' He threw a rope towards her. 'Here take this.'

She snatched up the bread, then took the rope and pulled it tight to stabilise the canoe. The man pushed his oar into the room, then grunted as he braced himself against the opening and climbed into the tower.

'Doesn't get any easier with practice, that's for damn sure.' he grumbled to himself. Angel dropped the rope, stepped back into the shadow, put the shard of glass down and began to tear at the bread with her teeth.

'I'm Jim. I've come to help,' he said as he picked the rope up, tied it to his oar and positioned it across the archway. 'I expect they're tracking you. We need to fix that chip.' He patted his left and then his right shoulder.

Angel touched her left arm where it was tender and hot.

'Here.' She was surprised by the sound of her own voice.

'We need to do it quick. It's your body ID and the way they track you.' He reached out with a piece of metal in his hand 'It's a magnet.' Angel stepped forward and let him sweep over her shoulder. 'This should do the trick, but if you want to be sure, we can take the chip out later.'

They both heard it at the same time. A splash! Someone was outside. It was the splash of a tired swimmer, slapping the water.

'Quick! under the big bell. Should be air in there.' whispered Jim.

Angel waded toward the bell, slipped into the water and ducked underneath. The water was a quarter of the way up the flank on the outside but level with the base on the inside. She thought for a second, she could hide in here, but she needed to know what was happening. Besides, they'd already tracked her to the tower, so there was no point in hiding. The old man didn't look much of a fighter.

She decided that if she had to leave, she would dive back down the tower into the church and surface behind the buildings further away. So, careful not to make waves, she slipped down out of the bell, tentatively felt for the top of the ladder with her toes and watched.

She saw Jim slip back into the shadows seconds before

the young man pulled himself up out of the water and stepped into the tower. He pushed his hair back and scanned the room. He was tall, his shoulders curved with muscle. The setting sun cast a halo of fire around his red hair. Jim stepped out of the darkness and stabbed him in the shoulder with a sedative dart.

'Sorry son,' he whispered as he caught him, dragged his limp body to the corner and leaned him against the wall. He tapped his knuckle on the star bell twice and said, 'Time to go.'

Angel rose smoothly from the water and stepped up on to the floor.

'We need to go, get your things. They'll have noticed that your tracker stopped.'

Angel picked up the foil blanket and bread then she walked over to the unconscious man, nodded to herself and said, 'Got a knife?'

CHAPTER THREE

Jim leaned forward and inhaled the steam from his mug. He was sitting next to Mary at a blistered Formica table that they had salvaged from the sea. Branches of scrub laurel scraped against the grey, glass windows of the conservatory.

'She carved an R in his face, you know. On the left side, just here …' He touched the flesh of his cheek. 'R for Reaper.' He raised his mug to his lips and thought for a moment.

'He can't go back to the boat; he'd be useless. Seems, he's the one that got her.'

Mary nodded. 'And he can't go to anywhere that's been reaped, they'd kill him. He's dead meat.'

'Absolutely …' Jim stood up and began to pack a jar of water, a foil blanket and a piece of paper, into the canvas bag that Angel had found the previous night.

'I'll take this back later,' he said.

'She's one to watch, you know …' said Mary with some admiration in her voice. 'If she's still here.'

Jim looked up 'Do you think she's gone? I wanted to talk to her.'

'Well she wasn't going to stop, least not until I gave her the key to the room so she could lock it from the inside.'

They both paused for a minute, listening for sounds of movement. The plastic roof of the old conservatory clicked in the morning sun. Mary pulled the empty mugs towards her.

'Are the others all gone? '

'Much better to do it in the dark,' Jim nodded.

'Let's hope they can't remember where we are.'

'I watched the boat break up against the pier about two this morning.' said Jim. 'What was left of the crew rowed the dinghy around the headland. I expect they'll join up with another lot of Reapers.'

'Not if I can help it!'

Mary and Jim turned to see Angel standing in the doorway. She had a blanket wrapped tightly around her body. She was tall, and broad shouldered, with long, silver-grey hair and ice blue eyes. Swimmers shape thought Mary.

'Morning, we weren't sure if you were still here.'

Angel tried to pull her fingers through her hair, but it was sticky with salt.

'I need to ask you how to fix this tracker,' said Angel touching her shoulder.

'Sure,' said Mary rising from the table. 'Drink and food first, though? That's the thing.'

'Yes please.' Angel stepped into the room. Her bare feet clicked on the old tiles. She walked to the door into the garden and tested that it was locked. Satisfied, she sat down at the table.

'I'm not sure if you remember our names from last night, you were exhausted. I'm Jim and this is Mary … We're Star People.'

Mary spooned porridge into a rose-patterned china bowl. 'I don't think you told us your name, dear?'

'Angel … I am *so* hungry! ' She took the bowl and a spoon from Mary, and then glanced up; her eyes were still red rimmed from the seawater. 'Where are we?'

'This is the edge of the new east coast,' said Mary. 'South of what was the Humber and north of the Wash, a bit inland from where there used to be a place called Humberstone.'

'There's a lot of good farming land out there,' said Jim, indicating the sea.

'Where are you from?' asked Mary softly.

'The Old Lakes.' Angel felt a wave of sadness rise into her throat. She ached to be at home with her stepfather, but just for the moment, it felt good to be here. The warmth of the porridge spread out from her stomach and for the first time in days, she began to relax. 'Thank you, I don't know when I last ate.'

Mary sat down at the table and watched; she wondered what it had taken to make this angel. When she'd finished the porridge, Mary took the bowl and pushed a mug towards her, 'Do you have family who worry about you?'

Angel looked at her for a moment. 'My mother died when I was little. Measles … but I do need to get home to my stepfather, though. He's going to be so …' Her words stuck in her throat.

Mary nodded in understanding and gestured to the corner of the room. 'That box over there's got clothes in it. Take your pick.'

'Thanks,' said Angel, 'but first tell me about the Star thing.'

'Haven't you heard of us?'

Angel shook her head.

'OK, let's see.' said Jim, 'have you heard of the Silver Thread?'

'No.'

'Well you've heard of the Super Elites?'

'Oh, yes, I know about them! They're the Offshores … live in cities on ships … big as islands.'

Jim nodded, 'They control the Harvesting. The Reapers provide the bodies.'

'Yes, but what's the Star for?'

'When it first started, they just hit the countries around the equator.' explained Mary.

'Starvation and drought led to catastrophic disruption,' added Jim, 'and who can keep track of millions of refugees.'

'But when the easy pickings dried up, the Reapers widened their net and started to take travellers and people on their own, and now they can scavenge pretty much anywhere they like.'

Angel nodded. 'But the Star?'

'Well, we heard that one of their cities has travelled further north.' Mary continued. 'The weather's been really, well … very odd and they prefer easy pickings, so it seems that we're their next big harvest zone.'

'But, please, the Star thing?'

'Yes, well,' said Jim. 'You know that they go after younger people, children, babies even?'

'Pregnant women are snatched up,' added Mary looking at Jim; he held her gaze sadly for a moment and then turned to Angel.

'They don't want us older folk or people who aren't so …
able. We can't do their work and hell; nobody wants our
body parts …'

'So, we're invisible, you see. Redundant.' Mary shrugged.

'And we've decided to resist. To make them think twice
about doing their dirty work here.'

'Because we're not afraid. Besides we've got nothing to
lose, and …'

'Somebody's got to do something or there'll be nothing
left,' said Jim banging his fist on the table.

'Resist?' Angel was amazed. 'But they'll kill you.'

'So, we die.' They spoke as one.

'The Star means regeneration, hope after dark times.'
Mary spoke softly. 'Like a morning star.'

'You church?' asked Angel suspiciously. 'I've heard of them.'

'No, they fell.'

'They didn't speak out when they should have.' said Jim.

'Well, we don't know for sure what they could have done.'
Mary's voice trembled.

'People didn't trust them. They got angry with a god or
whatever … for not stopping it all.' Jim leaned over and
touched Mary's shoulder. 'Started with the weather … I
suppose.' His voiced trailed away. A pigeon tapped across
the opaque plastic roof and plucked at a dead leaf in the
gutter.

'Anyway, the Star is for everyone. It has eight points like
the compass. It's a good symbol,' said Mary.

They watched the pigeon land heavily on a nearby
conifer.

'Well we need to think about what you're going to do next,' said Jim.

Angel pulled her attention back into the room. 'This chip in my arm, is it definitely dead?'

Jim looked at her arm. 'We can take it out if you want.'

Angel nodded 'I'll do it. Have you got a knife?'

They paused for a moment, thinking about what she had done with the last knife.

'I'll get the knife.'

'And I'll get a dressing.' said Mary.

CHAPTER FOUR

Angel held the knife out to Jim. There was a small tube of plastic the size of a piece of straw on the tip of the blade. A thread of blood ran down her arm, along her fingers and dripped on to the floor. Mary stepped forward with a bandage and wrapped it around her shoulder.

'I'll get rid of that for you.' Jim said as he opened an old woodstove door and flicked the chip into the fire. Then he held the knife over the flames for a moment to sterilize it. Mary gently took hold of Angel's hand and turned it palm up. Cupping her long strong fingers in her own veined hands, she looked into Angel's eyes and whispered, 'There's blood on your hands, sweetheart. You should clean up.'

Jim settled a pan of water on top of the stove to warm. Water drops hissed and hopped across the metal hotplate.

'And I think it might be a good idea to cut your hair,' Mary added. 'You know; disguise yourself a bit. Make yourself harder to spot and easier to forget. You're going to be amongst strangers until we get you home.'

'And after what you did to their boat and two of the crew, they're going to be curious about you to say the least.'

Angel started to search through the box of clothes. 'I should go!'

Jim pursed his lips. 'Well, actually … I wanted to talk about something. We have an idea.'

Angel looked up, a pair of grey overalls in her hand. They were darned and patched where the buttons had been torn away. She pulled at the repair, testing its strength.

'What kind of idea?' She held the overalls up to her body. They were the right length, had intact pockets and were big enough for her to layer things underneath.

'Get dressed, I'll make you another drink,' said Mary.

Angel selected a multicoloured sweater from the bottom of the pile. It seemed to be made from different yarns, as if someone had pulled out the knitting of old garments and saved any bit of wool with some wear left in it. She slipped it on, it was soft, and it didn't smell too bad. The sleeves were long enough to cover her hands when she wanted. Next, she stepped into the overalls then found a belt strong enough to tie a knife to. She picked a black woolly hat, twisted her hair into a knot and tucked it in, and then knelt to search through the shoes. These were important. They needed to fit well enough to avoid rubbing, not to make a noise, but above all to stay on when she ran.

'OK,' said Angel sitting back down at the table and picking up her drink.

Jim sat opposite her. 'Well as we've said, they've moved closer and that they'll clear out our coastal areas like locusts, then move inland. On a small island like ours, if we let them build up to full strength, there'll be absolutely nowhere to hide.'

'We've had Star People watching them. We know how they work. They deal through markets. Blood, organs, bodies, and slaves are sold across the world. But there's also a high value traffic in healthy young people, for grafted transplants like organs, skin, eyes, eggs, scalps … things like that … well … it depends on their latest fashion trend. Some people, they hunt to order.' They watched Angel's face to see if she had realised where the conversation was going. 'You know … for recreation.'

'But the whole market's fed by the small boats, like the one that you were on,' said Mary bringing the conversation back to Angel.

'So, what's your plan?' asked Angel, beginning to feel restless.

'Well,' said Jim. 'The Star People … well, we've decided to close down the coastal network.'

'Block their supply chain.' Mary paused for a moment and then continued. 'But … before we go on, there's something you really need to consider.'

'What?'

'We think that you were stolen to order.'

'Me, why?' Angel froze with her mug half-way to her lips. 'Really. Why?'

'Well, look at it like this,' said Jim softly. 'They travelled a long way to find you. They didn't hurt you. When you jumped in the water, they didn't shoot you, and they sent two good swimmers to get you. From what we saw, well, we think they really want you alive.'

'But I …'

'And look at you!' interrupted Mary, touching Angel's cheek. 'You're perfect. Your hair shines like silver, your skin, well, it glows with health. You're long limbed, muscular, your teeth are strong.'

'Stop it, you make her sound like a horse,' teased Jim. 'Maybe they're looking for breeders? Perhaps someone paid for you? Somebody with the money to make a trip that far north, worthwhile.'

Angel's skin crawled as she remembered the woman on the boat stroking her hair.

'Word is that the Super Elites don't make pretty babies. If they've been "augmented" beyond recognition … they're not going to want a baby that looks like they used to … or if they want to keep all of their money in the family, they marry their sister or brother and have a breeder that looks like them.'

'It's a short life, being a breeder. But better than being farmed, I suppose,' said Mary thoughtfully.

'Even more reason for me to move on.' Angel put down her mug and started to stand up.

'Wait!' said Jim urgently. 'We couldn't help but notice what a good swimmer you are. If you help us close this bit of the coast down, we'll help you get home.'

'How's that for an offer?' added Mary reaching over and touching Angel's arm.

'Close the route?'

'Yep, then head for the hills and disappear just like that!' Jim snapped his fingers.

Angel looked at the elderly couple in front of her. What they lacked in strength they more than made up for in resourcefulness. The fire in their eyes was startling; she had never seen people with such fight, such fierce resilience. She remembered the horror that she'd felt when she woke up in that black hole of a coffin and knew that she was going to die. She remembered the agony of being imprisoned when her muscles were fired up to run or fight. People all over the world were suffering the same thing, knowing that their reality was a brutal animal death.

Angel nodded. She thought of her stepfather and her home in the lakes and her longing to be there took her breath away. He would be distraught. He had always said that there was no escape, no rescue, and yet, she had got away … and she had been helped.

Who knows how they were going to react, but she certainly wasn't going to risk leading them home. She knew they wouldn't let her get away with it. And what if Mary was right? What if someone wanted her? She looked up at them both,

'What do you want me to do?'

CHAPTER FIVE

Together they surveyed the old town. They memorised the layout of submerged streets and noted where the dangers were. Angel swam with the tides, and from his canoe, Jim mapped where the drag and pull of the current could catch a boat and draw it on to waiting posts or to tangle it in old power cables or a rusted chain link fence.

They took down the marker buoys that had been used by the previous boat and realigned them to mark out a channel leading on to the jagged, iron struts of the old pier. They pushed metal spikes into tree branches and the gaps between buildings, each set at an angle, ready to pierce the hull of an unsuspecting boat. They set low tide traps and high tide traps.

Mary had left on the morning after Angel's escape to get a message to other Star People. She returned on the fourth evening, looking grey with fatigue. She had heard that a Reaper transporter was due to arrive the next day, two days earlier than expected. She'd spread the word across the Star network that they needed urgent help. It was a tall order; and they would have to see if enough people could get there in time.

Angel left them to talk and walked down to the water's edge. The air was thick; it weighed heavy in her lungs. She listened to the feverish flop of the waves and searched for give-away disturbances on the surface of the flaccid water. The underwater traps were hidden, and there was no rough water to betray their handiwork. She just hoped that they had done enough.

• • •

Waking before dawn the next morning, Angel crept downstairs. The wind had changed direction in the night; the house felt different and she was uneasy.

She decided to make a drink, watch the sunrise, and try to find a moment of calm before the day began. She opened the kitchen door quietly, slipped into the dark room and closed it behind her.

'Ah, you must be her,' said an unfamiliar voice. She spun around, her back against the door. In the gloom, she could see a mass of faces looking at her. The room smelled muggy, of wet coats and mud. A candle was lit and pushed into the centre of the table.

'Relax, Mary told us all about you,' said a frail looking man. He had thick grey hair and a face that was sun-lined and spiked with white whiskers.

'We're here to help. Have a drink.' A large elegant woman pushed a cup towards Angel.

'Come and join us, we haven't had this much fun in years!' said another woman over the rim of her mug. 'They say you're pretty good in the water.'

'And with a knife!' added another. The room filled with laughter. Angel smiled, relieved that some Star People had made it. She relaxed and took the mug.

'You're here to help?' she whispered.

'Too right, the bastards took my grandson,' said a small voice from the back of the room.

'And my daughter. '

'My littlest.'

There was silence.

Angel counted fifteen people.

'We reckon the van'll be here in about three hours and the pick-up boat should come in with the tide.'

'Time for more breakfast then?' asked a man hopefully. Amidst laughter and cheers two plastic boxes of dried fruit and biscuits were slid on to the table. Angel dipped a biscuit into her drink and watched small gestures of kindness and solace settle the room.

Outside, raucous crows lifted from their treetop nests and moved inland. The breeze stirred and overgrown bushes tapped against the window. Purple and pink streaks bled across the sky. The day had begun.

Mary stepped into the room. 'Ah I see you've all met. Angel these are old friends … what we lack in strength we make up for in experience and …'

'Heart,' said Angel softly. A murmur of agreement and appreciation spread around the room. She felt a warm hand rest on her shoulder.

Outside, the bell in the church tower rang; the tide was turning.

• • •

The driver leaned forward and swiped condensation from

the windscreen with his ragged sleeve. Long dawn shadows stretched across what remained of the road. He swerved to avoid a deep hole partially covered by a mesh of tree roots that had fingered across the disintegrating tarmac. A low branch slapped the side of the van. In the container behind, someone called out in fear and pain.

'We might not make it,' said Gerry the co-driver leaning over and tapping the fuel gauge with a dirty fingernail. 'Fuel's low.'

'Hopefully they'll have some on the boat. We're burning oil too,' said the driver, looking in his remaining rear-view mirror at the trail of blue smoke left hanging in the morning air. 'Good job it's downhill.'

'This'd better go right. We don't want to end up like that last crew. They would've been better … well anything would be better than ending up on the farm ship. God, Dave! Imagine …'

'Don't want to. Let's just get this right eh?' The two men nodded, then leaned forward and peered into the lightening sky.

Five miles away a flashlight flicked on and then off. A message passed along the chain.

Twenty minutes later the truck manoeuvred around a bend; it was the last one before the sea. They sighed with satisfaction; they'd made it. Then a sparkle on the road caught the Dave's eye.

'What the–?' There was a spatter of loud bangs, the van rocked violently and began to skid. Gerry braced himself against the dashboard with both hands, eyes wide with horror. The driver fought to keep control, but the vehicle slewed and twisted. Then it settled low and then lower as each tyre, pocked with nails, shredded and flattened. Wheel rims groaned as they dug into the road surface. The prisoners trapped in lockers waited in terrified silence. The two men looked at each other, slowly reached for weapons hidden under their seats, then nodded the count, one … two … three … and leapt out of the cab.

They were twenty paces from the plastic and weed debris left by the high tide and hemmed in on both sides by dense shrubbery. They could hear nothing except from the hissing of deflating tyres and weeping in the back of the truck. Gerry turned to bang his fist on the side of the van and felt a smack on his neck. Ice spread through his veins, he fell where he stood, a dart hanging lazily below his left ear.

'Watch out for the nails!' Dave hissed, peering over the bonnet. Careful not to step on any himself, he stood on tiptoes to look for his mate, who from the sound of it had just dropped his weapon. A dart thumped him in the chest. Stunned, he looked down … the pretty feathers reminded him of something … He was dead before his head hit the road.

Four silent figures slipped out of the shortening shadows and began to haul the first man into the bushes.

'Good shot!' puffed one.

'Thanks, always thought I'd make a good a vet.' chuckled a plump woman as she grabbed hold of the co-driver's collar. 'Enough in those darts to kill a horse twice over.' Her long hair swayed as she used her knee to roll him under low hanging branches.

'Let's get them out of there,' shouted Jim as he reached into the cab and took the keys. A small wiry man with thin, jet-black hair stepped out of the trees with a crowbar in his hand and levered the rear doors open. Carrying a pair of bolt cutters, Mary helped to pull the doors open, then climbed up inside the van. It was dark and smelled of fear.

'No! No!' screamed a woman from one of the boxes.

'Shush dearie, we're here to help,' said Mary. She began to hum and then to sing in a low gentle tone, '*Amazing grace, how …*' She snapped the chain on the top locker '*Sweet the …*' she lifted the lid and tapped on the side of the box. 'Up you get sweetheart, we need to hurry.'

The young woman lay still for moment, shocked and afraid, waiting for a Reaper's hand to pull her up.

'*Sound …* Come on love. I need your help.' Mary rapped on the side again. She moved on to snap the locks on the other containers. The young woman sat up and looked over the ledge.

'You're helping us?' she whispered.

'*That saved a wretch …*' Mary nodded as she lifted the lid on the final box to reveal a young girl, no older than twelve, curled up with her back to the light. 'Come now, my lovely.' She laid her hand softly on the girl's cold shoulder. 'It's time to go home.' She moved around the van snipping plastic cuffs, reassuring with a smile and a gentle touch.

Bemused and afraid, people stumbled out of the back of the van into the kind hands that were waiting to lead them away. Mary followed on behind swinging her bolt cutters as she walked.

CHAPTER SIX

Angel watched the shaky trail of people being passed from hand to outstretched hand. She counted fifteen. One by one they disappeared into a gap in the dense bushes that led to a safe house. Moments later their guides stepped back into view, one carried a dart gun and another a crossbow. They slipped the handbrake and rolled the van forward, where waiting logs held it just above the water's edge.

Then she checked for signs of the boat. Heavy flat-bottomed clouds skimmed the horizon. Behind her, the rising tide moved the bells; she glanced at the largest one, the star was already covered.

She waded over to the landside arch and checked her tools. Leaning against the wall, was a pole with a blade bound tightly to one end and a coil of nylon rope at her feet. She tucked a knife into one side of her belt and a claw hammer into the other. Her long, silver hair had been expertly braided and tied up to keep it under control. She couldn't afford for it to get caught in any of the traps, or to get in the way in a fight. Satisfied that all was ready, she perched on the sill of the arch, opened a tin, took out a hazelnut biscuit and settled down to wait.

The tide was almost full when they got their first sighting of the boat. Angel heard two blasts of a whistle from one of the lookouts on land and moved into position. It had cleared the headland and was making its way towards the town. She glanced inland; two people were busy working around the back of the van. From a distance, they would look like Reapers preparing to hand over their cargo.

The boat passed close to the tower, carefully following the newly positioned marker buoys. The noise of the engine reverberated around the tower; the small bell hummed and then faded back to silent. She hid in the shadows and listened to the unsuspecting crew call to each other as they prepared to take on their human cargo.

Their wake slapped hard against the old stone walls. Angel moved to the landside arch, slipped into the water and moved around the walls of the tower. The noise of the propeller deepened as the engine reversed to slow the boat. A film of diesel smoke drifted across the surface of the water. She could see a man in a white boiler suit and sandals walk to the front of the boat, and stand wide-legged, ready to throw a rope to the van driver.

She took a deep breath and pulled herself under, waited until the hull had passed over a mass of tangled wire and cables, then used the claw hammer to knock loose a stay that had been pinning it flat to the seabed. The metal rose silently behind the boat. A steel fencepost that they had wedged into the doorway of a submerged house fell into position and nudged the boat side. It rocked gently on impact; the propeller broke surface, sending out a cascading spiral of bubbles.

The trap was almost complete. Just one more element remained. She swam back to the tower. Two people stepped from the bushes and began to throw petrol bombs. The first one smashed against the side of the boat, sending up a flare of orange flames. Some skittered across the deck, others smashed on impact. One exploded against a loose stack of nylon rope. Blood-red flames began to lick up the side of the melting blue coils.

Old rags and foam that had been packed into the lockers were now burning furiously. Two more people crept out from the cover of the bushes, pulled the logs away from the front wheels and scuttled back to safety. One heart stopping moment later the wheels began to turn. Gathering pace, the van rolled forward and smashed into the boat. It rose up and shot backwards. The metal post, already nudging the stern lunged into the hull. A scream from the propeller signalled that it had bitten deep into the wire. The engine stalled. The trap shut.

The man in the boiler suit was knocked to his knees. Angel watched him slide back towards the burning pile of ropes. Black-tipped flames slithered across the deck towards him as he scrambled to his feet and screamed at the crew. They were peering over the stern, horror on their faces. The man scrambled away from the flames and threw himself on to the roof of the van. It was white hot. A wave swept past the van and a curtain of steam rose around him. His high-pitched squeal cut through the air. He fought to rip his burning boiler suit from his body as still writhing, he disappeared into the cold water.

One of the Reapers ran forward with a fire extinguisher and began to spray the deck. A crossbow dart felled him. The flames spread silently around him. The extinguisher rolled into the water, caught a wave and floated towards the van.

With the crew's attention moving to the front of the boat, Angel swam to the back and cut through the rope that was securing the dingy. Sculling backwards she towed it to the church tower. There was to be no easy escape for this crew.

She saw a Reaper run to the cabin and emerge with a rifle. A crossbow dart pierced his shoulder; he jerked forwards and fell into the water.

Stunned, what was left of the crew watched him fall, then spun around to see where the bolt had come from; another fell mid-turn.

Angel reached the far side of the church and tied the dinghy to the copper lightning rod. She checked that the oars were secure and then moved back so that she could see what was happening.

The engineer stepped out on to deck and bellowed, 'Why aren't we moving?'

'Watch out! They've got weapons ... crossbow or something. In the bushes!' shouted a man in wellingtons and a plastic apron who was hiding behind some wooden crates. Angel saw him peer at the flames, now creeping up the cabin wall and then look at the turbulent water over the old town. He seemed to consider his options, then he ripped his boots and apron off, jumped into the water and set off for the shore. Angel reached into the tower took hold of her spear and shadowed him under the water. She waited until his arm was stretched forward, lunged the spear into his chest, then pulled it from his limp body and headed back to the boat.

She rested by the still propeller to catch her breath. She had counted five dead, just the engineer left on board. He had a rifle so she would be just as vulnerable in the water or out of it. But a part of the plan was to loot the boat, and it was burning; time was running out.

Angel pushed her spear on to the deck and climbed aboard. She crouched, searching for the last man.

'Not so fast! Drop the weapon ...' growled the engineer as he stepped out of the cabin, rifle raised. She dropped her spear and faced him.

In the corner of her eye she saw a flash of light from the hilltop. Didn't know we had a sniper, she thought. The engineer fell hard to the deck. She picked up his weapon and rolled his body into the sea.

Five minutes later she was passing supplies and a collection of weapons down to Jim in the dinghy.

'Let's go,' he said, looking at the pall of black smoke rising from the burning van and boat. 'They'll be able to see this for miles.'

'One last check,' said Angel. She stepped into the wheelhouse. There were maps and papers scattered across the floor. She walked over to a computer and touched the screen. She wanted to know the position of the factory ship and where the rendezvous was meant to happen. It would give her an idea how long it would take for the boat to be missed. The screen lit up, she leaned in. A message popped up. *WEBCAM ON ...*

'Shit!' She slapped her hand over the lens ripped the screen from the console, then turned and ran.

CHAPTER SEVEN

'Bigger. Make it bigger!'

The screen on the wall showed Angel leaning forwards, eyes down. Smoke drifted past the open door behind her. Her features were clear; hair pulled back, pale blue eyes, thick arched eyebrows, straight nose, mouth pursed in concentration. She glanced up and saw the webcam light. She mouthed a word. The screen went black.

'Again! Have we anything else?'

'No sir, she triggered it when she touched the screen. The other cameras were burned out.' The screen lit and showed Angel's face again.

'Freeze it there … no … go back …' He leaned forward to scrutinise her face. 'You think that's the one that escaped from the other boat?'

The image ran forwards for a few frames. 'Well if we look there … on her shoulder, you can see where we chipped her.'

'OK, I need to tell The City. Find out anything you can about her, will you? Did we test her? Did we inseminate her? Where did we find her? What did the Reapers know about her? We need her story!'

'Yes sir.'

The officer hung up, then he took a deep breath and dialled. He spoke softly. 'Yes sir, did you see that? We're pretty sure it's her, yes, the one who escaped. Samples? We'll find out … Drones? None in the area.' He checked his computer. 'Three hours, sir … OK … your eyes only. Understood.'

The line went dead; he sat back in his chair and studied Angel's face again.

• • •

'They saw you?' Mary was horrified.

'It had a webcam.' Angel's fingers trembled as she collected her things and pushed them into a backpack. The room was empty. The Star People had split into small groups and left as soon as their part of the plan had finished. Most of them took survivors, supplies and weapons. They would take great care to travel undetected. The events of the day must stay a secret, because revenge would surely follow.

Mary had stayed behind to make sure that Angel was safe and on her way. She had spread a piece of paper out on the table. It looked like a page from a book.

'We made this for you. See, we're here; the New Lakes are up there and the Old Lakes there. You need to head for this place. It's safe. We've sketched intact routes and seasonal paths around lost land and new rivers. Keep off motorways and major roads. People live on them, especially around bridges. They'll rob you and kill you. Follow country lanes, old salt routes, the hedges and the landmarks are still there if you look for them.'

'I can move fast. Where do you think I should go first?'

'Here's a safe place.' She pointed at a mark, north west of

the coast. 'Stay there for a few days, at least until the drones and heat seekers have gone over. Then move in behind them. Aim for here.' She pointed at a circle about seventy miles north. 'It's a safe community, a place of refuge. You can trust them.' She squeezed Angel's hand to make her point.

'Mary, which one of us had the rifle?' Angel asked quietly. 'They saved my life. Can you get a message to say thanks?'

'Rifle?' Mary looked surprised and shook her head, 'Nobody had a rifle. Just a crossbow and a dart gun.' She picked up a small box and emptied the contents on the table. 'We know you lost everything, so we had a collection. There's something from everybody. To thank you …' She fanned the contents out on the table. There were some bootlaces, a folded blue cotton scarf, a silver locket, a compass, some biscuits, spelt bread and some boiled eggs. Angel touched them gratefully.

'I didn't get to thank them.'

Mary gave her a knife and a silver foil survival blanket. 'These are from Jim and me.' She looked at Angel for a moment and smiled softly. 'Please sweetheart, cut your hair. It'll give you away.' She stroked Angel's earnest face. 'And be good … very good.'

Angel nodded, already sad to be leaving her. Mary's face held a generous and calm beauty. Then she whispered her thanks and put the gifts in her bag. She kissed Mary on the cheek, stepped out into the mellow afternoon light and began to run.

She stopped at the top of the hill and glanced back. The tide was low. The van and the boat were still burning; black smoke hung low over the bay. The shadows of the old town were just visible through the waves. Then she turned inland and set off running with a steady, economical stride.

• • •

Three hours later the sun was low in the west. After her efforts in the water and the run from the coast Angel's legs were leaden, she needed to rest. Deep in the long shadows in a thicket of trees, she saw the remains of a stone building. It seemed empty. The windows were broken, and the door had been kicked in. It looked like it had been looted. Parts of the ceiling had fallen in and a tangle of tiles and roof timbers were suspended through ragged holes.

She checked for signs of life, then she searched the building more carefully. There was a brittle plastic bin bag under the old kitchen sink, she picked it up and sat down in the corner. She had left in such a hurry, that she hadn't packed her bag properly, just stuffed things in. She needed to have her knife and water easy to reach and the rest needed to be better balanced.

Once it was better organised, she sat down and listened to the settling sounds of the evening. Satisfied that she was still alone she took off her shoes and socks and wriggled her feet, still wrinkled from the sea. She peeled the shell from a boiled egg and ate it slowly. Then she unfolded the map and began to memorise it. She would have to destroy it soon; it could lead the Reapers home and she wasn't going to allow that to happen.

Hunger satisfied, Angel spread the plastic bag on the floor in front of her and knelt forwards. Slowly, she unbraided her hair, still heavy and damp from the sea. It was silver, and it reached her elbows. She had a fleeting memory of a bedtime story, her stepfather's voice, just a whisper … 'Angel, Angel let down your hair …'

Angel gathered a handful of hair, brought it to her face … kissed it … then she twisted it into a tight ponytail behind her head and sawed through it with her knife.

She cried as she cut. She cried for what she had lost and what she had become. She cried for her stepfather who must think that she was dead, and she cried for the sleepy silver-haired little girl in her imaginary tower. She systematically worked around her head until it was short enough to just pinch between her thumb and fingers. Angel shivered, just the memory of the weight and touch of her hair remained. It felt like a ghost.

With trembling hands, she put her shoes and socks back on, and dug a hole with her knife and the edge of a roof tile. She buried her hair under the hard, dry earth and pulled some of the roof timbers down on top to cover the marks. Then she gathered dry leaves from the corners of the building and scattered them over her footprints, picked up her bag and stepped outside into the twilight. Resting her hand on the wall she looked at the first evening star, then swiped a tear from the side of her face, found her direction and ran.

Angel guessed that she had already covered at least ten miles and after her rest she could probably do another five before she needed to sleep. She ran on, alert to the sound of people and animals, for lights, signs of habitation or the buzz of drones.

She developed a steady rhythm, two steps for every breath in … and two steps for every breath out … she was alert and yet able to allow the landscape to become a blur. Time ceased to have any meaning.

The full moon had risen to her shoulder height when she paused in the cover of a copse of tall beech trees near the top of a hill. The route that she had been following, led on to a distant ridge. She crouched low to avoid being silhouetted against the skyline and scanned the area. The sea was out of view, and the moonlight picked out the straight edges of the building of the two abandoned villages that she had skirted around. Tarmac remnants of old roads scarred the landscape like silver stretch marks.

Angel was tired and needed to rest, she knew that the mental and physical impact of the last few days were starting to catch up with her. She stumbled over a tree root. Her head had cooled; she shivered and pulled her collar up to her ears.

In the distance, she could see a section of broken drystone wall. Prevailing winds had bent shrubby trees over it to form an overhang. Drawing on her last fragments of energy, she set off towards the wall.

She found her spot under low-hanging hawthorn branches and dragged some loose rocks over to make an enclosure on the ground. Then she spread her plastic bag out on the damp ground and made a pillow with her bag.

Cold now, she wrapped herself from head to foot in her foil survival blanket, pulled her sleeves down over her hands and fell instantly asleep.

• • •

She woke to the sound of distant humming. It was still dark. She froze, hoping that the drone would not recognise her shape through the tangle of branches and that the foil blanket would blank out her heat signature.

She stirred again at dawn. A blackbird was chattering angrily at something near its fledging chicks.

The third time she woke with a start, sure that something wasn't right. She didn't know what had woken her, but adrenalin was pumping through her body.

There was the smell of bruised grass and … a presence. She felt for her knife, whipped the foil blanket away and leapt to her feet, hoping to catch whoever it was off guard. She frantically searched the area, ready to sprint forwards or to scramble back over the wall and hide. But she could see nothing, no people, no boar, no wild dogs, no raptors.

She checked again more carefully and then slipped her knife into her belt. Shielding her eyes from the early morning sun, she scanned the land, the trees on the hill, the wall behind her, the tall grass bent over by the wind, and the stark blue sky. Something wasn't right. She looked again and caught her breath. There on the wall, close to where she had been sleeping was a small red apple. A shiver of fear ran through her body; someone had been that close!

She leaned forward and studied the lines of the wall, the trees on the hill, looked for footsteps in the morning dew, or shadows in the grass … Nothing.

She checked the hedgerow; there was no apple tree, tangled in the hawthorn. Nothing … her heart pounded in her chest as memories of the events of the last few days rose up.

Angel carefully reached out and picked up the apple. It was fresh, had a few marks on the skin but no bruises. There was no dew on it, so it couldn't have been there all night. Who had put it there? And more importantly, how on earth had she allowed herself to be so vulnerable?

She sniffed it and then took a small bite, instantly the sweet juice lifted her energy. Perhaps one of the Star People had left it for her as they passed. She took another bite. Whoever it was they were good people!

Angel scattered the seeds along the edge of the wall where saplings would be protected from the elements, then stood up and scratched her scalp. Her head was dizzyingly light and cold. She took her scarf out of her bag and wrapped it around her head to protect it from the wind. Then she packed her plastic bag and blanket into her rucksack and set off running at a steady pace. She had to get as far away from the scene of yesterday's action as she could and much more importantly, she needed to be much more careful.

CHAPTER EIGHT

'Closer. Let me look at the eyes.' Two men stared at the image of Angel. They were sitting on white calfskin chairs, leaning forward, elbows resting on a deeply polished ebony table. A large screen in front of them showed Angel's face with pinpoint detail.

'More,' said the older man. His hair was silver white, his eyes the colour of a winter's sky. His suit was of the finest lambswool and his cuff links caught the light as he stroked his soft cheek.

The younger man pinched and spread his fingers on a pad in front of him. The screen showed the empty wheelhouse, black smoke curled past the door. Angel's face moved to the centre of the screen. He pinched and spread his fingers a second time. The screen zoomed in to Angel's eyes just as she looked up at the flashing green light. They were pale, grey-blue. They checked her head, hairline, forehead, eyebrows and ears.

'Now show me that picture of Lilith again,' said the older man.

An image of a young woman appeared next to Angel's face. She was tall, had silver blonde hair and strikingly pale blue eyes. Her arms were folded, and she was glaring at the camera.

'Can you match them?'

The young man dragged an image of Angel over Lilith's face. The hairline, the forehead the arch of the eyebrows and the colour of their eyes matched. The nose and mouth didn't.

'Course, Lilith might have had surgery before she disappeared,' said the older man thoughtfully. 'Do we know if this one would have been evolved?'

'Not in the field sir, nobody gets it done.'

'Ah yes.' He leaned back in his chair. 'They don't have drugs do they … So, this photo is … em … natural?'

'Yes sir.'

'So, what are the odds on these … similarities appearing on their own?'

'Slim, sir. Since the Fall, everything is so dislocated … transient … but …'

'OK, so did we get bloods?'

'Don't know sir, everything was lost with the boat.'

'The crew?'

'Dead sir, we killed them.'

'Oh yes, got to set an example. Did we inseminate her?'

'Possible. We normally do it in the van.'

'OK.' The older man scratched his ear.

The younger man pursed his lips, unsure of the wisdom of what he had to say next. 'Em, strange thing sir, the transit records were encrypted. We're working on them, but we think that this Reap, hers, was commissioned.'

'Commissioned?'

'Yes. Procured … to order.'

'Whose order?' He sat up and slapped the table with his

hand.' I want answers! Who did it and who let it happen? Is somebody trying to hijack us? Get me answers!' He held his hand up, to show that his was the last word.

The young man gathered up his papers and tablet and started to move towards the door. 'One last thing.' The young man paused mid-step. 'Are we tracking her?'

'Working on it, sir.' As soon as the door had clicked shut and the lock engaged, the older man leaned forwards and tapped a key on his desk pad. An elderly woman answered.

'Mother. It's me. I think we've found Lilith's daughter.'

• • •

Angel travelled northwest. She took animal tracks and bare ground where she could to avoid leaving a trail in the wet grass. The terrain had become more rugged and it was harder to keep up a good pace. She pushed on, determined to have much better shelter by nightfall; she couldn't risk spending another night in the open.

As she climbed, the air began to cool, the wind stiffened, and it started to rain. She pulled the plastic bag out of her backpack and tore holes for her arms and head then slipped it on over her clothes and carried on moving.

She was stepping between waist-high rocks when she caught sight of a star scratched into a boulder. It shone white against the limestone and moss.

Her muscles were stiff, and her shoulders were sore where the backpack had rubbed; she slipped it off and groaned as she rubbed her neck.

Squatting in front of the boulder she traced the star with her fingertip, something about it caught her attention. She leaned forward to take a closer look. One of the points was deeper and longer than the others. The star was freshly cut; there was white dust in the cushion of moss beneath it. Someone was pointing out her route. They knew she was coming! She stood up, alert, energized and ready.

Her first impulse was to be cautious, find her own safe place, perhaps a cave or an old building, and take the time to observe this person. Then she remembered the apple and how easily someone had got close to her. In her heavy heart, she knew that she needed help.

She looked back to the far horizon and wondered if the others had got away. She hoped that they had, especially Mary. A bank of dense cloud was moving towards her, the rain was going to get worse. She took a piece of bread out of her bag and bit into it. The crust was hard, but it was tasty, and she needed the energy.

Angel unwrapped the scarf from around her head and rubbed her scalp. Unaccustomed to the lack of weight, the roots had become sensitive. She closed her eyes and let the wind cool her scalp and then wound the scarf around her head to form a tight turban. It still had slight traces of the perfume of roses, she smiled; this was from the woman with the dart gun. She glanced at her water bottle; it was half empty. Taking a measured drink, she resolved to start looking for clean water. Then shouldering her bag, she checked that there was no trace of her break and set off to follow the star.

She guessed that she was on an old country lane, the hedge had grown wild, but the line was still visible. Tree roots had fractured the concrete road surface. There had once been a ditch at the side of the road, but reeds, almost shoulder high, had filled it. Angel knew that this meant that any water that she might find would be filtered clean. But she couldn't see any way to get between the reeds, densely packed brambles and buckthorn. Filling her bottle would have to wait.

An hour later it was raining hard, she stopped at a fork in the track not sure whether to go left or right. On one side there was a large, lattice-barked chestnut tree with a hollow at the base of the trunk. She glanced up, the branches fanned out over her head, their leaves glistened in the rain, but underneath the ground was almost dry. It wasn't ideal but she could sleep there if she needed to.

Down the track she saw an old wooden gate leaning against the bushes. She walked along and looked at the gatepost; it was riven with cracks, and spongy when she pressed it with her finger. It smelled sweetly of fungal decay. There were remnants of painted letters on the top bar, she guessed that they might have once said *Danger*. She checked the other bars, feeling for a star sign, and then she leaned over to look at the back. She almost missed it, but there, newly scratched into the back of the hinge, was a star. Did they mean for her to go through the gate or to keep walking? Being off the track would be safer, she supposed.

Angel looked at the dark and tangled woodland ahead, then back to the chestnut tree. She thought for a moment, then decided that she would walk into the woods for ten minutes; if she didn't find somewhere, she would turn back, sleep in the tree and decide what to do in the morning.

She shrugged her bag into a better position and began to walk. The ground started to slope downhill and became softer underfoot. She glanced back to fix the return route in her mind. The sky had turned a deep slate grey. The trees sighed and then stilled as she moved deeper under the canopy of branches. There was a whisper of running water to her right. She ducked below low arching brambles and her scarf snagged on a thorn. The feeling of cold rain on her scalp was a shock, she stopped to pull it free.

'Ah there you are!' a man's voice echoed.

Startled, she spun around and peered into the shadows. She could just see a tall, thin man leaning against a large rock. His long dark hair was tied back, and his face seemed drawn with pain. He raised his hand to beckon her towards him. Then he picked up his stick and leaning on it heavily, moved forward.

'Got the word to look out for … Well I suppose …' He looked at her carefully, concern in his voice. Before he could speak a snarling black dog, knee high and solid, ran between them. He clicked his tongue and the dog stopped, and moved back, still growling and ready to attack.

'What's your name?'

'Angel.'

'They said you had long hair.'

'Cut it off.' She held her scarf up and moved her head to show her hair.

He thought for a moment, then he pushed the dog forward.

'Angel meet Leila, she keeps me safe. Leila meet Angel, we're going to hide her. Welcome to my quarry.' He gestured for her to follow him.

As her eyes adjusted to the light, she could see that the quarry bed had grown wild; ferns, buddleia and brambles filled fissures in the rock. Willow and birch grew in the spoil heaps. An old green shed had been pushed up against one of the walls. The man picked his way between the rocks, the dog walked by his side, occasionally glancing back to make sure that she was keeping up.

'What's your name?' Angel asked.

'Mac.'

He stepped into the shed. It was low and dark. Ragged curtains hung at the window, limp and heavy with dust. Soiled and faded work charts were still pinned to the walls. He waited until she had stepped inside and closed the door. She wondered if they were going to stay in the shed.

'Follow me.' He pushed the back wall. It opened into what looked like a small hollow. A gap in the quarry wall had been hidden by the building. They stepped into a cave. Candles backed by pieces of mirror lent a sparse light to some sections. It was impossible to see how big it was, but it sounded enormous. Leila walked briskly over to her bed and lay down with a grunt.

'Girl, girl! Come here.' A woman stepped out of the darkness. 'Let me give you a hug!' Angel found herself enveloped in one and then two pairs of arms.

'Thank you, thank you, thank you,' said the women behind and in front of her. They rested their heads on her and wept. Angel felt shocked. In their warm embrace, she felt jagged and hard.

'How can we ever repay you?' said the first woman, cupping Angel's face in her hands.

'Thank you, bless you.' The woman behind sobbed gently into Angel's shoulder. She could feel their warmth; it was a lifetime since anyone had held her. She lowered her face, her throat hurt, and she felt the sudden need to sit down.

'Let's give her a chance to breathe, shall we?' said Mac gently. 'Angel this is Aris, and this is Jen.'

'Are there more?' she whispered. Mac shook his head. Angel looked at the two smiling women as they stepped back. Aris was tall and muscular, her skin shone dark in the candlelight. Jen was smaller; her dark hair, tied into a knot on top of her head framed her more angular features.

They both smiled through their tears; Aris folded her arms across her chest and tapped her foot impatiently as if trying to control the urge to step forward and hug her again.

Angel thought that they both looked familiar and then she remembered them from the boat. They were escapers.

'Did you two jump the same time as me?' asked Angel quietly.

'Come here,' said Aris, unable to contain herself any longer. She wiped a tear from her face and then took hold of Angel's shoulders. 'Let me look at you.' She shuffled them around so that the candlelight illuminated Angel's face. 'There,' she whispered as she wiped away another tear.

'Thank you from the bottom of my heart.' Then she took a deep shuddering breath.' Do you want to sit down?'

'Are you hungry?' asked Jen.

'Do you want a wash?

'Or to sleep?' Mac added.

Angel looked at them, unsure which question to answer first. They looked at each other and then laughed. 'Let's start with a sit down. Mac, you put the kettle on,' said Jen, as she and Aris led Angel deeper into the cave.

'Your mother will be so proud of you,' said Jen helping to lift the bag from Angel's shoulder.

'Would be,' said Angel softly. The three women sat down, close together on an old sofa and watched Mac as he brought food. Flat bread, bean butter, goat's cheese, dried cherries and hot mint tea reminded her how very hungry she was.

'Thank you; I've just had a boiled egg and what I could forage. I'm really hungry.' She paused for a minute; 'Oh, and one of the Star People left me an apple on a wall while I was asleep.'

Mac raised an eyebrow in surprise. 'Not sure who … well never mind … you're here now, and you're safe. Probably best to stay here until we can spread the word a bit wider. For a day or two at least.'

He stood up to collect her plate. 'They've probably got drones and stuff searching. Once they've passed over us, you can tuck in behind.'

Leila yipped in her sleep. Angel looked around the cave, it was warm and surprisingly dry. She yawned.

'Where are you from?' asked Aris.

'A village in the Old Lakes; just a small place. You?'

Aris looked at her and sighed, 'Near Warwick. You know, I reckon I was set up.'

'Really?'

'Yep, that man of mine has wandering hands. We had words. If I get home and find a new face in my bed, he'll beg the Reapers to take him!' She laughed and then she looked sadly at Angel. 'Nobody raises my babies but me.'

Angel turned to Jen, who was quietly picking at a thread in her jacket.

'What about you, Jen?'

Jen sniffed a tear away. 'I'm from Nottingham, my family won't take me back. They think obeying the rules keeps us safe.'

'Why, what did you do?' asked Angel.

'I … I spoke to someone … a stranger. She had a little girl and a new baby … it was screaming. I talked to the little one, while she fed her baby.' She looked down at her hands. 'We're taught to turn a blind eye. You never know … what about you?'

They turned to Angel expectantly. 'Me … I was at a market. I'd found some parts for our generator. They don't come up often, so we always get spares if we see them. The trader was the one who snatched me.'

'So, you weren't in trouble?' said Jen.

Angel shook her head.

'Was it revenge?' asked Aris.

'No knowledge of Reapers in the area?'

'No, they've never made it that far, it is pretty rugged country.'

'How many did they take?' asked Mac.

'Just me, I think.'

'Sounds to me like you were caught in a trap.' Jen touched Angel's arm.

'I don't know why,' said Angel almost to herself, searching for anything that would make some sense of it all … then she drew a deep breath. 'I need some air. Is it dark outside?'

Mac called Leila from her bed and told her to take Angel outside. The dog nudged her hand and led her outside.

Darkness had fallen; it was a soft, watchful night of stars and shadows. The wind had dropped, and she could hear water dripping from the quarry walls. She stretched and took a deep breath. The sky was ink blue and the moon hung low over the trees. She shivered. A wave of calm rose up from her feet as the horror and fear of the last days began to melt into the gentle night. She took another breath and let it go.

Here, she was safe; she could lower her guard and let her fear rest … for the moment at least. Her eyes blurred with tears; stars melted into a kaleidoscope of colours. Snatches of memory flashed into her mind. Images of the people that she had killed … the muscle memory of the blows, the throws … the taste of blood in saltwater. Had she been quick … efficient? Taken no pleasure in it … no satisfaction. Because that was the way she had been raised.

She could hear her stepfather's voice telling her to hide … to run … to fight … to kill … and if all else fails, she shook her head at the thought … to die. She would have killed herself before the factory ship got her. She missed him so much, and her heart ached for the pain that he must be feeling. She wanted to go home. But would it ever be safe to go back?

She remembered Mary telling her that the machine parts at the market were bait. On balance, she agreed with her. It probably wasn't random, and she knew that she needed to get to the bottom of it. She couldn't go home until she knew what was going on.

She felt calmer now. But there was still something, a half-thought that wouldn't let her rest, something that she couldn't quite grasp … something important. Leila padded out of the undergrowth, leaned against her leg and sighed. Angel looked at the bushes and remembered a flash of light in the trees. A gunshot that had killed the engineer. But Mary said no one had a rifle. A shiver spread down her spine. If they had been aiming at her, why didn't they take a second shot? If not … did someone save her? But who?

CHAPTER NINE

She woke to morning sounds, turned over and stretched in the ever-burning candlelight. She had slept hard and deep and now her joints and muscles ached. Her bed had been a layer of blankets; her pillow her folded clothes. Someone had placed a mug on the floor close to her head. Chestnut coffee, her favourite, and it was steaming hot! With a groan, she raised herself up on to her elbow and picked up the mug.

She could see Aris and Jen working on the far side of the cave. Boxes and crates had been stacked up against the wall to make a random shelving system. Branches had been suspended across gaps between the boxes. Strips of meat were hanging down to air-dry. On another branch, herbs and fruit were drying.

'Morning.' called Aris. 'You slept well.'

Angel sat up and pulled her blanket around her shoulders.

'We thought that you might want a wash, so we've been heating water. Come and see.'

Standing in a corner near the kitchen area was an old bath behind a screen made of old doors. Jen tipped the last bucket of water into the bath and placed it on the floor, ready to be used to sluice the water away later. They went back to their work to let Angel have some peace. She slipped her blanket off, stepped into the soft, warm water and lay down with a sigh. Leila appeared from behind the screen, licked her shoulder, and curled up close by. A block of rough soap sat in a saucer by her toes.

'We've found some scissors. We thought we might tidy your hair up a bit.' Aris called from behind the screen. 'What did you use to cut it?'

'My knife.' Angel ducked below the water.

'Figures,' said Jen.

The water was cool when she finally emerged, wrapped in an old towel, Leila by her side.

'She's taken a proper liking to you.'

'Just ignores us.' Aris shrugged as they led Angel to a stool. Jen gave her some bread and goat's cheese to eat while they assessed her hair.

'I can't decide if it's blonde or if it's grey,' said Jen.

'Grey, it went like this when I turned sixteen. Apparently, my mother was the same.'

'Well it's beautiful,' said Aris.

'We thought we could cut it so that it looks … well … less like a hedgehog.'

'And we could teach you how to make things with your scarf, like a turban or a face veil.' Jen inspected the blue fabric. 'Then we can have a look at your clothes and make them easier to wear.'

When Mac returned a few hours later Angel had short hair that looked intentional and her overalls had been cut into trousers and a jacket.

They had found a leather belt and a pouch to hold her

knife and compass. Mac stepped into the room and nodded his approval.

'Thank you. I think I might go for a walk. Stretch my legs.' They stood back shoulder-to-shoulder and nodded in approval as she walked past them. Leila fell into step at her side.

'Stay in the shadows,' called Mac.

Angel and Leila stepped through the shed into the open air. She wanted to find higher ground to get her bearings and to plan an escape route, in case her pursuers got too close. The three, kind people living in the quarry didn't deserve to be mixed up in her problems.

Gravel crunched under her feet as she crossed the flat expanse of the quarry floor. Brambles tangled and coiled around the walls. There was a shallow pond in the far corner. Up on the ridge out of the shelter of the quarry, leaves hissed and sparkled in the breeze. To one side she could see a rough pathway that disappeared behind a curve in the rock. She glanced down at the dog and then strode over to explore. Familiar with the route, Leila trotted ahead and led her up a narrow scramble between rocks.

At the top, Angel stood in the shade of the trees and looked around. Nose down, Leila picked up a scent and wandered off. Quarry workers had dug deep into the side of a hill. Standing on the highest part of the ridge she could see for miles. To the east, she could see her route from the coast disappear over the rocky outcrop where she had found the boulder with a star carved into it. To the north all that she could see was miles of forest. A wide, brown scar snaked through the tree canopy. Angel assumed that it was where a river had drowned the trees. She wondered if it was on her map.

She was turning to look the other way, when she heard a low growl. She snapped around, her hand already on her knife. The growl erupted into a deep ferocious bark. Angel started to move forward, but Leila moved in front of her, hackles up, aggression bristling along her body.

'What is it?' Mac shouted from below. Angel scanned the woodland and saw nothing, but then, perhaps, deep in the trees, a flash of russet. A branch moved and obscured her view; when it swayed back … it was gone.

'Here Leila,' she whispered as she turned and quickly moved towards the path. Leila continued to bark, placing herself between Angel and the point of alarm until they were close to Mac.

'What did she see?'

'A fox?'

'Don't think so, she usually chases them,' said Mac scanning the ridge. 'You go inside, I'll have a look.'

• • •

For the rest of the day Mac sat in the shed doorway, checking the quarry every half hour. At dusk they barricaded the entrance and he moved his bed next to it. Once Angel had stopped pacing, Leila stayed at her side, yipping and snarling in her dreams. She reached down and gently stroked the dog's velvet ear.

Aris spoke softly of her plans to return home, but Jen was going to stay longer, to help Mac to prepare for the winter. He had injured his leg in a fall and was struggling to set aside enough food and wood to see him safely through the wet season. Angel had noticed that they smiled at each other and spoke quietly as they worked. She doubted that Jen would be leaving at all.

Mac told her how the trees had died. The river that scarred the north of the forest was a new one, an unnamed tributary of the Trent; it looped around for about fifty miles. The last tidal surge had caused a massive back up of floodwater. Years later when the land had finally drained, a network of new channels had been scored out of the land. Roads, railway lines and houses were gone, swept away. Maps were useless.

By the end of the evening they had agreed that travelling on water was the best idea. He explained that people mostly used the river because the forest tracks were often blocked by changing water levels; it was dangerous to lose your bearings in the forest … you could drown. And at least on the water you were safe from the packs of dogs and wild boar that roamed the countryside.

He agreed to arrange for someone to collect her and take her to the next safe place on her map.

• • •

At dawn Angel pulled on one of Mac's old coats, and a weather-beaten hat. He handed her a stick, and Leila walked over and sat by her side.

'Are you sure she knows the way?'

'Better than I do.' replied Mac, handing Angel her rucksack.

'And the way back too, she'll be fine.' Aris adjusted the hat. 'From a distance you'll look just like him.'

'Just be safe, OK?' Jen said softly, then she stroked Leila's head, 'and you come back soon.'

She was sad to leave the safety and comfort of the quarry, but yesterday's incident had left her restless and edgy. She reached down, patted the dog's shoulder, whispered that it was time to go. She had enough food and fresh water to last her two days. Mac had arranged for her to be collected from the riverside. It was well over twenty miles away and they needed to make good progress.

The rough ground near the quarry soon gave way to heavy thicket and then dense woodland. Dense leaf litter cushioned their steps but hid roots and fallen branches. Leila walked confidently along a path that was only known to her and Mac. Angel learned to watch her carefully and follow in her footsteps.

The temperature dropped as they moved deeper into the forest. And as the day slipped by, the air became damp and heavy. Nightfall found them curled up under a large oak tree. Angel hung her bag high in the safety of the branches. She stretched Mac's coat over them both, and slept, confident that Leila would hear any danger, long before she did.

• • •

A woman of indeterminable age peered at the screen. She could see stills of Angel's face. Her son watched her from a thumbnail image in the top right-hand corner.

'Well she's got Lilith's ears and my mother's hair. But it's hard to tell much else under all that ugly flesh.' A minor wave of distaste crossed Katrin's features. 'Remove the surplus, make her look normal.'

A technician remodelled Angel's image to minimise muscle bulk. Her cheekbones, chin and collarbone became instantly more angular and the shadows deepened. The woman leaned forwards, the light from the screen illuminated thin parallel scar lines around her hairline.

'More like it!' She sniffed in approval, tilting her chin up to squint at the screen. 'Don't know who the father was?'

'No mother. Lilith didn't tell anyone. At least no one who survived our questioning,' Charles added quietly.

'She's got a good proud stance. Even if she isn't blood, I think we can do something with her. What do we know?'

'We don't know if tissue tests were done in transit, the files were corrupted, and the boat destroyed.' He glanced at his mother to see if she was going to ask for an explanation for the file damage.

'Where is she from?'

'Not sure, the North, somewhere. It's sparsely populated up there. That's why she's managed to stay hidden from us for so long.'

'Do you think there might be brothers … or sisters?'

'Our people are searching. We will find her,' he added with forced certainty.

'Make sure you do. She could be very useful.'

'The board will have a report …'

'I see it first!' interrupted Katrin. Then with a minimal nod, she flicked his face off her screen. She looked at Angel's face. 'I found you Lilith. You didn't really think that you could stay hidden from me forever, did you?' She whispered softly, 'We're coming to get you. No escape now, my run away girl.'

• • •

In his office, Charles was checking through his report for the board. He called a number on his touch screen.

'We razed the place where the transit boats were attacked, right?'

'Yes, sir. The whole town's rubble, above and below the water. Nothing remains of the boat or the van. No one will ever know.'

'And do we know who the ringleaders were?'

'No sign of anything organised. Perhaps the ones who escaped from the first boat, took out the second.'

'Lets hope so.'

CHAPTER TEN

'This is it then?' she whispered. The place seemed to require quiet. There was no bird song, and no wind in the trees. A river stretched out in front of them, a hundred paces wide. It ran slick and black. A line of drowned trees, almost halfway in, indicated the original bank.

In a far corner she could see an abandoned house. The walls, windows and the trees around it were curtained by a high-water mark of black mud. She stepped back into the cover of the trees and moved toward the house. It was just as Mac had described. The front door was leaning against the wall; its hinges ripped from the doorframe. The river must be a beast when it floods, she thought. The contours of a small star had been scratched into the paintwork. 'Seems so,' she whispered to Leila.

It was an emergency shelter used by travelling Star People. Mac had warned her to sleep upstairs and be ready to move into the roof space; the river could rise to waist height in an hour. Angel glanced at the water's edge, made a note of its position, then glanced up to check the sky. High feathery strands promised change; she would need to keep an eye on it.

The smell of fox and rotting wood met her as she approached the door. Leila stopped, hackles raised.

'Go seek.'

With her head down, and tail straight, Leila scented the walls and the mud-covered floor, then disappeared into the house. There was a high-pitched squeal, and a flurry of movement. A large rat ran out, closely followed by Leila. Where there's one there's a family, thought Angel as she stepped cautiously into the house. The floorboards were springy and soft. The mud was probably two days old; the only footprints were small and animal.

With her back against the mildewed wall, Angel climbed the spongy stairs, testing each tread in turn. She paused at the top, checking for signs of habitation; it smelled sour, but dry. Through tatters of wallpaper that hung down from the ceiling, she could just see a low slatted bed in one room.

There was a sound of movement downstairs, she stepped away from the stairs and reached for her knife. Leila yapped, Angel smiled, clicked her finger and the dog bounded up the stairs, into the bedroom, and curled up in a corner. As she followed, her bag brushed against a wallpaper tendril and loosened a shower of cobwebs and plaster on to her head and shoulders. Angel took the hat off, shook it, lay her coat and bag on the bed, then straightened up and stretched.

Next the loft. Mac had told her that there was an emergency stash of food hidden up there. She found the access hatch in the gutted bathroom. It gaped open, dark stains blossomed across the ceiling. The bedframe was too awkward to move, so she was going to have to jump. She hoped that the roof timbers were going to be strong enough to take her weight.

She bounced on the floor to test its strength then crouched low, jumped up and caught hold of the wooden frame. Then she kicked hard and pulled herself up into the roof space and carefully stepped on to a beam.

A fallen branch had taken down the corner of the roof. She inched over, steadying herself with splintered cross beams. The metal box was exactly where Mac had said, tucked under some broken tiles.

She sat on the bed to inspect the tin. There was a snow scene on the lid. Children were playing and behind them was a stout man made from snow, wearing a hat and scarf. She touched the raised writing across the top of the lid; the paint had worn away. Her stepfather had told her about snow-time games although she had never played them herself. The memory of a song that he used to sing teased her … just out of reach. She hummed quietly as she opened the tin. Inside was a flint, some dried fruit; apple, pear, berries and some dried vegetables. Her rations were low and there was enough here to make soup. She paused by the front door for a moment to check that she was alone and then went into the woodland to gather dry weed from the low branches close to the house, and dead wood from where the ground was drier.

• • •

Leila's barking pulled Angel out of a fitful sleep. Throwing off Mac's coat she picked up her bag and ran to the head of the stairs. The dog, half in half out of the door, was barking viciously. Back in the bedroom Angel cleaned a circle on the window and saw a long-limbed woman pulling a canoe on to the bank.

'Leila, girl you know me!' laughed the woman, pushing her thin hair out of her eyes. 'Hello. Anyone there?'

Angel got her knife out of her bag and ran down the stairs and out of the door, standing behind the now growling dog.

'Ah, good. Are you Angel? I'm Cheryl … come to collect you?' Angel nodded in agreement. The woman walked toward the house and gestured toward Leila who inched forward a few tentative steps. 'Come here girl.' When the growling subsided, the woman stepped forward slowly, holding out a small apple. Leila accepted it and padded indoors.

'I've brought some things to leave in the loft.'

'Can I help carry things?' said Angel, pointing at the canoe.

Cheryl stopped to look at Angel, smiled and shook her head. 'You can help pull the other one up. Are you any good in a canoe?'

'Oh, yes!' Angel held her hands out to show the hard skin on her thumbs and index fingers.

'Great, that should make things a whole lot easier.'

Light was fading when they moved into the house. Cheryl squatted in front of the fireplace, reached into her bag and pulled out a tin can with holes punched in the sides and a short candle; she lit the candle and turned the can over it. Once it was hot, she placed a metal plate on top and began to cook. Angel watched her work, each movement swift and smooth.

Cheryl looked up and cleared her throat. 'Right here's the thing. They're searching for you hard, and they really seem to mean business. There's a reward and they want you alive … that's a first. They're using drones to search the open land. And they're asking people to look out for a tall girl with long ash coloured hair.' She scrutinised Angel for a moment. 'So, we need to get you to the Beguinage quickly. Then we can hide you there for as long as it takes. We're a semi-closed community. You should be safe with us, or at least as safe as you can be anywhere.' She leaned forward. 'What puzzles us is why they want you so bad. It's a big effort to catch one escapee; besides you weren't the only one to get away.'

Angel shook her head. 'I don't know either.'

'Bit of a mystery then … tell me about your family. Are they powerful?'

'No, my mother died when I was small. My stepfather farms and does some trading. We live in the Old Lakes.'

'OK,' said Cheryl as she passed over a mug of mint tea. 'Better start early, if we catch the tide right, we'll be there by night fall.'

'Where is it?'

'Probably best that you don't know. Now are you OK on the floor? I need the bed.'

CHAPTER ELEVEN

Leila left at dawn, with a star scratched on her collar.

The two women set off a few minutes later, their canoes whispering through the water. The restless shadows of the trees made the river look like wrinkled black tar. The current was slack, and it was smooth going. They kept under the cover of the low, overhanging branches and made good progress.

Cheryl had made the journey many times and rowed with a steady, economical pull. Angel followed behind, matching her stroke for stroke. She knew that Leila would get home OK, but she wasn't so hopeful for Aris and Jen and she hoped Mac would be OK. She stretched her spine, took a deep breath and relaxed.

Two hours later they had left the tributary, moving out into the main, much wider confluence of the Trent and the Ancholme. The current was taut like steel. She had been warned that they might see other people from here on, so she pulled her hat down to cover her hair and tucked in behind Cheryl's canoe. The river was littered with debris. They manoeuvred around a tangle of trees, ripped from the earth and impaled headfirst into the riverbed, their bare roots clawing the air.

'Watch out,' said Cheryl indicating to her right. 'Container ship. Current can push you on to it.'

Angel glanced at the complicated turbulence and followed Cheryl's line further left.

The landscape was low, flat and flooded as far the horizon. The sky mirrored in the floodwater seemed endless. They skirted around the sides of isolated bridges and slid above drowned fields. Below the surface, Angel could see the ghost of hedgerows and fences, and the shadows of winding country roads. In the distance on a small island to her far right, she saw a crooked wooden windmill standing stark against the sky. Its slatted sails were redundant, the fields where the wheat used to grow were beneath her.

Cheryl slowed down and rested her paddle across her knees. Angel bumped alongside. 'From here it gets hard,' Cheryl said. 'We're going to pull out into the Humber. Three miles wide. Fierce current. Watch for a sandy line to the left, that's where we're heading. It's what's left of Read's Island. We need to get to it quick, then wait for the tide to change.'

'Ok then what?'

'Soon as it changes, we get ourselves across to the other side as fast as we can.'

Angel nodded and peered into the waters ahead.

'If we play it right, we get a rest on a sandy beach.' smiled Cheryl.

Angel pulled her hat off and splashed water on to her head to cool down.

'I'm OK … really. I do this a lot at home.' She smiled at Cheryl's anxious look. 'But a rest would be nice.' She could feel the river tugging at her canoe and pulled on her oar to keep her position. The muscles in her arms were glowing.

'Right then, let's go for it!' Cheryl turned and sped out into the wide expanse of the Humber. The wind became gusty as they moved out into the open; Angel had to use all of her strength and speed to move forward.

'Go right!' shouted Cheryl zipping to the side. Too late, Angel saw that the water ahead accelerated as it was forced between the bank and the island. She realised with horror that it was undulating right in front of her. The canoe dropped violently and then kicked up. One wave and then another and another bounced across the front and slapped against her body and face. Each time she gasped and shook her head to get the water out of her eyes, put her head down and fought the river with all her strength. But, try as she might she was losing ground and being pulled back. She turned her face away from another wave, caught a glimpse of Cheryl who was leaning forward and powering diagonally into the current, using it to push herself across at an angle. Angel pulled hard to get closer, at first it felt as if she was stationary but gradually, she began to make progress. The island was getting closer.

As soon as she felt the sandy bank beneath her, she threw herself from the canoe and hauled it out of the water, gasping for air, muscles on fire. A blast of wind nearly blew her over, so she lay down on her back and fought to control her breathing. That was hard, she told herself, pushing away thoughts about the rest of the crossing.

Angel lifted her head, 'How come this doesn't wash away?'

'It does but it grows again. It's silt coming down river,'

said Cheryl. 'There are other ways to cross but this is the quickest.'

'What's down there?' Angel indicated the riverbanks downstream.

'There was a city, a bridge and a lot of industry; it was low lying, so you know … there's not a lot left. On the other side, there was a massive oil refinery, but some people tried to loot it … big explosion … there's just tangled metal and chemicals now, you don't want to go there. Out there at the mouth of the estuary, there used to be a long sand spit, but it's gone now. Beyond that it's open sea.'

Angel nodded 'How far to the …?' She had never heard of the type of place that they were going.

'Beguinage. It's an old name for a community for women. You'll be fine there.' She handed Angel some bread and a curl of fruit leather and smiled. 'We're about halfway.'

The two women sat and watched the water race past their feet.

'You could get dizzy, watching this.'

Cheryl nodded. 'Best not to look, just close your eyes and feel the wind. When it starts to drop… we're off.'

She gazed at the vast expanse of water still to be crossed. 'Be careful, even with the rising tide, if you fall in you'll be out to sea before you come up for air … deadly undertow.'

'Where are we aiming for?' asked Angel scanning the far bank.

Cheryl pointed out the mouth of the river that they were aiming for; it looked like a silver gap in the inky silhouette of low-lying land.

They waited until the wind eased and the river slowed.

'Aim for the sun, it's in the west now, go upstream of the entrance to the river and the current will push you right down towards it. Good Luck!'

• • •

The sun was at late afternoon when the two women, laughing with relief, slipped into the lower reaches of the River Ouse and headed north.

'Perfect!' said Cheryl. 'We'll be there by midnight. Are you OK? Do you need a rest?'

'No. Let's keep going.' Cheryl nodded in approval and they moved on upstream.

The full moon cast their shadows across the river. Cheryl paused to point out the dark outline of the City of York as it began to rise in front of them. She beckoned to Angel to catch up.

'You need to be my shadow from here. Absolutely no sound.'

The noise of the city closing down for the night crept along the river towards them. 'They're shutting the gates,' whispered Cheryl.

Angel looked around; the large stone walls butted right up to the edge of the river. A stout black gate closed off an ornate metal road bridge. She could smell wood smoke and rotting food.

She had never been to a living city before and she was curious. Everywhere she looked there were houses. Some of the buildings were enormous and one had two … no … three square towers. But just one building dominated the night sky, it loomed tall and black. An ancient stone tower stood brooding on a perfectly round hill. Angel shivered and looked away.

She could see that the Ouse had claimed many of the river-fronted houses. They stood in water up to their gutters. Their roof tiles had been salvaged; and some of the timbers were gone too. They didn't look burnt, so she supposed that they were being used to repair other buildings.

They glided silently into the shadows between walls and houses. Cheryl tapped Angel's boat to catch her attention and indicated that they should move left. Bumpy water ahead meant that they were passing over submerged obstacles.

'Now hang on to my stern and lie back,' whispered Cheryl.

From what she could see, it looked like they were going to crash into a solid wall. Angel caught hold of Cheryl's canoe and held on tight. Then she realised, it wasn't a wall, it was a bridge, free standing and almost completely underwater. It stood alone, resisting the rolling waves that curled against its sides. They lay back, flat, and let the current take them. The arched roof cleared her face by inches, she breathed out and the air misted.

On the other side of the bridge she paddled like a whisper. The sounds of the city were muffled by the brooding presence of buildings that were only flooded to their ground floor windows. The water was becoming shallower.

They turned left into a narrow space between two buildings, then moved silently into the deep shadows. Angel lost sight of Cheryl. She heard two clicks from the pitch black on her right and tentatively eased herself over. There was another click, closer, something moved her canoe. She was pulled forward then turned sideways. She raised her oar ready to defend herself, it was grasped and pulled away from her.

'Easy,' Cheryl whispered.

Angel put her hand down and found herself hard up against a wooden platform. The sound of her breathing seemed to be amplified, her canoe dipped and then rose as the water bounced against her side and she realised that they must be inside a building. Cheryl touched her shoulder. She climbed stiffly out of her boat on to a platform, wiped her hands against her legs and stretched her aching shoulders.

'This way, quietly.'

She followed Cheryl across a bridge that spanned a gap through a window into the next house.

CHAPTER TWELVE

Angel had been led straight into a room by the entrance. The windows were small and close to the ceiling. In the candlelight the grain in the wood-panelled walls seemed alive. She could hear a baby crying somewhere in the building. This was her welcome to the Beguinage and she was exhausted.

'I'm Miriam. Please take a seat.' The woman smiled and gestured to a vacant chair. Her long black hair was held back by a strip of cord. Her eyes were deep brown; and her olive skin deeply scored with lines.

'Around the table, we have Cheryl, our messenger, who you've met, and our four other founders.' The four women nodded, as she said their names. 'Ivy, Rena, Olayah, and Fenna.' Miriam continued, 'Our values are equality, trust, industry and community.'

'Community comes first,' said Cheryl.

'Everyone contributes equally. All skills are equal, all lives are equal, and we have a mutual responsibility to each other. We are a community,' said Fenna.

'And for that reason,' Olayah spoke firmly, 'we allow no men, just women and children.'

'And no religions,' said Rena, 'and nothing else that can destabilise.'

'Now you pose us something of an unusual problem,' said

Olayah, 'and you need to know that we've had a bit of a difference of opinion.'

Angel held her breath, surely they weren't going to turn her away?

Miriam leaned forward, 'This is what we know … you are somewhat … unusual. We know that they are looking for you hard … and there's a ransom … a big one. We've never heard of that before. It's clear that you matter to them. So, just by being here …'

Angel nodded miserably; she knew they were right.

'If the Stars hadn't asked us to help you, we would have turned you away.' said Fenna.

'To our eternal shame,' said Miriam checking the faces of the others. They murmured in agreement. 'And so, we are going to offer a welcome with open hearts … but troubled minds.'

'Oh, thank you,' said Angel, overwhelmed with relief. 'I hope I don't cause you trouble. Although I can't promise … ' Her voice trailed off.

'We're trying to find out what's going on,' said Cheryl.

'We have listeners out and about,' said Ivy, 'and we've contacted the other Beguinage, but it'll take time to get a proper answer'

Cheryl smiled. 'Word of mouth is slow but safe. Old women are useless and invisible so we can move about easily, nobody notices us.'

'We listen as we go,' laughed Fenna, 'and we *tidy up*!'

Angel watched the women look at each other and smile. She got the sense that they were a formidable team.

'So, we've decided that until we work out what's going on, we need to keep you hidden,' said Miriam.

Angel's heart sank, 'You mean lock me up?'

'No … just isolate you. The women here need preparing …' said Rena, with some kindness in her voice.

'This place used to be a school and we have an old chapel that we use as an isolation ward. Hopefully we've done with this year's wave of scarlet fever, and for the moment at least, the infirmary is empty,' said Miriam.

'Clean but empty,' nodded Cheryl.

'Our women and children give that area a wide berth; too many bad memories,' Miriam continued. 'We won't keep you there a moment longer than necessary.' She rested a hand on Angel's shoulder, it smelled of soap and cooking. 'Just until we know what we're dealing with.'

Angel nodded, she wasn't in a position to refuse, but she felt trapped, her voice wavered; 'Can … can you get a message to my stepfather, to let him know I'm …?' She was going to say safe but changed her mind. '… alive?'

Miriam nodded. 'We can try. Now let's get ourselves settled before the early risers start moving about.'

The women quietly pushed their chairs back and each took a candle from the table.

'This way,' said Rena.

It was only when the candles were moved that Angel realised that they had been arranged in the shape of a star.

• • •

Her shoulders and neck ached, and her hands were blistered. She kept getting flashbacks of the journey … the smell of Leila's fur … sitting on the island watching the river barrel out to sea … a row of cormorants basking in the evening sun on an almost submerged school roof, and York's silhouette against the sunset. She had set off with no idea of what to expect, but it wasn't this. Had she just been locked in another box, she wondered, and if so, what was she going to do?

She rolled on to her back and opened her eyes to the cool dawn light, this was her first proper sight of the infirmary; it had been dark when she had arrived. The wooden ceiling was high, arched and supported by carved beams. There was a raised platform at one end; she could see marks on the wall where plaques or statues had once been fixed.

The room was cool; light seeped in through simple stained-glass windows. A rainbow of light traced time on the red-tiled floor. In the far corner a stack of bed frames and mattresses leaned against the wall. Her bed stood alone, close to a large oak door. A jug of water and a cup stood on a small table by her side. She rolled on to her stomach and drifted into a fitful sleep.

Outside, a bell rang and the sound of children playing fell to a whisper. Angel listened intently; the children didn't sound frightened, just organised.

There was a knock on her door, she sat up, and Olayah entered.

'Morning. Well, it's afternoon actually. I've brought you some food. We don't know what you like so I've brought you a range of things. There's cheese, soup, bread …'

'That all sounds wonderful,' said Angel suddenly aware of how hungry she was. Olayah placed the food on the table and stood back smiling.

'There's a washroom through the small door on the platform. You'll find a towel and a few other things in there.' She looked at Angel and smiled. 'Try to rest, and don't worry, nobody knows you're here.'

Angel wasn't sure if this was a good thing.

'What can I do while I wait?'

'What are you good at?'

'Oh, outdoor things, mainly. Do you have leather? I could do with a new scabbard for my knife, or I can make belts for people. Or if you have wood, I can whittle. What do you need?' She paused to think. 'Wool? I can spin with a drop spindle. Anything really.'

'Let me think.' said Olayah moving toward the door. 'Eat and rest, for now.'

• • •

Angel had watched colours from the stained-glass windows stroke across the floor through three full days. She listened to the music and chatter of children playing in the evening. In the distance, she heard geese protesting at some intrusion in their space and the delighted squeal of children.

A tray of food lay on the end of her bed. Inactivity was affecting her appetite. Hanks of spun wool hung over the stacked beds, and her fingers were sticky from the oils in the fleeces. She'd paced the room and tried to loosen her aching body. She hadn't been so inactive since her time in the locker and her discomfort was growing. They came to her at night, when the building was quiet, to talk and reassure her, but they had no news.

She had tried reading a book that she had found in a cupboard, but the language was difficult to understand. There was a cross on the front, like the mark on the wall.

There was a faint tap on the door and Cheryl stepped lightly into the room.

She held something to her chest as if it was a treasure. It was a piece of paper. She spoke softly. 'Angel, we managed to contact your stepfather.' She held the letter out with trembling hands. 'Here … I'll leave you.'

Angel held her breath, if this was a dream she didn't want to wake. The door clicked shut and the key turned in the lock. She gazed at the envelope as if it might contain her stepfather's voice, his smile … his bear-like hug. Then she held it to her heart. She could imagine him squinting as he wrote, reading aloud to himself to make sure it was clear, she saw his large sun scarred hands smoothing out the paper. She carefully opened the precious letter and read:

Angel, my heart,

They tell me that you are alive. I've hardly allowed myself to hope that it could be so. They tell me that you are safe, for the moment. This is wonderful news. I thought that I had lost you and now I swear that I am even smiling in my sleep. Are you well? Are you hurt? Are you with friends? I have a thousand questions, but they must wait, because, right now, I need to tell you something.

First of all, it was Jay who led them to you. They took her baby to blackmail her; she didn't get him back. She's paid a heavy price and we are trying to console her. Forgive her, please. For who would not have done the same for their child? I certainly would have.

Now, my sweet, there are things that I should have told you a long time ago. I hope that it isn't too late and that you will forgive me for not telling you sooner. I hope that what I say now will help you to keep safe.

Your mother Lily (Lilith) ran to me when she realised that she was pregnant. I think you knew this, but this next part is very important.

She never spoke about your father and I didn't ask. I knew that her family was rich and ruthless. They hunted for her, but everything was in such turmoil. It was easy for us to disappear. We ran to the Lakes and hid.

As time passed, she told me little bits about her life. Her family were the first financiers to lead the Offshore movement. When the world started to fall into chaos and they couldn't trade on the markets, they moved into open slavery.

I wish that I could see your face when you read this next piece.

They are looking for you my sweet Angel because you are family. You have your mother's eyes. Her hair was silver, too.

They are the Alphas, and you are theirs. I don't know why they want you now, after all this time but I doubt that it will be for good reason.

Don't worry about me; we have closed the community down. It is fenced and guarded. The entrance is where you used to swim …

My heart rejoices that you are safe; my head rages that I may lose you to those people. I will imagine you hiding better, running faster and fighting smarter than any angel ever could.

I wait for you.

My sweet girl, my heart, my Angel …

She read the letter until it was too dark to see the paper; and then she waited for the moon to rise, so that she might read it again.

CHAPTER THIRTEEN

Angel woke at dawn, still holding the letter. Someone was unlocking the door. She sat up quickly and tucked the letter under her pillow.

'Things just keep getting better and better!' muttered Fenna as she hurried towards Angel. 'There's a man here. He's insisting on speaking to you!' Angel peered at the indignant woman. 'You didn't tell us that there was a man!'

'There isn't! Is there?'

'Well there is now, and it changes things; we told you the rules. Miriam's with him in the guardroom. I'm to take you there now.'

Angel pulled her shoes on and followed Fenna out into the unfamiliar corridors. Their footsteps whispered on the tiled floor. It was just light outside; she could hear a child singing to itself in one of the rooms. Further along the corridor, a baby cried and then hushed as its mother spoke softly to it. It felt as if the building was listening.

Perhaps her stepfather had come to get her? She walked faster. She needed to talk to him about the letter, Fenna's shoes squeaked as she turned the corner towards the main entrance.

'Here we are,' she whispered, pushing the heavy, wooden door with her shoulder. Angel took a deep breath and stepped into the room.

The smell of drying clothes met her. Boots and wet coats were stacked against the far wall next to a studded dark-wood triple-locked outer door. She could see Cheryl and Miriam standing on her left. The high windows behind them were barred.

'Ah, Angel, do join us.' said Cheryl.

A hooded figure sat in the darkness at the far end of the table. He was looking down at his hands. She couldn't see his face. Ivy was standing next to him. Angel knew at once, that it wasn't her stepfather; he would have looked up.

'This man says that he must speak to you,' said Miriam indicating the figure in the shadows.

'But I don't know ...'

He looked up at her and she gasped.

She hurled herself at him, knocking Ivy aside and grabbing for his coat. He leapt to his feet.

A chair spun and crashed against a wall.

Arms grasped at her. She felt herself being pulled back. She fought to claw at him.

Hands held up defensively, he backed away. His hood slipped.

A shock of honey red hair framed his face. An ugly red wound shaped like an 'R' disfigured his left cheek.

'Steady!' said Miriam, as Ivy and Olayah dragged Angel back. She fought to reach him.

'You tried to kill me!'

'I saved you twice.'

'You're a Reaper!'

'I infiltrated them to ...'

'You snatched me!'

'To protect you!'

'That's ridiculous!' spat Angel.

'Please, let me explain.'

Angel stood glowering at him, over Olayah's shoulder. 'We heard that the Reapers were excited about finding someone, so I joined them to find out what was going on.' He paused when Angel said nothing and continued.

'I told them that I wanted to catch you and swap you for my sister. They thought I didn't look like a Reaper and could maybe get close to you without too much of a struggle ...'

'But!'

'They had orders not to hurt you.'

'Why?'

'Not sure ... we had an intercept crew set up further along the road, but they slipped up. It went wrong. I was trying to work out how to get you off the boat when you jumped. So, I played up the chaos, pushed some more in and distracted the guards for as long as I could.' Angel was listening now. 'I volunteered to chase you when the other one ...'

'Stopped.' said Angel flatly. He seemed different to the man she had seen in the tower; his face was grey and tired. The edges of his wound had begun to heal but the rest was puckered and angry.

'I didn't know that you already had help when I climbed into the tower.'

Miriam and Fenna were watching intently as the atmosphere in the room began to calm.

'Do I have you to thank for this?' he said touching his cheek.

'Well, I could have slit your throat.'

'Thanks, for that.' He nodded.

'And you followed me?'

He nodded. 'I needed to talk to you. To ask for your help.'

'No. We're even!' said Angel emphatically.

'When you were fighting on the deck of the second boat … it was me who shot the engineer.' He indicated to the corner where a rifle was leaning against the wall. 'I left an apple on the wall, that first sleep.'

Angel nodded slowly as the events of the last few days shifted into a new perspective. She glanced at the others in the room.

'Well, I think that we should have some breakfast after that!' said Miriam cheerily, looking relieved that the anger had subsided. Ivy picked up the overturned chair and handed it to the visitor, then she and Olayah left the room, their whispers could be heard as they walked toward the kitchen.

'Now why don't you two sit down?' said Miriam.

'It was you at the quarry when Leila went crazy?'

He nodded. 'I lost you along the river for a while.'

'Did you follow me through the forest?'

Miriam looked at Cheryl and raised an eyebrow.

'No. We waited and picked you up as you crossed the Humber.' He glanced across at the two older women.

'They could have stayed hidden in the forest?' said Miriam.

'Not safe.'

'Followed the river down to the coast?' said Cheryl.

'Too dangerous, they would have been swept on to what's left of Hull, or worse, out to sea.'

'Upstream?'

'We would have spotted you.'

'OK.' said Miriam nodding. 'Why York, why here?'

'That took longer. In the end word started to filter … someone's in isolation … a stranger. They're worried about getting sick.'

Miriam sighed and looked at Cheryl.

The man turned to Angel and spoke softly. 'You're not safe here. If we can find you so can they.'

'I'm sorry.' Angel looked into the Cheryl's troubled eyes. 'Hiding me here isn't working, I'd better go.' She began to stand, but Miriam raised her hand.

'Eat! First, we eat, then we think.' There was a tap on the door. Ivy entered the room backwards, pulling a trolley with a fluttering wheel. Olayah followed with a handful of ointments and a dressing. Angel saw Miriam raise an eyebrow at Ivy who responded with a slight nod of the head.

'So, tell me about yourself,' Ivy said as she poured a mug of hot milk and pushed it across the table.

'Thanks. I'm Raph,'

'Handy with the 'R' then!' said Olayah sitting down at the table.

'Pleased to meet you Raph.' Miriam nodded. 'Who is this "we" that you keep talking about?'

'We're a group of … we work within their IT systems,

computers, data; you know spy and then sabotage what we can.'

'Never heard about you.' said Fenna.

'That's good. We didn't know about the Stars until the last few weeks. Or you, come to that ...'

'Fair enough,' Miriam acknowledged.

'Thing is, they have blind spots a mile wide and they don't, well, obviously, they don't see them ... but we do.' Raph picked up a piece of cheese and broke it in half. His hand was shaking. Angel wondered if he was tired. 'But it's early days,' he added.

'It's hard to organise any kind of resistance,' said Miriam. 'People are beaten down ... hopeless.'

'So much poverty,' added Fenna, shaking her head. 'Disease and poverty.'

'But now we know that they want, Angel, we have their attention and they're not looking elsewhere ... We have a chance to do something ... something big,' said Raph.

'You're not using Angel as a decoy, she came here to be protected and we're not beaten yet ... unless she wants to go, of course. Do you?' Miriam paused. Angel shook her head. 'Right then, we all need to talk; us, you and the Star People.'

'We decide where,' Cheryl added.

'Do you have somewhere to stay?' Miriam asked. Raph nodded. 'Good, then, first we're going to patch your face up and then we need time to think.'

CHAPTER FOURTEEN

Ted's empty seat at the table was invisible. That was the rule. Charles looked at the men waiting for him to speak. They all wore this month's cut of business suit. Trouser cup-and-lift panels were not built for sitting, more the power stand. They were beginning to shuffle, and he was making them suffer … because he could. They were his board and they would wait until he was good and ready.

He admired his reflection in his screen, he had his mother's jawline, it was rich and proud.

Long past, The Family had divided the Primary Asset … the planet … into exploitation zones; Underground, Ground, Sea, Air and they were a fraction away from re-achieving Space. It was a good split. Each zone was represented here in front of him, except for air. Ted was away on his annual augmentation break.

Obviously, The Family ran comms, intel and the top line overview. Nobody … absolutely nobody did anything without his say-so. He glanced across at John and noticed how his stubble – just long enough to suggest high testosterone and contoured to emphasise a square jaw line – glistened with perspiration. John had the Underground Portfolio; coal, oil, gas, tar, minerals, metals and pretty much anything else that he could find. The name of the game was to get it before the other Offshores got it. John was good; they had a monopoly on Underground.

Next his eyes rested on Brad, and he pursed his lips in distaste. Charles knew the others well, after all he had known them since school, but Brad was different. He was here because of what he knew, rather than who he knew and that made people nervous. Brad was an IT wizard; they had poached him from another city, so he brought a lot of insider knowledge. But he still hadn't got their eye for the politics of clothes. And he'd better get it … fast! The lighting in the room didn't work on him either, it was meant to make people look thin, angular and white, but most of all it was meant to pick out their augmentation scars. They were badges of honour and belonging. The sooner Brad got some of those, the sooner we can all relax, thought Charles.

He looked out of the window and saw tall palms bordering a beach of sparkling, white sand. People were busy clearing away the wreckage of what had been a particularly wild party. Behind the beach there was a half size replica of the old canary wharf, pre-surge, of course. Screaming gulls circled behind the ship, anticipating the next discharge. He'd never seen so many fat birds.

'Right gentlemen,' said Charles. 'Sorry to drag you away from your work, but we've got a bit of an issue.' The men sat up straight, relieved that the meeting was finally starting. 'I'll get right to the point. We've had two failed reapings along the eastern coast of the British Isles. The natives clearly don't know how to behave.'

'And so, we need to teach them a lesson,' Andrew snapped. His Ground Portfolio included the sentient assets. There was a dwindling of good stock availability and he had been forced to search wider afield. It was getting costly, and resistance to reaping would be a major problem; an expensive one. He would come down on this very hard.

'Normally, I would say yes, Andrew. But we have, by chance, spotted something of great value to The Family … and therefore to all of you.' He looked at each man in turn. An image of Angel appeared on their screens.

'Tasty!' said Brad, throwing his pen down on to the table. Charles looked at him in distaste.

'We have reason to believe that this is a family descendant, my niece, in fact.'

An almost inaudible sigh of satisfaction circled the table, the men nodded vigorously, to make sure that Charles knew that he had their full support. Brad picked his pen up and studied it carefully.

'You may not all be aware that my sister disappeared some years ago. We had almost given up hope of finding her. This young woman is very much like her and we believe that she is her daughter. We want them back, both mother and daughter … and any other siblings that there may be. The woman in this picture was connected to the reaping … em … issues and so we know that she was on the East Coast. We have tried to locate her, but she has so far eluded us.' He looked at them all, silently counting to ten, waiting for the silence to smart. The men sat, trying to look both eager to begin their search and at the same time intent on listening to his instructions. 'This, gentlemen, is now your number one priority … move heaven and earth, find them! It need not be said, that it would be a disaster if she should fall into the hands of one of the other Offshores. We want her home in the bosom of her loving family, intact, unharmed and fast!'

• • •

Outside, Angel could see children playing. One small group were sitting in a circle listening to someone reading a book, and solemnly acting the story out as it unfolded. She thought that perhaps it was about a spider in the rain. One small boy perched on his brother's knee. They both had the same shock of dark curly hair. She noticed them because it was unusual for a mother to have two surviving children. At least she hoped that there was a mother. Angel brought her attention back to the room.

'Keeping you hidden isn't proving so easy,' said Miriam. 'We would understand if you wanted to go. There are other places that we could send you.'

Angel had been feeling restless since Raph's visit. 'Do you want me to go?'

'No dear,' said Fenna. 'We are just going to have to have a rethink, especially about the things that Raph said. As far as we can check, he was genuine, but we can't be sure.'

'What he said was true … but it might not have been all of the truth.'

'Are you sure?'

'He's been where he said he was. I just don't know why. I know that he could have shot me when I was on the boat; or any time afterwards, come to that. I don't know if he helped me to escape, like he said, but he's definitely a good tracker.'

'Yes, but was he going to kidnap you in the quarry?'

'I'm not sure, but it would have been much easier for him to do that when I was sleeping by the wall, but instead, he left me food.'

'OK,' said Miriam. 'For the moment we are neutral, but if anything, leaning cautiously towards believing him. Right?' They nodded their heads. 'Well, we shall know more tomorrow, one way or the other. But for now, we need to bring you out of isolation.'

• • •

Fenna led her out into the fresh air and instantly, Angel felt brighter. She stood in the sunshine, closed her eyes and felt the caress of the breeze on her skin. She had never been indoors for so long before; even in the worst of winters she'd always worked outside.

As they walked, Fenna explained that the Beguinage had been a derelict school when they first moved in, over a decade ago. It was situated within the ancient city walls of York. One of their first jobs had been to make the place safe. They'd added high fences and viciously spiked gorse, holly and buckthorn under the perimeter trees. They had built a gatehouse, but it was now mainly used for storage. The river ran nearby, and regularly broke its banks. She said that only the older women knew about the entrance that Cheryl had used for Angel's secret arrival.

Angel could see that the school grounds had been turned into vegetable and herb gardens, an orchard and animal pens. They had goats, ducks, geese and chickens.

'We chose these because they can get to safety when the river floods,' said Fenna, 'and the geese are as vicious as guard dogs.'

Angel stopped to look at the main building, it formed a V shape, two floors high, with the lower windows half bricked up.

'We lost the roof a few years ago,' Fenna explained, 'so we converted the upper floor into a water capture system. It works pretty well, feeds the kitchen and bathrooms.'

Angel could see that they had taken bricks out of the walls at roof level and put in spouts so that surplus water ran away rather than soaking into the rooms below. She was impressed by the women's ingenuity and hard work.

'We sell goat's milk and cheese as well as medicines and we buy wool, which we spin and weave into cloth. We have a network of suppliers and buyers. We get by … so far anyway.' Fenna shrugged.

As they walked past women working in the garden, Fenna introduced Angel as the traveller who had been in quarantine. She explained that she had been near an outbreak of scarlet fever a few weeks ago and had chosen to stay for an extra-long isolation, just to be sure that she hadn't got the deadly disease.

The children clung to their mothers' skirts. The little boy who had been sitting on his brother's knee, made a serious wide-arced wave. Angel waved one back.

'That went well,' said Fenna leading her back. 'They won't be in a hurry to talk to you and the mystery person is revealed.' When they were closer to the building she whispered, 'You are going to get a bit more serious questioning when the others get back tonight.'

'Others?'

'Yes, our sellers and buyers are due back tonight. They … mm … take less shelter from us. For various reasons, they don't have children, but some have men outside. We suppose that they like the life in here. They're respected by the other women, because they deal with the outside world and do our buying and selling.'

'What shall I say?'

'Say that you had a fever when you woke up the first morning, but that it was nothing. Now we need to find something for you to do so that they can see that you can contribute.'

'I'll try anything.'

'OK, but first there's something that I need you to see.' Fenna took Angel behind the main school building, where there was a single storey structure. It looked like a wreck, but Fenna said that it was being used as a store. One wall was lined with stacked and chopped logs, seasoning in the sunshine. Sheets of opaque plastic that might once have been the roof were being used to form a lean-to hot house on the south facing side.

A glass door at one end led into the building. Inside, the floor was lined with stacks of wood, metal and reclaimed building materials. Fenna stepped over some sacks of potatoes and slipped behind an old door that was leaning against the end wall. Angel peered into the unexpected darkness. She could see a hole, the top of a metal ladder and Fenna's hands moving down the rungs. The rasp of her footsteps echoed strangely. Angel edged forward and looked down. Fenna looked up at her and whispered for her to follow.

Angel found herself in a strange rectangular room, it was tiled and had a bar running along the top of the walls, near the roof. She looked to the far end; the floor seemed to slope uphill. It seemed possible to stand up for about a third of the length but from there onwards, the ceiling was too low.

'It used to be a swimming pool, 'whispered Fenna. 'We covered it over after it was pretty much wrecked by a storm. We use it to store anything that we can scavenge, but it's also a good place to hide.'

Angel looked around; the roof wasn't dipping with the weight of the building material that was stacked on top of it, the floor was dry. She thought that if need be, she could hide in amongst the stacks of clothes and old shoes up at the shallower end.

'Have you ever needed to hide here?' She felt honoured to be shown their place of safety.

'No but we practice with the little ones. The older ones would stay up there and … you know. I just wanted you to know about this, just in case …' Her voice trailed off to a sigh.

'Thanks,' said Angel pushing a pile of desiccated leaves with her foot. 'I hope that you never need to use it because of me.'

CHAPTER FIFTEEN

Fenna was right, the women who returned that evening, were much more curious. From Miriam's room, Angel watched them return in twos and threes. One group pulled a flatbed trolley piled high with bundles of fleeces.

Miriam had told Angel that York Beguinage was well known for its dense woollen felt. They made it through the winter when there wasn't much to do in the gardens. It was more water and wind proof than other wool and their dyes were fast. They bought the fleece from hill farmers with the money that they earned from selling surplus food and herbal medicines at the market in York.

In the evening, Miriam and Fenna took Angel to the empty refectory. It had once been the school gymnasium. Wood had been stripped from the walls and the plaster painted white. Long, rough-wood, trestle tables ran across the room, lined by an assortment of chairs and benches.

At one end of the old gymnasium, hung a large patchwork tapestry. It almost covered the entire wall. Angel noticed that it was still unfinished at the sides and each patch was unique. It gave an impression of chaos; and she sensed, a heavy feeling of sadness.

Miriam spoke softly. 'We ask each woman who joins us, to make a square. Most of them use a scrap of fabric that's special to them.'

Angel walked across to look at it in more detail; some patches were made of rough cotton, others thick wool, but each one was carefully stitched. Women had decorated their squares, some had written or sewn words and pictures, some had attached small items like a button or a milk tooth. One woman had lost eight children; each one was meticulously named in thread. No square was bigger than a child's palm. It carried such a weight of sorrow; it was almost impossible to be so close to their pain. She stepped back and put her hand to her mouth.

As she turned Miriam and Fenna nodded. 'It's still growing. We have two women sewing theirs now. We find that it helps them feel that they belong.'

'Yes, and it's a lucky mother who has a memorial for their children these days,' said Fenna softly.

Angel looked along the bare walls and wondered if in time they all would be covered.

Miriam touched Angel's arm; they listened to the sound of people approaching. Fenna opened the door. Ivy and Cheryl wheeled two trolleys of food and dishes into the room and set them up against the wall. Hungry women and children followed noisily behind. Angel recognised two of the traders at the head of the queue. They saw Angel standing with Miriam. The queue fell silent. Oblivious, two small girls ran gleefully to the trolleys to see the food. Soup and dumplings steamed in large pans on one trolley, potato bread and goats' cheese sat on a wooden board on the second.

'Let's join the queue, shall we?' asked Miriam cheerfully.

As she ate her soup, Angel could feel the women traders

looking at her. When she looked up to acknowledge them, they looked away. One woman, about her age, was too slow to avoid eye contact; her expression was distant. Her curly blonde hair was tied back and held by a tight band. Light blue eyes shone from her deeply weathered face. Angel watched her rise and walk over to get another piece of bread. She moved slowly as if her legs were too heavy. Angel could see a small bulge; the woman was pregnant. Miriam saw her watching and leaned in to speak quietly.

'Zette has lost two children. We think it was dysentery. Her husband was killed a couple of months ago, she's no one left. It's not long since she came out of isolation and the sight of children is still very raw.'

Once the noise in the room hushed into a satisfied hum, Miriam stood up to speak.

'Sisters, good evening to you all, I am glad to announce that our produce has raised enough money to buy sufficient wood to heat the main building this coming winter. We already have enough raw wool to keep us more than busy through the dark days and nights to come …' She glanced around smiling; but there was an unmistakable tension in the room. 'And I would also like to introduce our newcomer … Angel. She came to us several days ago and has been in isolation. We are glad to say that she is well. She will be sharing the single women's room tonight. I trust that you will all make her feel welcome.'

Angel looked around the room, some women were tending restless children, others looked at her with open interest. The women on Zette's table were talking quietly.

The trader who had been at the front of the queue lifted her eyes to Angel and gave her an ice-cold look.

At dusk the children helped to release the geese into the area around the perimeter fence. Their raucous indignation subsided long after the children had returned.

Angel collected her few belongings from isolation and moved them to her new, shared bedroom. She wasn't looking forward to it at all. When Miriam had said that she was moving in, no one looked at her or smiled and no one spoke to her after the meal. She had taken the precaution of giving her father's letter to Miriam for safekeeping, she didn't want any of the women to read it. She needed time to come to terms with its contents first.

The room had six beds, each with a chair. At the end of the room there was a door leading to a washroom. The sinks were rectangular with cracked rubber plugs. Green stains blossomed from the plugholes to the tap. In the corner a large flat sink contained soaking clothes. Angel heard a noise, someone had come into the bedroom. She returned to the sleeping area to find Zette sitting on the edge of her bed, sewing a square for the tapestry.

'Hi, what are you making?' Angel was hoping to break the ice, but Zette ignored her. 'It's OK, I know I'm not infectious, there's no need to worry.'

Zette looked up slowly, 'Worry? I know who you are … the others told me … You're the one they're all looking for.' Angel froze. 'You're not infectious, but you are dangerous.'

'What? I don't know what you mean.'

'Silver hair, blue eyes, scar on your shoulder, travelling

alone; you're not safe and you didn't ought to be here. We've had enough trouble.' Her voice cracked. 'There's a big reward out for you and a lot of people are looking.'

Without another word Angel left the room. She found Miriam and Fenna in the kitchen. 'You should be OK, we've closed down the perimeter and everyone's locked safely inside, so news can't get out tonight. We'll decide what to do after tomorrow's meeting,' said Miriam.

'And if in doubt, head for the place that I showed you, stay there until we come and get you. OK?' added Fenna.

Angel looked from one to the other of them. Suddenly she felt no safer than she had when she'd been sleeping under the hawthorn scrub, but she had no choice this time. What would they say if they knew about the content of her stepfather's letter? She was glad now she hadn't confided in anyone.

When she got back to her room, Zette was pretending to be asleep. Angel heard her sniff and wondered if she had been crying. She slipped her shoes off and tucked them into her bag, got into bed fully clothed, and stared at the ceiling, waiting to see what the night would bring.

About an hour later she heard whispers from the corridor. The other women were preparing to come into the room. Angel closed her eyes and breathed slowly and deeply, as if she was asleep.

'I'll just open this window,' said one woman, as if to an audience. The other women giggled. It was a large window close to Angel's bed. She felt a cold draught press down on her head.

'Yes, let the bad air out!' added another, as they moved to the washroom and then silently got into their beds.

In time, their breathing lengthened into sleep rhythms. Zette snored quietly in the corner. Angel couldn't sleep. The moon cast a blade of blue light across the far wall. She watched it track across to Zette's bed then pass on out of sight. The room darkened. She picked her bag up, and quietly slipped through the door and out into the dark and silent corridor. She made her way to the refectory, planning to sleep on a bench or a table. Moonlight illuminated the heart of the tapestry. She walked over to have another look and reached up to touch it.

Her hand froze.

The geese at the perimeter suddenly made a loud and angry chorus of alarm. Intruders! She knew, immediately, that this was about her. She caught sight of the names of children on one of the squares and wondered, with dread in her heart, if any would die that night. She heard doors banging and a child began to scream. The intruders were inside. It was too late to run to the pool.

Angel pulled the corner of the heavy tapestry away from the wall and slipped behind. Her heart beating in her throat, she worked her way along the wall, hoping to get to the darkest corner. She flinched as her outstretched hand touched something cold.

It felt like a ball. No, it was a door handle!

She grasped it and held her breath, pleading for it to be unlocked! The knob turned stiffly, but it opened into a cold dark space. She stepped in and quietly closed it behind her.

The room smelled of dry wood and old carpet. The sound of crying and shouting had been muffled when she'd closed the door, but a wisp of a draught near her bare feet told her that someone was in the refectory. Angry male voices shouted above the sounds of the women and children. Angel could hear heavy footsteps as the men walked around the room. She could hear furniture being knocked over.

'Where is she? Give her up and no one gets hurt.'

'Who?' Miriam was trying to calm the men down.

'You know! The one they're all looking for. We know she's here,' a man's voice growled.

'I don't know who you mean,' said Fenna.

Angel's was sure that if they stopped talking, they would be able to hear her heart pounding in her chest.

'Enough time wasting! Get everyone in here. We're going to search the whole place.'

Angel could hear cries of dismay as the message was passed along the corridor. The refectory filled with frightened women and crying children. She felt in her bag for her knife and stood with her ear against the door, listening for the sound of a struggle or of people being hurt.

After what seemed like an age, it became quiet. Outside the geese raised the alarm. Someone stepped back into the room. There was a murmur of relief.

'They're gone.' Miriam spoke angrily.' They searched everywhere … including your rooms. They took some of your things.' There was a moan from the women, 'And I had to pay them to leave!' There was a pause for the women to absorb the news.

'They seem to have got in through an open window in the single women's room. If it weren't for the geese, they would have come and gone without us knowing. And Angel would have been on her way to the Reapers.'

'She shouldn't have been allowed here in the first place …' shouted one woman. The room was silent.

'Sisters! Friends! This is a sanctuary. A place of safety,' said Miriam.

'Every one of you has reason to be here,' added Cheryl.

'We didn't select you, we didn't turn you away, no matter what your circumstances were,' said Olayah.

Some of the women murmured in agreement.

'And yet … and yet one of you … or some of you, put us all in danger tonight.'

The women shouted in disbelief, and then they started to murmur Angel's name. The call grew louder.

'No! Not Angel … Think!' Miriam' voice rose over their clamour. 'The ones who opened the window … the ones who told their men friends about her … the ones who told them where she was.' She paused and then spoke with real menace. 'Because they knew all right.' The room was silent. She took a deep breath. 'As of now … friends … sisters … I am declaring this a closed community. No one will leave or enter without my agreement. The gate is closed. If you go out without permission, you will not be allowed to return. I suggest that some of you … seriously consider leaving.'

'No!' one of the women shouted.

'You can't!' called another.

'I can and I have.' Miriam spoke more calmly. 'We'll trade

at the gate; we will secure every inch of the perimeter. Consider your positions, my friends. Goodnight.'

Angel heard the door close as Miriam and Olayah left. The room filled with noise. Cheryl began to speak, calmly and with authority.

'We know that this is a bit of a surprise but listen … the Offshores have moved closer, big time. Up to now they've just been testing the water. But it's going to get a whole lot worse. Believe me, if you thought that you knew about reaping before, you're in for a nasty shock.' She paused, the room was silent; 'Our only hope is to be invisible, to hide, to keep our heads down, to fade into the background. Gossip will attract Reapers and their collaborators to York. We've been exposed tonight. And that's made us a part of the problem. And people in York will point them in this direction, to protect their own people. Who could blame them?' Angel could hear murmurs of agreement.

'Our only hope,' said Fenna calmly. 'Our *only* hope … is to raise our defences and to lower our profile. And this is exactly why we are closing the community.'

'I suggest that you spend tonight working out what you want to do … stay … or go,' said Cheryl.

Fenna and Cheryl left the women alone in the room. After the door closed there was silence for a second and then the noise grew. Angel sat exhausted on the floor and listened to the tears, the cries of protest and dismay. Over what seemed like hours they gradually subsided into silence.

Dawn broke as the last of the women went to their beds. Angel curled up against the door and slept.

CHAPTER SIXTEEN

'Are you there?' whispered Fenna through the tapestry.

Angel gently tapped the door with the handle of her knife.

'Stay there. We'll come and get you later.'

They had breakfast in the quiet of Miriam's office. Some of the chairs were damaged and a picture had been smashed. Angel was subdued and very aware that the trouble was her fault. Fenna and Cheryl sat with her.

'How did you know where I was?' she asked quietly.

'I noticed that a corner of the quilt had moved. Not many people know about that old storeroom.' said Fenna.

'We were hoping that you hadn't gone.' said Cheryl softly.

'How many people left?'

'Five, everyone but for Zette from your room. She hasn't been outside the community yet, so we know she wasn't involved. One from another room went with them.'

'Willingly?' Angel asked, surprised that they hadn't taken Zette with them.

'Mixed.'

'I'm sorry,' said Angel quietly.

'It's OK, things are different outside now. We would have needed to change things sooner or later.'

'By the way,' said Fenna. 'We've spoken to York about becoming closed after last night. They're talking about repairing walls and tightening their own security; they don't want Reapers or bounty hunters around any more than we do. With luck we might be a closed community in a closed city.'

'Did you tell them about me?'

'No, just that some people had jumped to conclusions, stirred up trouble, and now they're gone,' said Cheryl. 'I think they believed us.'

'Are you sure? Rumours aren't that easy to stop.'

'It's OK, we've been here a long time and they need us.'

'Are you all ready?' Miriam asked opening the door and beckoning for them to follow her. 'Our visitors are here. We're using the pool.'

Angel stood up. 'Won't the others wonder what's going on?' She was eager to hear news of Mary and the other Stars, but worried that the Beguinage couldn't take much more disruption.

'No, they're catching up on their sleep, and we've asked them to clear up the mess left by last night's … visitors,' said Miriam.

'And Ivy and Olayah are going to work with them to cook a good meal. We want to celebrate our first night as a closed community,' added Cheryl.

'Not goose though,' said Fenna. 'They're worth their weight in gold!'

• • •

Angel stepped down into the old swimming pool. Seats had been arranged in a line against the deep-end wall. Lanterns had been hung from the handrails. Long shadows cross-hatched the tiled floor.

She saw Mary standing with a group of Star People and moved over and touched her shoulder. It was a delight when Mary turned and hugged her, they held on to each other tightly and then Mary stepped back and touched Angel's hair. 'I'm so glad you did this. Are you OK?' Angel nodded and asked, 'How's Jim?'

'Fine, they all got back OK, and Mac says hi.' Mary squeezed her hand and introduced Angel to her group. Miriam joined them and kissed Mary on the cheek; the two women walked into the corner for a quiet conversation.

On the other side Angel, could see Raph, he looked a bit more relaxed and there was a fresh dressing on his face. Angel suspected that was the work of Ivy. Next to him was a tall woman. She had long, red hair and freckles on her face and arms. The woman appraised Angel seriously, their eyes met, but she didn't acknowledge her.

Behind them, Angel could see that maps and charts had been taped to the wall.

'Shall we begin,' said Miriam, 'perhaps with introductions?'

The woman with Raph introduced herself as Mani, and her other companions as Peta and Asta. She explained that they were representatives of an underground resistance movement that was embedded in the Offshores' IT systems.

She stepped towards Angel. 'I hear that you spared my little brother's life. I probably wouldn't have done in the same circumstances but thank you anyway.'

Angel wasn't sure if she was being thanked or criticised.

She nodded her head, but Mani was already walking back to her group.

Mary introduced herself and her group. Angel listened carefully. She had thought that the Stars were a small group, but in fact they were a wide network that covered the whole country and large parts of northern Europe.

In turn, Miriam explained about the Beguinage movement and how there were small hidden refuges, some closed, others partially closed. They were mostly for women and children, but some were for men.

They all turned to Angel; she cleared her throat. 'Hello, my name is Angel. I was born and grew up in the northwest. I escaped from the Reapers ... with all of your help.' She took a deep breath, looked at the floor, and spoke quickly. 'And I've recently learned something that might explain things a bit ... I'm sorry but there's no easy way to say this ... I've learned that my mother, Lilith, was a daughter of one of the Offshore families ... the Alphas.'

The atmosphere in the room turned to ice.

'They must have recognised me from some CCTV footage from one of the boats and they want me back. That's why there's a reward.' Angel looked around at the stunned faces. 'That's all I know ... sorry ...'

'Oh, poor you ...' said Mary, the first to recover from the shock.

'You can't help who your parents are,' said Miriam. She turned to the room. 'But let's make the most of this, we might not get a second chance.'

'Agreed,' said Mary, 'let's hope our dying days are over.'

'OK,' said Mani. She stepped forward to speak. 'First things first, we can make your locations disappear; they'll be invisible; like they've never existed.'

'My stepfather, he's vulnerable.' said Angel.

'I can put a blackout shield around your home, erase it from all e-maps, make it as if it was never there, and we can interrupt information going in and out. The only leakage would be on foot.' Mani turned to Miriam. 'The Beguinage network will cease to exist as soon as we know their locations. Can you limit slippage?'

'We are all about to close our gates.'

'How do you all communicate?' Mani asked.

'A mix of communication tree and ham radio, some places still have the old land line telephone connection, it's all below their radar, I hope.' said Miriam.

'Stars use CB radio, we use gardening-based code, oh and word of mouth,' added Mary.

Mani nodded. 'Nothing satellite? No Internet? No cell data?' The others shook their heads; she nodded in approval. 'You are totally beneath their current level of scrutiny. I can provide one comms machine per organisation. We'll keep our communication, transparent. If we use financial codes, they won't notice.'

The meeting broke down into smaller discussions about how the new communication system would be used. Angel knew that the Beguinage and the Stars knew each other, but she wasn't so sure about Mani. She saw Raph looking at one of the maps and walked over. She could see three Offshore cities positioned in the North Atlantic.

'Are there others?'

He turned to see who was talking and moved so that she could get a better view. He pointed to another city in the Pacific Ocean. 'There was one near Australia, but we believe it's moving to the South American west coast. There may be more, they squabble and split up, you know. Most of the global resource stripping is on the Atlantic side. But we think they may be going to open up new ground in what's left of the Pacific Island states.'

Angel studied the large world map, it had been marked, and shaded, and wide areas had been blanked out.

'Why are some countries shaded grey?'

'Near total collapse, either significantly under water, infrastructure not strong enough to maintain life, turned to desert or just as likely reaped out.'

'And this wide red band, right around the globe?'

'New desert. It was the belt where we grew all the rice, maize and corn … the world's staple food. It's where the first mass migrations started; they were starving. And, you know … all of those dispossessed people …'

'The industrial scale reaping started there?'

'Yes.' He nodded. 'Mind you, they put up a good fight. It was touch and go for a while.'

They stood shoulder to shoulder; Angel pointed at a series of areas that were coloured purple.

'Slave plantations, opencast and deep mining, body farms …' His voice trailed away.

'The whole planet is their factory …'

'Indeed,' said Mani, who had walked up behind them. She turned and clapped her hands for silence.

'And now I need to tell you about our opportunity. This season's first major block of extreme weather is building; it looks like it's going to be a monster. We've already set their weather monitoring systems to forecast good weather for at least another month.' She gestured towards the map. 'And if you look at this map, we have the three Atlantic Offshore cities heading north for their biennial Peace and Prosperity Summit. The further north they are towards the Bay of Biscay, the more vulnerable they are, when it strikes. Together, we have the best chance for more than a generation to end this. We must get it right; retribution will be total.'

'So, let's do it right.' said Mary.

• • •

Cheryl and Angel walked along the corridor leading to the refectory. Miriam and the others were going to join them when the visitors had left the grounds and the geese had been let out. The sound of people celebrating could be heard along the corridor. They expected the noise to level to drop to one of suspicion and disapproval when Angel walked in, but it didn't. She filled a plate of chicken stew and vegetables, sat down in a space next to Zette and began to eat.

'Hi. Are you OK?' asked Zette, her blue eyes searching Angel's face.

'Fine thanks, are you?' she responded.

'Yes thanks, I'm relieved, to be honest. I knew they were

up to something, but if I'd known what, I would have told you.'

Angel was taken aback by the look on Zette's face. Her candour seemed genuine. 'Can't have been nice for you, having those men burst in through the window,' she said softly.

'I was terrified. You should have seen them search for you. The women, I mean. The men were furious.' Zette paused. 'Where did you go?'

'I hid,' said Angel taking a drink of water.

Zette thought for a moment and then asked quietly, 'Why is there a ransom out for you?'

'I escaped from the Reapers, sank a boat, and killed some of them.'

The room went quiet.

'God no! You are so brave,' Zette said.

Angel looked up, the rest of the room was looking at her in surprise and admiration.

'Not really, I just don't intend to die any time soon.'

Angel collected her empty plate, stacked it on the waiting trolley and picked up a pear to eat later. Miriam opened the door and followed her into the corridor.

She leaned forward and whispered into Angel's ear, 'The seed is sown.'

CHAPTER SEVENTEEN

Knowing that Angel had managed to escape from the Reapers, gave the women in the Beguinage new hope. Their sense of what the future might hold for themselves and their children, fractionally shifted. With new hope came new energy.

They threw themselves into the changes that their closed community needed. The perimeter was repaired and strengthened; the only entrance was through a secure gate into the city. The pool bunker was prepared for greater numbers and there were regular practice evacuation drills for the children.

With less contact from strangers there was a reduced risk of infections or disease. So, the infirmary was moved to a smaller space near the gatehouse and the old chapel became a schoolroom. It was a place for everyone to learn.

Mani made sure that, one by one, their scattered places of refuge slipped from the grid. It was as if they had never existed. Angel's home in the Old Lakes melted into the mountains, roads were re-routed, and the lakes swelled to hide villages and towns.

Computer loops of fine weather were created, ready to replace storm warnings. Repair and maintenance schedules for the Offshores were downgraded and records falsified.

• • •

Angel opened her eyes at a gentle touch to her shoulder and found Cheryl signalling for silence with a finger to her lips. Angel blinked at the cold grey dawn and nodded to say that she would follow. They walked silently to Miriam's room, where they found her standing with Fenna and Raph. His hair was longer, and he had the beginning of a beard that would probably hide most of his scar. He nodded to Angel and moved towards her.

'There's a plan to kidnap you … they're coming tonight.' He stepped closer and added softly, 'I can get you out if you come now.'

Angel shook her head, 'No I can't just leave the women here to fend for themselves. They wouldn't be in this mess if it wasn't for me.'

'True, we can hardly tell people that she's gone, so you can cancel the raid, can we?' said Cheryl.

'Especially since we've gone out of our way to deny that she's here in the first place.' added Fenna. 'They'd never trust us again.'

Raph shook his head in exasperation. 'This is a mess. They're coming armed, this time. People will die.'

'Not if we kill them first,' said Cheryl over Angel's shoulder. Miriam and Fenna nodded. 'And if we make an example of them, it'll stop anybody else from trying it.'

'It's time to flex a muscle,' said Fenna.

'OK …' said Raph, reconsidering, 'but just how do you plan to stop them?'

'Oh, my dear, we have been very busy!' said Miriam with a smile.

• • •

A honey-yellow moon slipped behind the tips of a line of poplar trees close to the river. Angel was waiting high in an oak tree, near the perimeter fence. The city was closing down for the night. It stretched only a mile and a half between the walls, and sound carried. Doors closed and a dog barked in the middle distance. She could hear a child complaining about having to go to bed.

It was a still and quiet night; the moon shadows stretched far across the pastureland. She expected that the kidnappers would wait until the early hours when it had set, and the city was asleep. She settled down for a long wait.

Raph had managed to discover that it was going to be a two-pronged attack, a decoy one at the main entrance and a larger group aiming to breach the perimeter fence.

A clock was chiming half past the hour when a flock of screeching parakeets burst out of the shrubbery, flew over to the roof of the old building, and settled noisily, among the water tanks. Angel held her breath and listened.

The bushes below her stirred. There was a low cursing. She watched a man force his way through backwards. He was caught on thorns. He clutched a rifle in one hand while he yanked at his jacket with the other. Angel slipped down out of the tree, knife in hand and landed, silently behind him. One clean movement, and he fell, dying, into her arms.

'Nice!' whispered Raph stepping out of the shadows. She wiped her knife on the dead man's jacket.

They both heard it at the same time … the sound of struggle … a woman cried out. Angel turned and sprinted towards the noise.

From the darkness under the trees, she could see a writhing shape on the floor. Two women were locked in a fight with a large man. A second stood hands in pockets, rifle by his side.

'My turn next, girls … when my friend's done of course, only polite.' He snorted. Angel could see the women's weapons, garden blades lashed to poles, lying on the floor behind the standing man.

No, it's my turn, she thought. An arc of blood rattled on the holly bushes … it shone silver and black in the moonlight.

The women called for help. The man, who they were wrestling with, was fighting to get to his feet. He punched one of the women, then set off across the moonlit grass. Angel threw one of their spears in a perfect hissing parabola and he took just three more steps.

'OK?' asked Angel to the two women, who were looking wild eyed at her.

'Move them to the bushes and cover them with leaves, then clean and check your weapons.'

She touched one of the women on the shoulder and then ran back to the oak tree.

There was no sign of Raph, but she could see the body in the bushes. Two loud gunshots rang out from the direction of the gatehouse. Let that be two more of theirs, she hoped.

Moving swiftly and soundlessly toward the shots, she heard grunting and the crackle of leaves. Through the darkness she could just make out the shape of Raph moving another body. She hurried forward and scooped leaves over a leg and unshod foot, Raph threw a shoe into the darkness. She wiped her hands on her trouser legs and whispered, 'Three here, two over there, how many more are we expecting?'

'Maybe three, maybe four.'

'OK, do you want to see if the rest of the women around the perimeter are OK, I'll go to the gatehouse?'

Raph nodded, picked up his rifle and walked into the night.

Angel heard laughter coming from the gatehouse. It seemed incongruous on such a night. She tapped on the door and it opened a fraction and then Cheryl opened it wider, meat cleaver in hand. Miriam was standing by the outer door.

'Come in!'

'What's so funny?' asked Angel.

'There were three of them, but what with the rifle shots and the sight of us with our knives, they had a sudden change of heart.'

• • •

As dawn bruised the morning sky, a bell rang inside the Beguinage. Women and children came out of their hiding places and made their way to the refectory. With a touch on the shoulder or a smile, they honoured the line of fighting women standing in front of the tapestry. Their night's work had left them exhausted and dirty, cut and bruised. One woman had a black eye and her arm bound across her chest. Their faces sombre, and their words unspoken, said: It is done. Don't ask.

Angel stood at the end of the line watching them sharing empathy and grief and their strength of resolve grow. She cleared her throat and said quietly, 'Sisters we are tired.' The spell broke and together they moved into a new day.

• • •

Later that day Miriam and Cheryl returned from an angry meeting with the city leaders. They had gone to complain about the attack on the Beguinage and to demand that they stopped. The shamefaced elders agreed to spread the word that an attack on the community was an attack on York. They told Miriam and Cheryl that they would arrange for the dead to be collected by nightfall.

That evening Angel and Miriam stood in the gatehouse doorway and watched two rain-sodden men pulling a straw-covered cart containing the bodies back to the city. They didn't greet them or look up from the ground, just kept their eyes down and moved quickly.

'They're afraid of us.' said Angel quietly.

'So am I, a little,' replied Miriam with a sigh. 'You know, Raph said something before he left last night. It made me think.'

'Oh?'

'He said, that watching you fight … he really believed that you could have killed him when you cut his face … and that you chose not to. You're not squeamish, or bloodthirsty, you're balanced, somewhere in the middle. He said that you act with honour. And I think he's right.'

They watched the lights over the city fade then they barred the door and crossed over to the main building for their evening meal.

They collected their food and sat at the end of the long table. Angel was about to put food in her mouth, when the room went quiet. She paused and looked up from her plate; everyone was looking at her.

'Angel, we want you to sew a patch for our tapestry,' said Zette standing up from her seat. Angel glanced at Miriam and Ivy and saw their surprise. It felt as if the whole room was holding its breath.

'But I haven't lost anyone,' said Angel softly.

'No, we know.' Another woman stood up. 'But we think … we think, that in that whole wall of grief … there should be a space for a little hope. We want you to make a patch for us. A small part of you and a little bit of hope.'

'Are you sure?' she said, the immensity of what they were asking burning her throat. Every woman in the room nodded.

• • •

Angel lay awake long into the night, thinking how everything that she knew about herself and her life had changed. Her life had become so much more brutal than she could ever have imagined. Her stepfather had protected and taught her so many skills. He must have been preparing her for something. But after all the things that she now knew that she was capable of doing, she wondered who she actually took after, her mother's family, or her real father, whoever he was? And was there any of her stepfather's influence left? She was so different now.

She sighed … could she ever go home?

She recalled when Mani had said that she would have killed Raph if she had been in Angel's position in the tower. She played through her options. He was defenceless and she had an escape route. He was no immediate risk to her. Sure, he might have drowned if it had been a high tide, and she didn't know how much sedative Jim had given him. But no, Angel was sure that it was the right thing to do. Mercy has its place, it must. She didn't like the person that she would have become if she had killed him. She rolled over on to her side and looked at the night sky. She really, didn't want to be that kind of person.

What's more, she needed to keep an eye on Mani, because she was clearly a very ruthless woman.

CHAPTER EIGHTEEN

'One of our drones was lost last night.' Brad was reporting to the Alpha management team. 'The signal got patchy over the Isle of Man and it ditched. At least we assume it went down in the sea, between there and the Lake District.'

'OK, and you are telling us this because?' said Charles with a sarcastic sigh.

'I was thinking that maybe John could get any ships in the area to look for it.'

'And exactly why should I do that?' said John, taking his cue from Charles.

'Well,' said Brad reluctantly. 'It's the third. Must be a bad batch. I need the recorder to work out what's wrong, and then I can sort the supplier out. We can't afford for this to keep happening.'

'We? Who's the "we"?' said John, with a cold grin on his face.

Charles paused just long enough for John's words to sting. 'For God's sake, deal with it!' He tapped his screen and the next item on the agenda appeared.

'Gentlemen, I have been contacted by Nova. They and Eden are steaming north to join us for our scheduled PAP summit.' He looked at Brad and spoke slowly, 'Peace … and … Prosperity.'

On the screen in front of them, the men saw an image of the Nova Megacity. It was bigger than Alpha, more than two miles long and a mile wide. Its fifteen deck levels curved to create a crescent moon shape. A waterfall cascaded from the aircraft landing area on the top level, down into a series of beach pools and reefs then through the roof of a casino deck to the lower portion of the city where it was pumped back up skyward. Beachside palm trees moved gently in the breeze. Nova was a rest and recuperation city where needy and deserving executives went to let their hair down and behave badly. The upper decks were augmentation centres, hospitals and spa levels. Much of the global restorative and enhancement practices took place there. The old saying was that other cities reaped, so that Nova could sew.

Charles looked at the images disdainfully and then turned away. 'Apparently, they have something special to talk to us about.' He looked around the table at the expectant faces. 'And Alpha says, bring it on … yes … gentlemen clear the decks, it's full steam ahead!'

The other men smiled brightly at the tired joke; Charles strode out of the room. He waited until the door slid shut and tapped his earpiece.

'Did you watch them?'

'Yes, Charles.' said his mother.

'I didn't see anything, and their biometrics gave nothing away.'

'So, what you're telling me, Charles in your usual roundabout fashion is …'

'It's none of us. Its external! My money's on Nova. I am sure they're the ones that discovered her. Don't forget they have the capacity to scramble our systems and down our drones. They're racing here for a PAP because they've got a devious little plan.' He stopped to draw breath and wipe spittle from his chin.

'Let me make myself clear, you can do anything with Nova. But first I want my daughter and granddaughter here, with me, alive.' His mother's voice was clinical in its clarity.

'Yes.' Charles tapped his earpiece and walked along the corridor, his face a mask of calm.

• • •

Angel worked on her patch for two days. Cheryl had let her select a piece of felt from the store. There were sheets of brown, green, red and yellow, but she chose a square of natural fabric.

'Sewing isn't my thing,' she confessed quietly to Cheryl.

'Just put your heart into it.'

And so, she did. It was a star, the size of her palm. It had eight points, four long and four short … like a compass. She embroidered it with tiny spirals of black thread and in the centre, she stitched the silver locket that had been given to her by one of the Star People on the coast. She had polished it until it sparkled. She drew a teardrop on a piece of paper carefully torn from the corner of her father's letter and placed it inside the heart-shaped locket.

On the third evening, she asked the women where they wanted her to put it. They crowded around her to look at it and then after a moment one of the women said they should make space in the centre. There was a murmur of agreement, so she pulled up a chair and with infinite care, moved a patch to the side. They watched Angel sew her star in place. When she stepped back, they all gazed at it in silence.

'They gather around your star … our lost children …' whispered one woman.

'Telling us that it's time for things to change,' said another.

• • •

Angel began to feel that it was time to move on. The Beguinage was well defended, and York was rebuilding its walls around them. She spoke to Miriam, who offered links to other communities where she could hide, but Angel declined. She had decided to ask Raph to come and get her.

On her last morning, the women led her blindfolded into the refectory. She could sense that they were nervous. Hands positioned her, then took away her scarf, she opened her eyes and gasped. A slender line of thread radiated from her star to every single patch. The effect was of a massive starburst. It powerfully connected her to every woman and every single lost child.

'Do you like it?' asked Zette, breathlessly searching her face for approval.

'I have never been more honoured or proud,' said Angel. 'It's beautiful, thank you.'

'Will you come back?' asked one of the small children touching her hand.

'How can I not. My heart is here.' The star blurred as tears filled her eyes.

CHAPTER NINETEEN

Raph and Angel stood on a towpath, knee deep in canal water and lifted their canoes over their heads. She peered into the fog. Her breath dampened her face. They were in the centre of Leeds, or so Raph had said, but she could see nothing of it. The sweat across her shoulders cooled and she shivered. He indicated that she should follow him. They moved along the canal side then turned and waded to the left.

Gradually, shapes began to solidify. What seemed, at first, to be a wall on her right, transformed into boarded-up arches. The tops of the brick parapet ran higher than a house above her head and stretched far out into the mist. He said that these were the units beneath the viaducts where the city's trains used to run, but that when the world stopped refining diesel, trains had stopped rolling. Long before then, being amongst strangers had been a contagion hazard; without medicine, it had become deadly to travel at all.

He led her over a roughly constructed footbridge and whispered that it wasn't far now.

'I'll show you the city or what's left of it, in the morning.'

They continued to climb up a gentle gradient; the canal water receded into shallow puddles. He unlocked a wire mesh compound gate in front of one of the arches, waited until she had stepped through and then locked it. Raph indicated that she should put her canoe next to his near the wall and hid them with a sheet of tarpaulin.

A barred and bolted panel of sheet metal and wood filled in the high curve in front of them. Saplings had nestled themselves into the broken tarmac and soil along the base of the wooden infill. He pushed the thin branches aside, unlocked a door and stepped through.

'Step high, there's a flood shield at the bottom.'

Angel stepped over the barrier into the darkness and then he locked and bolted the door behind her. The building smelled damp and sour. Raph lit a lamp and held it up for her to see. The space that they were in was ten strides deep, and half-full of brick rubble and scrap metal.

'Welcome to number sixty-nine.'

'Thank you,' said Angel unsure of what to say. She supposed that at least they were undercover. She looked at him. 'Why sixty-nine?'

He smiled and shrugged, 'There's a sign on the wall outside. Follow me, it gets better.' As they moved behind the pile of broken bricks, she noticed that the fallen rubble had been shaped to form a strong defensive barrier. The floor was broken, and dusty concrete crunched as they walked.

Above, the roof was too dark to see, but she could smell bats. He stepped through a hole in the wall into the next archway. He paused to light another lamp, hung it on the wall then moved on to light one more. In the half-light, Angel could see that he had draped curtains like a tent, across the roof to lower it and make it easier to keep warm. There were strips and patches of carpet on the floor. Two sofas were positioned around a woodstove and a jumble of old furniture was stacked near a pile of firewood. In a far corner against the wall was a garden shed, standing on stacked bricks; high enough off the ground to deter rats, she supposed. She could see the sparkle of broken glass underneath the base.

Angel shrugged her backpack off and put it by the sofa, then walked over to peer through the shed window. He had hung up a lace curtain, so she cupped her hands and leaned forward. It was full of food; stored and dried. She heard a click and turned around. Raph was lighting the fire.

'Better dry off before you get chilled,' he said as he pushed scraps of wood kindling deep into the belly of the stove. The glow from the flames made his hair look like it was on fire. He turned and caught her looking at him, she looked away, and he smiled.

'Put your wet clothes on this rack. There's a blanket on the sofa to wrap yourself in, until the place warms up.' He placed a kettle and a pan of porridge on the stove top. Then he pulled a wooden chair from the pile of old furniture waiting to be burned, tested it, and indicated that she should come and sit closer to the heat.

• • •

She slept well on the sofa; it was long enough for her to stretch out and the armrest made a good pillow. She woke to the sound of running water and birdsong. Pulling her blanket around herself, she sat up and saw that her dry clothes were stacked on a chair close by.

The stove had gone out, but there was light filtering through a curtain hanging in the corner of the room. Raph was nowhere to be seen. She dressed, then pulled the curtain aside and stepped out into his garden.

A ladder was leaning against the wall. Looking up she was curious to see that, there were about ten old washbasins hung on the wall in a zigzag pattern. She walked over to take a closer look. They were bolted to the brickwork and painted black; pipes ran from each basin to the one below. The top ones were fed water from a pipe running over the top of the parapet. Underneath the basins, standing on the weed-riven tarmac, were a row of baths, irrigated from the lowest basins and some rain butts.

Raph had planted hanging trailing plants in the sinks like strawberries, tomatoes and beans. Tap-rooted plants like carrot and parsnip as well as cauliflower and potatoes grew in the baths. He'd also dug out holes in the concrete at the bottom of the wall and planted fruit trees. Cordoned apple and peach trees spread their limbs out against the warm south-facing wall. Raspberry and blackberry canes grew wild in the patch beyond the baths. Angel was impressed; he had built himself a vertical garden. She reached out and pinched a raspberry from one of the canes and savoured its perfume before tasting it.

Raph's head appeared over the top of the parapet wall, he smiled and beckoned her up.

'So, this is where the apple that you left me came from, is it?' she said as she stepped from the ladder on to the railway line. The wind was brisk and cool, she pulled her jacket tight around her body. Raph turned off a tap that had been running from one of two large tanks of rainwater into a conduit that ran over the parapet into the basins. She could see that it would seep slowly through on to the next and the next until it had reached the baths and trees on the ground. On the far side of the track five solar panels were leaning against the wall. He had planted herbs between the rusted train tracks.

'Help yourself to gooseberries, they need eating.'

She picked a handful of plump purple berries and put one in her mouth. It popped when she bit into it, then filled her mouth with a fragrant sweet pulp. She was nipping the stem from the next one when Raph spoke.

'You like sour?'

'I like fresh berries; they remind me of home.'

'I've got fresh strawberries in that tub over there, but the rhubarb is past its best.

'Clever stuff. Don't people steal your food?'

'Nope. I don't have neighbours.' He looked up and smiled; there were white lines in the sunburn around his eyes, she hadn't them noticed before.

'Show me Leeds?'

He stood next to her and pointed out the canals, the station, the wharf, the buildings standing in water, and the tower blocks and scrubland that marked out the old road system. She could see where invasive tree roots had broken up the tarmac on the roads and car parks; making ways for other opportunistic plants to move in and begin to create a city centre forest. She'd never been in a big city before it must have been so noisy.

'Can't people see you?'

'Nobody to see me. There's the occasional looter, but they wouldn't be able to see up here unless they went into one of the tower blocks, but they're really not safe.'

Angel looked at the tower blocks more closely. Sheets of cladding hung from the tower blocks like waterfalls. He explained that extreme and relentless rain had penetrated and destroyed the fixings. She asked Raph, why the top floor windows in the tower blocks were all smashed out.

'Heat islands,' he explained. 'Hot air built up in the city centre and rose up the towers like chimneys, there was no way to ventilate the top floors. Plus, the tower walls themselves absorbed masses of heat from the sun. The people up there died when the power stopped. No lifts, no air con … they cooked.'

He told her how quickly the city had died; no transport meant no food was brought in, or fuel for cars to get out. People stopped going to work, they couldn't get there, besides there was no pay and nothing to buy. Everything stopped and the lights just went out. At first it went quiet, then people realised there was no help on the way, and they got scared. Then the fighting started. Some people just walked away, but there was nowhere to go, it was the same the world over.'

'That's when the big pandemics started, I suppose?' said Angel.

'Yes, measles, whooping cough, flu, cholera came in waves. On top of that people were dying of starvation.'

'My mother died from complications of the measles, I was only small,' said Angel. She looked at him for a moment and then asked, 'Where are you from Raph? Why are you here?'

She watched him pull a strapless wind-up watch out of his pocket and hold it up to his ear.

'Quick, we need to speak to Mani.'

He led her down the ladder and back inside, instead of going into the living area he stepped into a cold dark room in the next arch. The floor was strewn with dead leaves and dust. Rusted machinery as if from an old car repair shop littered the floor and walls.

He walked into the darkness, trailed his fingers against the flaking paintwork, and caught hold of a piece of rope that hung down from the roof. It had been tethered to a nail in the wall. Angel's eyes adjusted to the light and she watched the rope run through his fingers and a grey leather brief case slide into view. Raph flicked a switch on the far wall. A blue-white electric light flickered and clicked, then cast a cold light around the room.

'Save you falling into the pit!' he said indicating a deep rectangular hole in the floor behind them.

'Good hiding place,' said Angel peering up into the darkness of the archway roof. Two racks were suspended from the ceiling on ropes and pulleys. Jointed and salted meat hung curing from one, the other held a bicycle and what looked like camping gear.

Raph lifted a battered tablet out of the briefcase. He disconnected an auxiliary battery and nodded to Angel, indicating that she should come and stand next to him.

'Mani wants to talk to us at midday. We're a bit late.' He touched his thumb on a sensor and the tablet woke up.

'Good, there's something I need to ask her.'

Raph glanced up at Angel and raised an eyebrow.

'She intercepted messages that said someone was interested in me. That's why they sent you to help, right?'

He nodded as he typed Mani's code.

'If it was my relatives, I think that they would have just come and got me, I mean why involve Reapers? So, if it wasn't them, who was it who found me and why were they looking?'

'Good question, let's see.'

'Do you know?'

He turned to look at her; 'My sister doesn't confide in me. She never did. Besides the less we all know the safer the network is. I just do my part, but it's a good question and we need to know the answer.'

Mani's face appeared on the screen.

'Morning you two! What prompted the move, Angel?'

'Felt right.'

'Just as well. The good leaders of York just insisted on searching the place again. Apparently, they demanded it before including the Beguinage in the city's final defence plan. Your friends are locked in safe and sound now. Nowhere better.'

'That's good, how are the plans for-?' began Raph.

'Mani, who found me?' Angel interrupted.

'What? He did.'

'No, I mean who found me in the first place?'

'Ah … we monitor all of the Offshores' comms. One of the other Elite groups had been looking for you.'

The hair stood up on the back of Angel's neck. 'But why?'

'Don't know. Blackmail? Trade? Power? What else is there?'

'So, I was going to be a weapon to use against my family?' Just like now, she thought.

'Got to go,' said Mani abruptly. Her face disappeared.

Surprised and exasperated, Angel looked at Raph; he held his hands up in submission.

'Never talks for more than ninety seconds. Drives me crazy!' He closed his tablet. 'Often less than that. We'll get more out of her next time. Let's eat,' he said with a smile.

CHAPTER TWENTY

'You're going to do it aren't you?' Raph asked gently. They were sitting together on the sofa watching blue-tipped flames lick the air above a glowing piece of wood. Their feet were stretched out toward the stove and they were sleepy. Sparks blossomed and vanished as the log collapsed into the heart of the fire. Angel turned to face Raph, 'How did you know?'

'I just sensed it.'

'Well if Mani had lied to me, I would have left two days ago.'

'And you think she didn't?' he asked softly, resting his hand near hers.

'Do you?'

'No, that was her telling the truth, or as much of it as you need to know.'

'That's what I thought.' She lifted his arm up so that she could curl in against his side. He stroked her microchip scar. It was shaped like a crescent moon. He kissed her shoulder.

'Sorry, I couldn't stop them chipping you. Not all of the Reapers knew that you were different. The factory ship did, they were waiting for you.'

'It's OK.'

'I managed to stop them inseminating you, though.'

'What!' She sat up and looked at him.

'Well, it's normal, if they think you might be a breeder, they take one shot in the van … sometimes with a syringe … if that doesn't catch, you get pumped with hormones and have one more chance on the ship. And if that doesn't work, you're parts.' He leaned forward, gave her shoulder a whisper of a kiss and pulled her back towards him. She rested her head against him.

'He broke his neck falling from the van.'

'Who did?'

'The one who was going to …'

Thank you,' she said staring into the fire. 'I'm sorry about your face.' The top arch of the R was still visible over the line of his beard.

'It's OK, I'll never need to shave again.' Raph kissed the top of her head.

Angel closed her eyes and thought that she had never felt more safe … or in more danger.

• • •

It was a cold morning; Venus hung inches above the derelict brewery that ran parallel to the viaduct. Dew hung from the chain link fence. A message had arrived the previous night; Angel was to be ready to go at dawn. She stepped into the yard and took a deep scenting breath; it was as if she were fixing the location in her mind. She had arrived in darkness and was leaving in darkness. She doubted that she would ever find her way back again.

Raph moved close to Angel's side and slipped an apple into her palm. A fleeting smile passed across her face. He nodded to the driver who was standing next to an idling car. It was black, and the headlights were slits of light focused on to the road. The driver beckoned her forward, told her to get into the back seat and pull the heat screens down to mask her heat signature.

They had said their goodbyes.

Angel looked out of the window for Raph; but he'd gone, the door was shut, all that she could see was a row of arches.

She watched in silence as they picked their way through the city. She couldn't believe that it could have been so big, and yet have died so completely. There were wide lakes of stagnant water. Buildings had been robbed out and gutted. Whole areas had been burned to the ground. It didn't look like there had been riots, just that closely packed buildings had been caught in a firestorm that couldn't be controlled. Roofless buildings had been taken over by trees. They pierced walls, ripped away gutters and leaned out through broken windows. People seemed to have just evaporated; the city was dead. But what surprised her most of all, was the silence.

• • •

'We're ready for you now,' said a young red-haired beauty technician. She reached around the door and held out a long silver-blue gown. Angel stood up and took it from her. It was astonishingly light, almost without substance; like water. She stepped into it and pulled it up, the halter neck and cut-away shoulders flattered her shape but left the scar on her shoulder clearly visible. The young woman fastened the clasp at the back and tied a blue and silver scarf around Angel's head, trailing one end over her shoulder. It hid her short hair and made her pale blue eyes seem even more startling. Finally, she was handed her a pair of heeled shoes to strap on. Walking was impossible. So, they agreed that she could just carry them. She led Angel into the next room.

Angel was asked to walk in front of a large blue screen, gazing into an imaginary distance. A fan blew her dress and the tail of her scarf out behind as if she was in a stiff wind. She was told to smile, wave and frown and to hold up a thin-stemmed glass. As the morning progressed her costumes and the locations on the blue screen changed. Finally, the dress was ripped. Her face was painted to look bruised and swollen, and her lip to look as if it was bleeding.

'Well that should do for now. All we need is some DNA and some hair and we are done.'

• • •

'We got what we needed.' Mani told Raph. 'But she's quite an innocent, is our Angel, we had to coach her.'

'Are the pictures good enough? Will they work?'

'Yes, we should be able to use then.' Mani peered down the webcam. 'I still would have preferred actually getting her on to Nova. It's unmistakable.'

'No, it's too …'

'I know … dangerous. We don't want her in the hands of another bunch of Elites. But, remember, it's still our backup plan if this doesn't catch her family's attention.' Mani pressed a key and her face disappeared. Raph sat looking at the screen for a long moment, then with a sigh, he walked out into the night and stared at the crescent moon.

• • •

Angel was shown around her new hiding place. Salma her guide, hummed as she walked. She said it used to be a hospital, and Angel had to take their word for it; she had never seen one before. The building was four floors high and built in the shape of a capital H. All the long rooms had been totally gutted. The ceilings had been ripped out; there were piles of rubble where wires, pipes, doors and cables used to be. She could detect the unmistakable sweet oily smell of cockroaches and see piles of brown egg casings in dark corners.

She had been worried about meeting other people, but Salma assured her that it was unlikely. They had learned to stay away, there were no drugs, and no care, the only thing they took away from these places was death and disease. People had believed that the hospital labs were the source of anthrax and smallpox. It wasn't true, but they didn't take any chances.

They followed a yellow and green stripe on the wall. The corridors seemed to go on forever. Salma indicated that they were going into the last room on the right. A large piece of paper was stuck to the door with cracked brown tape. It was a price list for hours stayed, collections and deliveries.

'It's the mortuary.'

Angel stopped walking.

'Relax it's been empty since well before the crash. People couldn't afford the fees.' She held the door open for Angel. 'Damn viruses wiped out hundreds of thousands, staff and patients alike. In the end, nobody could pay, they had to burn them right here. They even had to dig mass graves for the ashes.' She gestured to a weed-strewn mound outside. 'And then, when it got worse, they just dumped them.'

'Is it safe?'

'Yes, well, as safe as anywhere. The exit's through there.' she gestured. 'We thought we could use the relatives' room … still got chairs.'

Ragged curtains let shafts of sunlight stroke the floor, dust motes drifted slowly across the room, disturbed by their entrance. Angel could see a massive hole in the wall where storage units had been ripped away.

'OK, if you need to get out quick, use that door.' said Salma.

'Are you expecting trouble?'

'Well there is still the ransom … but we need to stay here, until we see if they bite and how hard. No point in roaming about.'

'Anything I can do?'

'Mani wants me to teach you how to paint your face.'

'Whatever for?'

'In case we need to repeat the pictures in a hurry, and … for plan B.' Angel looked at her quizzically. 'In case the photos don't hook them, and we have to get you on one of their ships.'

Angel learned how to make her eyes look bigger, deeper, bluer, wider, whiter; her lips look riper, fuller, wetter, swollen; her cheeks look redder and her skin look like it had never seen daylight. She stuck on lashes, nails, jewels, masked her vitality and her youth and in the end, herself.

'I need fresh air!' she said wiping, pulling and stripping off attachments and coatings from her hands and face.

'Careful, it took months for me to find this stuff. Give it to me!' said Salma holding out her hand. Angel ripped off the last nail and flexed her hand into a strong fist.

'I'm sorry, I just hate it, my skin crawls. It smells like dust and old flowers.'

'That's perfume!'

'What is it supposed to smell like?'

'Don't know, but they expect it. The more unnatural they smell the richer they are!'

'I cannot believe that I am related to these people!'

'You'd better.'

Angel walked out into the corridor and punched a door handle, a vertical bar slid down and the door opened on to a quadrangle. It was almost completely full of a tumbling mass of thorns. Years of dry leaves had made a crust on the concrete slabs. To her right, she noticed that a dog rose had fought its way to the top of the blood-and-rust tipped brambles. Its simple white flower and golden heart was seeking the late sun. She reached up and cupped it in her hand; its fragrance was simple, sweet and light. She plucked a petal and popped it in her mouth. It lay cool and fresh on her tongue; she took a deep breath and went back inside.

CHAPTER TWENTY-ONE

'They're scanning us sir.'

'What? Who is?' Alistair Groves, the leader of the Nova Offshore city, put his coffee down and tapped his screen. It came to life and showed the face of his head of security. They were steaming north to rendezvous with the Alpha and Eden for their Peace and Prosperity summit.

His head of security was not a man to overreact, and Alistair was instantly alert. His screen flicked to a map of his city. He could see the curve of the decks and the iconic waterfall, plummeting past floor after floor of entertainment levels. Treatment suites were on the other side, with calming, healing views out to sea.

'They're scanning us top to bottom. They spent some time checking out the main city and now they're focusing on one of the themed recreation areas. They've done riverboat, titanic rail and tea clipper levels in real close up and now they're on the ocean liner level ll.'

'What are they looking for?' The screen zoomed in to the fantasy liner deck levels.

'Don't know, people hire whole levels for parties. And as you know sir, it can get wild and nasty. Do you think they're planning a special party?'

The screen showed a long sleek deck of dark wood and fresh white paint; elegant rails ran around the outer edge, topped by polished wooden handrail. Low steamer chairs lined the deck. Matching cushions and blankets were folded neatly and stacked on each seat. Doors opened from the balcony on to softly lit rooms.

'We let the rooms on that level by the hour.'

'Have they ever scanned us before?' asked Alistair.

'No.'

'Why now?'

'New toy, sir?'

'Let's hope so. Keep me posted if they get more intrusive.'

Alistair put the head of security on hold and touched an icon in the top right corner of his screen. His screen turned unexpectedly white. Curious, he leaned forward and listened to the sound of whispering. Then he shouted, 'Turn your camera round!' He heard scuffling, steps and a door being closed. 'Turn your damn camera around!' The picture jerked and then settled on a face.

'Mayor speaking,' said a flushed middle-aged man.

'I know who you are! I damn well called you!' barked Alistair.

'Sorry sir, what can I do for you?' said the mayor as he brushed his hand across his cheek to check for moisture.

'We dock with Alpha tomorrow morning; Eden is right behind us.'

The mayor nodded, he knew about the convention plans and wondered where this was going. 'Alpha's been scanning us. We don't know if they're testing our security or just got a new toy. Either way it's beyond our protocol agreement, it could be hostile, and I don't like it. Be alert and ready. All of your staff need to be briefed and on guard. See to it!' Alistair ended the call.

The mayor checked the time on his screen, turned it to the wall and messaged his visitor to come in and finish the job.

• • •

'She's gone sir, scanners can't find her,' said Brad. 'We can see where she was; there by the railings looking out to sea. Her scarf was blowing out behind her.' The two men studied the image of Angel in a silver-blue gown, holding on to the railing of the liner deck.

'You sure it's her?'

'Biometrics match and you can see the tag scar on her shoulder.'

Charles ran his hands through his hair in exasperation. 'How the hell did Nova get to her before we did? Come to that how did they know about her at all!' He looked more closely. 'Is she all right?'

'Well she looks nervous; she smiles like she's been told to. She's got a drink but she's just holding it. I'd say she's worried about drugs.'

'Show me the last one again.' Brad flicked through images of Angel, the final one showed her curled up on the floor, face bruised and swollen, dress ripped, and fresh blood running from her lip and nose. The carpet was deep blue and had a large golden letter N inside a ring of laurel leaves, woven into the pattern. This was his niece and she was being violated on Nova.

Charles stepped into the corridor and pressed speed dial on his phone.

'Mother, we know where she is.'

'Good, is she well? Can I see her?'

Charles closed his eyes and spoke quietly. 'Nova's got her. We've managed to intercept some photographs of her.'

'God no! How?'

'They're playing it clever; they haven't let on and they don't know that we know. Mother, we've scanned their ship and we're narrowing things down.'

'See you do … no matter what state. We need her …'

Katrin hung up and then softly added, 'DNA,' to her image in the mirror.

• • •

Alistair pushed his chair back and walked to the window. The sky was so heavy it felt like it was pressing down on the flat sea. He felt hot, and the air conditioning didn't seem to help. Forecasts for the weather in the next few days predicted sunshine and light breezes; it was just a matter of this evil weather moving on.

Spread out in front of him, the roads of Nova shone white like well-healed suture scars. Growth and self-improvement sprang from every corner of his city. His family had conglomerated medical, health and fitness interests, from cradle to grave. Moving to Offshores had allowed them to go up market and off the legal page. Now there were no limits. They were the 'go to' place and he wrote the rules … well he would, if he felt like it.

He stretched, took a breath and focused on mindfulness for a second. He wondered how bookings were going. These conventions allowed people from other Offshores to get their fixes; it was his busiest time of the year. He kept a swift and efficient supply of donors and the best skin, best noses, best hair, lips, livers, kidneys, ovaries … whatever … the list was endless.

He was thinking of the long game; it was obvious that sources would dry up eventually. Malnutrition, disease, ignorance and over reaping would mean that supply would get degraded. And this was where his new idea, a revelation for his conference showpiece would really make an impact. In the search for the perfect, the flawless, the enhanced body of the future, Nova was beginning to plan how to engineer the perfect donor. He would soon have a supply of the perfect products for this fashion season … hell, for this month. Each one genetically identical to the customer, so no rejection, no drugs.

Alistair smiled at the sky, he was a proud man, and he deserved to be. He stretched his shoulders and thought about his competition. Alpha was his main source of parts, they dominated the land and sea, and ran the reaping squads. They'd always been one step ahead: the first to feed conflict to bring down a government, the first to depopulate, the first to move into industrial-scale trafficking. But not this time, and he couldn't wait to see their faces.

He paused to consider Eden, the third element. It wasn't in the same class as Alpha or Nova. They ran manufacturing and production. They had slave enterprises on the main continents. True they fed, clothed and fuelled the elite world, but that was 'service' for god's sake. Nova was moving up a notch, and soon he wouldn't need the others, but boy were they going to need him. Nova was his city, his family business, and he was ready to make a game-changing move. With no waste, no shoddy goods and total control over the supply chain he was going to make a killing. He smiled to himself. After all, a hostile takeover is always good for the soul. God, he loved success, it made him feel divine.

A transport helicopter buzzed past his window and interrupted his reverie. They had been bringing in supplies and extra staff all morning. He could see an army of people moving along the decks with linen, cleaning materials, and food supplies. Then he caught his reflection in the window and blew himself a half kiss of appreciation; it was difficult, because his lips were newly bee stung. So, he sighed instead.

CHAPTER TWENTY-TWO

The narrow Cornish roads were like green impenetrable tunnels. The driver had dropped Angel off about thirty miles away. She walked through the night arriving for the dawn chorus.

The air was still and humid, she wiped her forehead, and looked around. A kingfisher darted across her eye line.

She was standing at the end of the road. Her shadow almost touched the water's edge. Small fish played in the warm shallows over a concrete causeway.

Rocky cliffs rose on both sides of the inlet and curved around the bay. This place felt more like home, it was wilder, fresher and never having been highly populated, there was less human desolation.

She saw a small stone house on a beach on the opposite bank. An elderly woman was dragging a rowing boat down towards the water. She waved to Angel, and then set off rowing across the bay.

Angel turned around to look at the small village that lined this side of the bay. The tidemark was level with the first-floor windows; the spring high tide must be really dangerous, she thought.

A movement in an attic window caught her eye. She saw the round face of a small child. It raised a hand to wave, just seconds before it was pulled back into the darkness.

The boat was close, Angel pulled off her shoes, waded into the shallows and took hold of the oar that was held out to her. The small fry darted into the shadows.

'Hello, I'm …'

'Best not to say.'

Angel put her bag in the boat.' You want me to row back?'

'No. You need to act like a passenger, I still ferry a little.' The woman waited until Angel was settled then she pushed off against the concrete slipway and began to row across to the house. Looking back, Angel could see the small almost deserted town clinging to the base of the cliff. Ahead, there was just the woman's house, sheltering against a backdrop of dense woodland. Out to sea, distant rocks pierced the sea, sending wide V's of white-lace froth racing towards the shore.

'The town hasn't died?'

'Almost. Those who are left scratch a living off the sea.'

The woman beached the boat on the firm wet sand and tied it to a long rope that was tethered to a stout tree trunk higher up the bank.

Three stone steps led them into the ground floor room of the cottage. A small fire burned in the hearth and beyond that in the corner Angel could just see stone steps spiralling up to the first floor. She brushed sand from her feet and pulled her shoes back on. The place smelled of cooking and woodsmoke.

'I keep the fire on to try to dry the place out. Bet you're hungry?'

Angel nodded vigorously; the food smelled good. Her

eyes gradually adjusted to the half-light and she could see metal hooks fixed high up on the walls and ceiling. Plastic folding chairs and a table hung like dead wood. The woman lifted two chairs down, then moved into a small kitchen. She chopped a fish into chunks and tossed it into a simmering broth.

Angel walked over and touched one of the windows, the glass had been painted over. The woman explained that the river regularly rose above the ground floor windows and so nothing like curtains were any use. She didn't trust the people across the bay and so paint seemed to be the best solution. She turned back to her cooking, rubbed some flour and fat together, then dropped the dumplings into the stew to cook.

'When's the next big tide?' Angel asked, glancing out through the half open door.

'My father used to talk about storms of the century, and then we had storms of the year, but I can tell you, that there's one brewing that we'll remember forever.' She paused to find a lid for the pan. 'A deep, deep weather front is sucking up a massive storm from the west and tomorrow it's coming straight at us.'

• • •

'Are we ready to roll?' Alistair said to Nova's head of hospitality.

'Yes sir, we've just finished populating Whitechapel Lane. We've got "mop up" covered 24/7.'

'And the others?'

'Both Titanic and the cruise liner, sir? Already done.'

'That's good; they're on the same levels as the enhancement suites. We can wheel them round before the drugs have worn off.' The men laughed; 'We give the punters what they want, before they've even thought of it. We're the specialists!'

The head of hospitality left the room and Alistair stooped to check his reflection in the window. He was feeling so good about this.

• • •

On the ocean liner deck a woman in a cleaner's uniform stepped into cabin 632 and closed the door. She snapped on a pair of surgical gloves, took a piece of tape out of an envelope and used it to transfer Angel's fingerprints to the stem of a wine glass. She tapped it on the washbasin and the bowl separated from the stem. Careful not to smudge the prints, she tucked the stem behind the pedestal Then, she took a vial out of her pocket and using a small straw, blew wide arcs of blood splatter across the mirror and wall. Strands of Angel's hair were slipped behind the bed head. Then she put the rest of the broken glass and the vial in her bucket; half filled it with water then stepped out on deck and threw the contents into the ocean. The webcam inside 632 clicked back into action. She moved on to 633 and began cleaning.

An urgent email arrived at Alpha's security desk.

• • •

'Nova will be docked and locked first, Eden two hours later,' reported the ship's captain.

Charles nodded and leaned forward conspiratorially. 'Good, now listen carefully because this is a bit unusual. I want you to set the undocking system so that ours overrides theirs. They both leave, only when I say so.'

'OK,' said the captain cautiously. 'Won't they complain, sir?'

'If they behave, they won't know. If they don't, they'll have more to worry about than a prolonged "merger". Let me know when it's completed.'

'Nova *and* Eden, sir?'

'Yes, both. We have a surprise for them. Wake me, when you've got Nova.' Charles walked out on to the balcony. The night was heavy and starless; the cloud cover seemed to be backlit. It gave off a faint glow of amber. He noticed an electric tang to the air. It felt strange, but he wasn't worried; together the cities were five miles across, and they were so well stabilised that no weather could ever interrupt business. Besides, he knew that it would be clear and bright by morning.

2-30 a.m. His clock flashed and then buzzed. Charles asked sleepily if Nova was locked down.

'Don't know sir, this is security. Thought that you might want to see this.'

A stark image was projected on to his ceiling.

'What is it?'

'Looks like she was beaten up in the bathroom.' Images flashed on Charles' ceiling. 'We found this blood spatter, a broken glass stem with her prints on and strands of her hair. I would say that this is the room where the photos were taken.'

'How'd we find them?' Charles was wide-awake now.

'I got some people to infiltrate Nova's comms. We're going to find her, sir, that blood's not more than a couple of days old. And by the way, she's definitely yours.'

'Thank you, said Charles; the possibility of sleep was long gone, white-hot fury coursed through his veins. The image was gone but he lay glaring at the place on the ceiling where Angel's blood had been.

CHAPTER TWENTY-THREE

Angel borrowed the rowing boat to survey the bay. She wanted to see where survivors might try to land. She could see that cliff paths had already been blocked with boulders and tree branches. And at high, clear points, there were piles of rocks ready to be used as weapons.

She paused in the middle of the estuary and looked out to sea. The sky and the sea were charcoal grey; a thin black line marked the far horizon. As far as she could see white breakers raced towards land. Gulls shone silver against the dark sky.

The woman had said that, out in the Atlantic, a monster storm was brewing and the wreckage and survivors of the Offshores were going to be swept this way. Star people and volunteers were preparing a special kind of welcome.

She turned the boat and began to row back to the house. On her right, she noticed an unblocked animal track, hidden behind a thick tangle of thorns, and made a note of its position. Nearby, on the cliff top there was a dead tree, a marker for people looking for a safe place to get up the cliff face. She decided to walk along there and have a closer look.

• • •

Charles had watched the third city, Eden, being hydraulically anchored into place. It was the smallest of the three Offshores, a latecomer to the movement. It bought Alpha's raw materials, iron, oil, coal, uranium, stateless slaves, and used them to manufacture whatever was needed. They built the Offshore cities, made weapons, made the tools that he used to harvest his assets. Eden didn't go in for art or design, or commerce, because it had no style, no class. They endlessly rebuilt their city to reflect its business. This time it was a showroom.

There was a souk, a bazaar, a market, and for tomorrow, an exhibition and conference centre. Eden was just a floating shopping mall.

The three cities had merged just off the northern edge of the Bay of Biscay. Their decks dovetailed together, and all told they made an island that was five miles across and almost as wide. It felt solid and strong. In line with intercity agreements, all but essential functions and life support ceased, and a common computer steerage system took control. It wasn't as if they were going anywhere, they were home.

Charles touched his tie, and for a second the sun dazzled him, then slid behind a heavy mass of low cloud. He checked himself in the mirror, practiced a greeting smile, then picked up his tablet and stepped into the corridor. Game on!

He strode, calm and with purpose, to his car. Processional music calmed his breathing. He reclined his seat and pressed back so that it could better caress his spine. He closed his eyes and rehearsed his welcome speech.

Alpha was the first and the best Offshore, it was always the host, welcoming the others 'home.' His ear-com buzzed, and he tapped it lightly.

'Locked down, sir, no one seems to have noticed. We have search parties on Nova, looking for your niece, as we speak.'

'Good.'

'Sir?'

'What?'

'We have some reports of sickness, sir, sea sickness.'

'Don't be ridiculous, we're stabilised to hell.' Charles sat up to look out of the window, but the deeply smoked glass only showed his reflection. He tilted his head and ran his finger along his temple to lift and tighten his skin.

'It might be something to do with the anchoring being more "solid".'

'Say that it's a bug or bad food. Find a worker with a disease. That can't be difficult!'

'Will do. Finally, sir … the weather.'

The car crossed on to Eden and pulled up in front of the conference centre.

'I haven't got time to discuss the bloody weather! Sort it!' He slapped his earpiece and waited for his driver to open the door. He expected to see an audience crowding around the edges of the red carpet. But instead there was a solitary doorman. He could see a crowd of people waiting inside the sumptuous complex.

He got out of his car and strode across the carpet. The air was still and sticky, his lungs felt unnaturally hot. He looked again, the man was not a doorman, it was Brad! Charles tried to push him out of the way.

'Sir, we need to talk.'

Charles ignored the urgency in the man's voice and hissed for him to get out of the way.

'Sir there's something wrong with the weather …' Charles pushed him away, but Brad stepped back in front of him. '… forecasts. They're rigged, sir. There's a storm coming. We should break up and head for shelter.'

Charles stopped and looked at Brad, his collar wasn't right, his skin was too normal, he was sweating like a pig, and he had a scar where there had been a boil on his neck, for god's sake. This man was … and then he realised … a Nova spy! They knew that he had the photographs and the evidence. Brad was trying to play for time. They wanted to decouple and get away with his property!

He leaned towards Brad and spoke very low 'Get … out … of … my … way.'

Brad stepped aside.

'I'll deal with you later.'

Charles opened the door and swept into air-conditioned heaven and the embrace of his audience.

Brad watched Charles disappear into the building, checked his watch then turned and ran to the heliport.

• • •

Angel had learned that the woman was called Rina. Throughout the evening, they had taken turns to row across to collect their visitors as they arrived. By dark, the house was filled with tired and footsore people, ready and prepared to defend the coastline. Angel stood on the doorstep listening to the chatter and keeping an eye on the village in case any latecomers appeared.

Rina strode out of the trees nearby and slipped into the house. She gestured for Angel to follow her.

'I've just had a message to confirm that they're locked together and what they don't know is that we have the key. A combined Offshore is going to face the biggest Atlantic storm in living memory. We have control of both their steering and docking systems.' She paused for the cheers to die down. 'They haven't got a single sailor who can read the weather. They've been fed fine weather forecasts for days, and no-one has had the good sense to look out of the window!'

'Where will it make land?' asked a man standing at the back of the room. Faces turned to look at him and then expectantly back to Rina.

'We expect that the bulk of it will break up on the rocks off Finisterre, but survivors and wreckage could hit us anywhere along our south west coast, Ireland or South Wales ... possibly Northern France. And we're ready for them!'

The room murmured its approval.

Rina continued, 'You need to be in position well before the storm hits, it's going to be like nothing that you've ever experienced before. You might need to tie yourself to something solid, there's rope outside. Take everything with you; this place may not be here in the morning. Rest for now, because the tide is turning.'

Angel smiled as the room erupted into cheers, then slipped outside into the fetid evening air.

• • •

Charles smiled warmly at the camera. His speech was being broadcast, across all three cities. The executives of Nova and Eden stood by his side. He spoke slowly to allow the sound systems to stay with him.

'My dear friends ... and family ... it gladdens ... my heart ...' He looked around and nodded, all eyes in the conference room were on him. '... to see you all ... again ... Let's make *this* summit ... be *the* one ... the *very best* merging ... of our fine cities ... and let it be ... the one where we all ... look back and say ...

I WAS THERE!'

The room burst into applause. He raised his hand for silence. 'And I say to every one of you ...' He leaned forward and added an extra note of sincerity to his voice. 'Welcome home my friends!'

The sound of applause echoed across the empty city streets. The camera swept across the happy upturned faces of the rapturous, invited audience.

The Eden leader slipped in front of the microphone and said, 'Time to get ready ...'

Alistair from Nova stepped forward and added, '... to party!'

The three leaders laughed and patted each other's shoulders. They left the room as if they were the greatest of friends, going their separate ways as soon as the door closed behind them.

The audience filed away quickly. The first night ball always had a theme and tonight required a lot of preparation. It always commemorated a lost country. This year it was Bangladesh.

CHAPTER TWENTY-FOUR

The combined, top-level executive committee sat around a large conference table. They were being hosted on Alpha this year. Each man had in front of him, a large bottle of Arctic Ice Water and a small bowl of exotic and rare fruit; a banana took pride of place on top. They were surrounded by a 360-degree 3D film loop of the aurora borealis. A single spotlight fell on Alistair, leader of Nova. He was responding to Alpha's opening speech. His agenda item was snappily called *Let's breed for success.*

There had been a ruffle of unease when he had started talking. People had thought that he was implying that the City leaders were failing to breed effectively. But now they understood that he was talking about the selective breeding of clones, the audience were in the palm of his hand. He was proposing that they create a refined genetic pool in order to match industrial demands and workforce tissue compatibility.

The energy in the room was building to a window-rattling climax and the camera scanned the happy admiring executives. Their smiling faces tracked across the bottom of the presentation screen. Charles looked up from his keyboard, saw that the camera was on him, and quickly smiled. Concern registered momentarily on the face of the man next to him, but then he too realised that he was on camera and mouthed an enthusiastic, 'Yes.'

Charles looked down at his comms pad.

–HAVE YOU FOUND HER YET?

–NO, SIR, STILL LOOKING

–FUCKING FIND HER

–MOTHER ARE YOU WATCHING THIS CLOWN? THEY'RE TALKING ABOUT CLONES BUT I THINK THAT THEY ARE GOING TO USE HER TO BREED A REPLACEMENT FOR A TAKEOVER!

–TO US? TO TAKE US OVER?

–WHAT ELSE? THAT'S WHY THEY WANTED TO CATCH HER, BEFORE WE FOUND HER!

He looked up from his screen and watched the light show on the walls. He had to agree that there were some good points. Reaping was getting to be more of a problem; the indigenous further north were less biddable than he liked. They were feckless and yet they appeared to be putting up some pathetic sort of resistance. But they weren't starving … yet. That could be arranged. Selective breeding might make better transplant material, and then the native population could be left to go feral. He could push them into land that he had no use for, to freeze, bake, or starve, who gave a shit?

Loud applause interrupted his thoughts; he smiled broadly and stood to lead the obligatory ovation.

He counted to thirty and nodded, the applause died down.

As things stood, this girl, the daughter of Lilith was the end of his family's bloodline. Unless she had brothers, or even older sisters, she would inherit Alpha, and if she was under the power of this bastard from Nova, who knew what might happen. The camera was on him again; it scanned his smile, his perfect smile. Was he overdoing it? He didn't want to look like a threatened ape; he let the sides of his mouth relax a little.

A silverback, he thought. I shall be a silverback.

• • •

That evening, Charles and his mother, Katrin, were at the top table on the premium level of the banquet along with the heads of other Elite families. Her implanted hair was long and black, and she was wearing a royal red sari with a golden top. Her hands were decorated with an intricate henna pattern and her bangles were encrusted with gems. A large ruby bhindi glistened on her forehead. She looked like a queen he supposed, or at least like one depicted on the latest fash-web. Did they used to have queens in Bangladesh? He smiled to himself, of course they did!

The lower floor level was a kaleidoscope of fabulous colours and glittering jewellery. The performers were exquisite, the music divine. Turbaned waiters in white uniforms rushed between tables serving food fit for kings.

Charles picked up his wine glass and looked around; people didn't seem to be eating much food, although the wine was moving fast. He had to admit that the floor did seem to be moving a little more than normal. The seaward windows led on to a large balcony. From his position, all he could see was rain running down the glass. He made a mental note to personally throttle the weather girl.

He nodded to a servant and indicated that the blinds should be closed. The man moved over towards the controls, and was standing, arm outstretched, when the floor seemed to rise up. He fell, skittering across the floor.

Bottles and ice buckets tumbled; the orchestra struggled to hold on to their instruments. Music sheets scattered. Limping, the servant moved over to the controls and closed the shutters.

Everyone looked at the top table; Charles lifted his glass and took a sip of wine as if to suggest that the man was drunk. People laughed nervously and raised their empty glasses.

The orchestra gathered their papers and began playing more loudly.

Still smiling Charles touched his comms pad

–WHAT THE HELL WAS THAT?

–GETTING ROUGH. STRUGGLING WITH THE STABILISERS

–'FIX IT

He slapped his comms pad off; it was time to raise the stakes. He gestured for Alistair to lean forward and smiled broadly, but spoke with venom,

'I know you've got her, and I know what you think you're going to do with her. But believe me you are mistaken. Your ship is under my control and you are going nowhere until you hand her over!'

'Got who?'

Charles was surprised to see a look of puzzlement on

Alistair's face. He looked lost for words. Then he watched him slowly put his napkin on the table and leave the banquet without saying a word.

Once in the restroom Alistair braced his back against the entrance door and rang his chief of staff.

'Alpha's searches, where did they focus?'

'Sea liner, deck, 623. Why?'

'No matter, test the docking.'

Alistair pinched his phone between his ear and shoulder and washed his hands, he was shaking the water off when his chief of staff answered.

'Nothing!'

'Nothing wrong?'

'No, no response, my controls are dead.'

'Listen, Alpha's locked us down. They're searching for some woman; I don't know who. You have got to get us free. Do whatever it takes.'

The ship lurched violently, and his face smashed against the mirror. He pushed himself up back up and checked for damage through his face print on the mirror. Fuck, that was close, he thought, checking his perfect nose. Bracing himself against the pedestal he straightened his jacket and smoothed his hair; then using the walls to steady himself, made his way back to the banquet hall.

He threw the doors back, and smiled his entrance smile, only to be met by chaos. Tables and chairs had been knocked over by the violent turbulence. He could see people helping each other up from the floor. The orchestra was trying to play calming music.

Something didn't feel right. He pushed his way over to the blinds and pressed the control switch.

There, framed for all to see were clouds. Not just ordinary storm clouds. Evil sulphur and black mountains of fury were barrelling towards them.

The room went silent. Mesmerized he watched the clouds double in size, and then double again. He waited for the spell to be broken, for someone to say that it was a joke … a part of the entertainment. But no one did. He stood transfixed as nature at its very cruellest, rose up and dwarfed the mega city.

It seemed as if someone was moaning. A deep and dreadful sound of grinding metal filled the room. It grew louder. His whole body vibrated. He struggled to breathe. Chandeliers shattered like raindrops on his head. A terrifying roar grew through his shoes, his chest, his head. He put his hands to his ears and screamed. A flash of electric blue light sent him reeling. Followed by more – too many to count. Then a solid wall of thunder hit the city.

Alistair searched for Charles, but he was gone. Bastard! What has he done? He turned back to the window. The sky was black … blacker than space … Relief! A starless night. Then ice-cold dread rose through him. It wasn't the sky. It was a monstrous wave.

• • •

Charles ran along the corridor, tripped and rolled, buffeted by another crash of thunder then picked himself up and ran. He stepped aside, to dodge a fire extinguisher that was bouncing towards him and then punched a quick-release handle of an emergency exit. Three tumbling and bucking decks down, an escape boat waited by his private jetty. The pilot handed him a life jacket and helped him to pulled it on over his silk suit. He strode to his seat and shouted, 'Give my mother two minutes, then we get out.'

'Two minutes?' bellowed his mother, as she pushed her way into the cabin. 'Go now!'

The cities screamed in agony. Metal ground against metal.

Their orange self-righting escape craft shot from the jetty and out into the hell-dark night.

'Life jackets and helmets on! Strap yourselves into your seats so tight you can't breathe and prepare yourselves for your worst nightmare!' shouted the pilot.

• • •

The call to abandon ship rang out across all the decks. People stood in disbelief for a second, then as one they screamed, and punched and scrambled over each other out into the howling night.

'Alpha can't unlock us; there's something wrong with their control systems. Some kind of override's system's jammed it,' the Nova captain shouted to Alistair over the roar of the storm. 'We're trying to move closer to land, to shelter from this …' He was lost for words. 'May God save our souls!'

Alistair threw down his phone and calmly walked to the window. He watched wave after wave, each one dwarfing the towers of Alpha, stack up and race toward them. He could see the thundering waterfall on Nova turn horizontal, then crash against the palm trees on the beach, bowling them off the deck and out into the night. Tents from the souk billowed and somersaulted up into the sky. He felt calm. When nothing is left to be done … do nothing. The air around him turned ice cold and he saw his last breath mist in front of his face.

The ocean fell on to the five-mile long island, folded it in half then drove it into the waiting cliffs of Finisterre.

• • •

Charles ripped his comms earpiece out, threw it across the floor and pulled his helmet back on. He glanced at his mother. Her Asian hair fanned out across her shoulders and her smooth neck arched as she stared defiantly though the black front screen. She reached up and wiped a thin line of blood from her cheek, her ruby bhindi was gone. She had ripped it from her forehead. He tugged on his harness with all of his strength to test that it was secure then rammed himself back against the seat.

The boat plunged into the wild sea and away from Alpha. The mega-city seemed to have bled large and small crafts. The sight of his Canary Wharf towers being crushed was almost unbearable. He hoped that a skeleton of his organisation would survive. Not the staff, they were easily replaced, but he hoped that the intelligence, the data, the knowledge could be retrieved. After all there were so many opportunities for profit in disaster, especially for the cool headed.

A wave punched into the side of their rescue boat and shot it tumbling under the water. There was darkness and a roaring slow-motion roll, and then another. They lost count … so they just waited … and then, at last, they breached the surface and sped away.

• • •

Angel pulled her coat across her body and tied it with a piece of rope. She was the last to leave the cottage. It took all of her strength to close the front door. Taking a deep breath, she turned into the wind and driving rain. Grasping tree after tree, she moved along the clifftop path. The wind punched her breath away as she stepped up on to the open headland. She staggered back and found herself pinned against the trunk of the dead tree that she had seen from the rowing boat. It felt like her hair was being torn out by the roots. The rain was horizontal and as hard as iron. She fought for breath as she lashed herself to the trunk and leaned back to support her head. Above her, the branches writhed white against the streaming black clouds and the wind roared in her ears. She prepared to endure the storm of a lifetime.

• • •

Dawn brought shadows instead of light. Waves boomed against the cliff face close below her, and sent vertical showers of salt rain, arcing over her head. The howling wind abated for a moment. She heard a crashing sound below and the ground shook. She fought to untie herself and edged forward. It looked as if a piece of the lower cliff side had been gouged away. She shielded her face from the updraft and glimpsed boulders as big as houses emerging and then disappearing under the waves. A trail of chalky water ripped inland along the foot of the cliff.

A sudden terrible wrenching sound came from directly behind, and she threw herself into the undergrowth. A dark and silent shadow passed over her head. Angel flattened herself to the ground and waited, alert and ready to run. When she looked back, there was a space where the tree had been; another piece of cliff was gone. She moved closer to the edge and saw the dead tree, shining white against the sea, upside down, its blunt dead roots close enough to touch.

Angel silently thanked the elements, that she hadn't been tied to the tree when it went over the edge, then crept into the hollow left by the roots, wrapped her arms around her shivering body and waited for the storm to pass.

She must have fallen asleep in the relative calm in the hollow, but she woke, instantly alert to the sound of small rocks tumbling down the cliff side. The tree roots were scraping against the side of the cliff, and she thought that she could hear voices. She searched around and found a newly fractured piece of rock; it was sharp and clean edged.

She peered over the cliff. An orange boat was loosely tied to the dead trunk. The rise and fall of the waves were too much for the length of rope and with each receding wave, the tree was being pulled down further into the water. She could see a man scrambling through the slippery wet branches. Close behind she thought that she could see another person.

Angel waited until his head was level with the top of the cliff and swiped him with the knife-edge of the rock. He cried out and fell arching backwards into the water. The next wave smashed his body against the rocks.

Her rock had split in half, so she dropped it and knelt to search for another amongst the debris. She could hear the tree shifting under someone's weight. She was just about to stand up, and try to push the roots into the sea, when her hand grasped a large piece of rock. She stood, raised her arm, and found herself facing a dark-haired woman, who was looking at her calmly.

'That's no way to greet your grandmother!'

The world spun to black.

CHAPTER TWENTY-FIVE

'Good news or bad news first, brother?'

'Good,' said Raph searching Mani's face.

'The cities sank off Finisterre. Fifty years from now they'll be a reef.'

'Bad?' said Raph scratching his beard. Mani paused; Raph leaned forwards and whispered, 'What?'

'We've lost Angel.'

Raph slumped back in his chair.

His sister spoke quickly. 'We thought she would be safe down there …'

Raph tried to speak but his throat had closed, he couldn't say the words. He coughed, then looked at Mani. 'By lost, you mean …?'

'We don't know, she was seen being carried away by a man and a woman.'

'Who?' Raph glanced up at his rucksack hanging above his head.

'Don't know, but look on the bright side, if she was dead, they would have left her. They put her in a vehicle. We're tracking.'

His next question was on his lips, but Mani said she would get back to him. The screen went black. He stood up and kicked his chair across the room. Then he strode outside, powered himself up the ladder to the railway line and howled into the receding storm.

He ripped up branches that had fallen in the storm, secured his ladder, checked his solar panels and the wall fixing of the plant basins. He lifted the baths ends on to blocks to aid drainage, chopped and stacked logs. By nightfall he was exhausted. She was everywhere. She surrounded him. The wet forget-me-nots were the colour of her eyes, the foliage and fresh air smelled of her hair. He strode into the room and held the blanket that she had used to his face. This was unbearable. He turned and switched on his computer. Mani's face appeared; she looked tired.

'News?' he demanded.

Mani raised an eyebrow. 'Got it bad, little brother?'

Raph shook his head to clear her words away, then glared at her. 'News Mani. What's happening?'

'Oh, OK. Well the system is in lockdown. The cities crashed, and we think the leaders went down too. Without them, there's …'

'Angel! About Angel!' he roared, unable to bear it any longer.

'Angel, yes. An army vehicle picked the three of them up. Charles the Alpha Exec was found floating in the estuary. We think the woman was Charles' mother. We found blood … we're testing it.'

'Are you still tracking them? Mani, tell me, please,' he implored.

'Brad is working on it,' she touched her screen and disappeared. Raph roared in rage. He gripped his screen ready to throw it across the room when it flicked back on.

'Army truck took her to …' She paused and looked away to confirm what she had just heard. Raph could hear a man's voice in the background say, 'Chequers.'

'Where?'

Mani listened to the man as he explained and then turned to Raph. She looked shocked. 'Chequers. Apparently, we still have a fucking Prime Minister.'

• • •

Angel lay on her bed. She calculated that it was four days since she had been caught; well at least that, it was two days since she had been allowed to wake up. The bump on her head was only a little tender, so she suspected that she may have been there longer.

The building was old, it had thick walls and the broad wooden floorboards creaked when she walked about. Her bedroom window was screwed shut. The view was one of countryside; neglected farmland perhaps, with deciduous woodland in the middle distance.

She was in a small locked room. At one end there was a wardrobe as tall as the ceiling. She guessed that the wood used to make it was as old as the building. Some of the panels had shrunk, one rattled when she closed the doors. It was full of women's clothes. She had refused to wear any of them. She wanted her old clothes back. They said that they weren't going to let her out of the room until she got dressed properly. It had been a stalemate, but now they had raised their game. They were refusing to feed her until she put some of their clothes on. She looked at the glass of water by her bed and sighed.

When she had first started to come around, she had felt eyes searching her face. Her skin still prickled at the memory. Apparently, the man that she had hit with the rock, had been her uncle. The woman who was studying her face was Katrin, her grandmother, and she didn't seem particularly upset by her loss.

Angel had never seen anyone so emaciated who wasn't close to death. It seemed that it was deliberate. She had never encountered such vanity.

There was a fresh wound in the middle of her grandmother's forehead; Angel supposed that it had happened when she was escaping from the city. She had thin white parallel lines of scars along her hairline and behind her ears. Her hair was unnaturally thick and black. But Angel stared the longest at the pre-adolescent skin of her grandmother's face.

'Which part of you is real?' she asked bluntly. Her grandmother blinked.

'Eyes. Hmm … irises. Well, all of it is real, just not mine until I bought it.' She ran her clawed finger through her locks, from her forehead to her crown and then flicked her head. Her hair was long and heavy, and so thick that it should have hissed as it moved.

'You have your mother's eyes, her ears … her hair,' she said as she reached out and touched a spike of Angel's hair. 'How is she?'

'Dead.'

The old woman dropped her hand. 'Dead? My Lilith, how?'

Angel saw her eyes glisten. 'Complications from the measles, they had no drugs.' Her grandmother sighed and smoothed out a crease in her skirt.

'Do you have any brothers or sisters?'

'No, just me.'

'Father?'

'Never knew him,' said Angel flatly.

'Children?'

'No.'

'Well, it looks like we just have each other, then,' said her grandmother through a grim smile. She stood and quietly left the room.

Tom, the servant who brought her water was kind. He tapped on the door and waited for her to say, yes, before he unlocked it and came in. He smiled and nodded at her. He was small and his freckled scalp shone through his thin white hair, but his eyebrows were thick and black. He had no scars that Angel could see. She imagined that he was mid-sixties, maybe.

She sat on the end of the bed, wrapped in a blanket and watched as he moved a copper jug from the windowsill to dust underneath and then polish his fingerprints from the jug handle. He hummed as he worked.

'What did you do to your leg?'

'Hmm?' He stopped and turned. His right leg was shorter than the left and he never put his heel down flat. 'Broke it when I was a boy. Didn't heal properly, it grew wrong.'

'I'm sorry,' said Angel.

'Thank you. I'm used to it now, although my other leg's giving me gyp.'

Over the days, they had had quick and quiet conversations. Angel learned that she was in a house called Chequers, home of the British Prime Minister. She'd never heard of one of those, so Tom explained that he led the country. He had lived in London, but when people began to starve there'd been riots, and so he moved here. When people had realised that he'd been paid by the Elites to let them pull their money out of the country days before the crash, things had got really nasty and he'd asked the army to set up camp here. He told her that her grandmother still supported the Prime Minister, in recognition of his loyal service.

One day she had asked him why he was here; he had thought a while before answering.

'Where would I go? I get fed, somewhere to sleep …'

'What are they planning to do with me?' Angel asked Tom on the morning of her third day without food.

'It's time you got dressed, came down and found out for yourself.'

'Can you get my old clothes?'

Tom shrugged his shoulders. 'They burned them.'

'I am not wearing anything out of that cupboard. Can you get me some trousers and a top of some sort, please?' Tom nodded and left the room.

Angel walked over to the window and looked out on to the rough meadowland. It had been raining and the heavy-tipped blades of grass sparkled in the morning sunshine. A blackbird screeched low over a cat high stepping across the garden. She heard a noise behind her and turned, expecting to see Tom, but a small trim woman stood in the doorway holding a bundle of clothes.

'Your clothes, madam.'

'Angel. You are?'

'Jude. Your clothes, Angel,' the woman repeated, 'and something for your hair.' She stepped into the room and laid the clothes on the bed. Angel saw on top of the pile of clothes, a small hairgrip decorated with a star. She looked up, the woman's smile lingered for a moment.

'Yes. I'll wait outside until you get dressed.'

• • •

Dressed in dark blue trousers with a thin grey stripe, brown laced shoes, a white collarless shirt and a waistcoat, Angel slipped the hairgrip in her pocket and opened the door. This was the first time since her capture that she had been allowed out of the room and it felt very strange. Dull gold writing on the dark wood told her that the room had belonged to a Lady Mary Grey. She reached up to touch the lettering and asked Jude who she was.

'Story is that she was a woman who disobeyed her queen; married for love and was imprisoned in that room for three years.'

'What happened to her?'

'Did her time ... husband died before she got free.'

The deep blue carpet decorated with red and gold crowns muffled their steps. Morning light filtered through leaf-covered skylights, casting shadows across stern and forbidding portraits of dark-suited men. She paused to look out of a long window at the head of the stairs. There was a wide expanse of grass. She would be very exposed, but she might be OK at night.

'Do you know my grandmother, Jude?' Angel asked, 'I mean what do you know about her?'

Jude paused. 'Not much. She usually brings her own staff and we do the washing up.'

Lowering her voice, she asked, 'Are there Star People near here?' Wide eyed, Jude shook her head. Had she misunderstood, was the hairgrip just a gift? The hope that she had felt evaporated.

It was lighter in the main body of the building, and Angel could hear kitchen noises. Her stomach grumbled loudly. They stopped at some large double doors; Jude whispered that this was the library and that there was food in there.

Angel opened the door and slipped inside. The heat in the room was dense. She could see a log fire, burning fiercely, in a fireplace that was big enough for people to stand inside. Tall windows rattled softly, and the long curtains swelled then softened back into place as she closed the door. Two empty high-backed leather chairs were positioned side by side in front of the fire. Against the far wall stood a long table. She was disappointed to see an elderly man spooning food on to his plate. She had hoped to be alone.

'Jolly good, you must be Angel. Do come in and help yourself to breakfast.' He brushed his grey-blond hair back from his eyes and looked at her. His skin was papery, and sun marked, and he seemed breathless as he spoke. 'We have salmon, eggs, cheeses … just help yourself.'

Angel needed no second invitation and popped a boiled egg into her mouth. She chewed for a second, swallowed fast and picked up a large piece of cheese. There was a whole loaf of bread sliced up on a platter. It felt spongy like cake. She slotted a slice on to a fork and then pulled her sleeve down over her hand and began to walk toward the fire, to toast the bread.

'How quaint! We have a machine for that, here, look.' He took a slice of bread and slotted it into the toaster. 'You just pull the lever down and it pops up when it is done.' Angel took a bite of cheese and put some nuts in her pocket. The man raised an eyebrow. 'Must say, my old trousers fit you rather well.'

'Thank you,' said Angel looking down at her legs.

'I have other shoes, if you don't like brogues.'

'These are fine.' She took the toast from the machine and spread some butter on it. She moved over towards the window. An avenue of trees lined the road that led to the house. There were outbuildings in the distance. She could see activity around a parked vehicle. Escape wasn't going to be at all easy.

'By the way I am George, George Cummings, Prime Minister.'

Angel looked at him. He pushed his fringe out of his

eyes and looked at her, as if he needed her to recognise him.

'That's nice. How do you get to be one of those?'

His shoulders sagged a little. 'You get elected by … well, people vote. Buggered if I know how to stop. No one left to resign to, you know.' Angel took a bite of her toast. 'What do you think?' asked George.

'Oh, OK, I suppose, though I quite like the taste of the fire.'

She poured herself a glass of milk.

'So, what does a Prime Minister do?'

Angel heard a noise outside the room and hoped that it wasn't her grandmother. She drank the milk quickly and wiped her face with her sleeve.

'Well, you know,' he said, waving his hands around in vague circles. 'Govern people.'

Angel cocked her head to one side, 'How?'

'Lead, represent, control.'

'Lead who?' she insisted.

He was beginning to look uncomfortable, 'Of course it's not so simple at the moment … but … but I lead the way … people thrive …'

She couldn't believe what he had just said, 'People are thriving?'

'Well, not after that damned storm, they're not. It's going to take quite some time to get back to normal.' Angel looked at him, he wasn't joking. She picked up her toast and left the room.

She paused in the hallway, at least the storm has caused

some problems, she thought with some satisfaction, but I wonder how everyone is? She decided to search as much of the house as she could before her grandmother appeared. Escape was a priority but a place to hide might buy her time.

At the end of the hall there was a large arched doorway, it seemed to lead to the outside. She tested the door, but it was locked and there was no key.

She checked each room leading from the hall in turn, they were dark, and the furniture covered by dustsheets. The house was silent except for the solid ticking of a clock and the noise of wood being chopped outside. She followed the sound through a door that was hidden behind the staircase and stepped into a light and airy kitchen. A kettle moaned on a large stove.

Jude looked up from a piece of paper, took off her glasses and beckoned her in. She placed the paper on a well-scrubbed wooden table and smoothed it with her hand.

'Your grandmother has some very exotic tastes. We haven't seen food like this for years. What's she like when she's disappointed?'

'No idea, I didn't even know I had one, until a few weeks ago.' Angel looked around the room. There was a line of small bells attached to a strip of wood near the ceiling, each one labelled with faded card.

Tom was just finishing washing up at a low rectangular sink situated in front of a window. Worn pans hung from a wooden rack suspended over the draining board. Next to him a sturdy door led outside.

'Do you mind if I just step outside and get some air?'

'What's she like with rabbit stew? I mean it's years since I saw any rice.' said Jude ignoring the question.

Tom finished drying his hands and sat next to Jude.

'I could maybe catch some freshwater shrimps, or an eel, but what's calamari when it's at home?'

Angel shrugged her shoulders. 'How many people live here?' She started to move towards the door.

Jude paused to score lines through the list. 'He's lived here permanently since London drowned and there's … ' She was interrupted by a burst of gunfire. Angel froze.

'Is that fighting?'

'No, it's what's left of the army. They defend him.'

'What from?'

'Rabbits, mainly.'

Angel laughed out loud, and after a second they joined in.

'What's so funny?' asked a young dark-haired woman entering the kitchen with her arms full of logs. She dropped them into a box, then took off her gloves and turned to look at Angel.

'Angel, meet Steph, our granddaughter. She's stays with us quite a lot.'

Steph nodded then bent down and gave her grandmother's shoulders a squeeze.

'Oh, your hand is cold, come in and warm up,' scolded Jude gently.

A bell on the wall twitched and then rang. Angel glanced up; it was from the occupant in room number one.

'It's your grandmother. Better get moving,' said Tom. He

levered himself up from the table and left. Jude tucked the list in her pocket and started to prepare a tray.

• • •

Eleven o'clock found Angel standing in front of her grandmother. The old woman looked tired; her skin had a yellow tinge. The wound on her forehead looked swollen and angry. Her long dark hair was tied up in a tight ponytail. It swayed, as she shook her head, disapprovingly.

'I won't wear them because I can't move in them, I can't walk properly and they don't keep me warm,' said Angel firmly.

'But those are men's clothes.'

'They fit my body, they've got pockets and they don't stop me moving about.'

'Very well!' sighed Katrin, hands raised to defend herself from her granddaughter's strength of feeling. Angel realised that she might be getting Jude into trouble for getting the clothes for her and softened her tone. 'I'm used to trousers. I live outdoors.'

'When I introduce you to my ... when I find out who survived ... and start to put things back to normal ...' She glared at Angel to emphasize her words. 'You will be at my side, *dressed as a girl!*' Angel looked away. 'You sure you don't have any brothers or sisters?' asked the old woman wistfully.

'Yep.'

'Well then, surely, we should try to get on?' She patted

the cushion next to her. 'Now come here and sit down, I have something to show you that will make you smile.'

Angel thought that it was unlikely, but she moved around the table and stood by her grandmother's shoulder. A jab with a manicured finger on her tablet conjured up a map of the world; a pinch enlarged the image on the screen.

'Everything that you see that's red ...' Katrin gestured with her hand across broad bands of the southern hemisphere. 'We own. And by we, I mean you and me. The purple and the blue parts were owned by other Offshores. I'm trying to find out who's alive. Anywhere there's a gap, we step in ...'

Angel looked up from the screen in horror. Katrin touched her arm and she flinched. 'Remember, if not us, then who? If not now, then when?'

Angel stepped away in disgust and turned to walk towards the door; her grandmother caught her by the wrist. 'Oh, no you don't! You are not leaving me. I've learned my lesson. Your mother slipped between my fingers. I'm going to make sure as hell that you don't!'

Angel looked down at her wrist and twisted it free. Softening her smile, Katrin pleaded, 'I need you. I can give you everything.' Angel opened her mouth to reply, but before she could speak her grandmother held her hands up in a prayer gesture and said, 'Go for a walk and think about it. I'll get someone to walk with you.'

'I don't need anyone to walk with me!'

'Yes, you do. The perimeter is land mined. I sorted it for the PM years ago. Too many needy voters.'

CHAPTER TWENTY-SIX

Angel and Steph leaned against the fence and gazed out across the fields. The woodland looked denser than it had from her bedroom window. A pattern of ridges in the rough grass marked out the shape of what Steph said was once an ornamental garden. Behind the house there was a vegetable garden, with a long greenhouse, leaning against a south-facing wall. Steph said that her grandfather looked after it all.

Angel glanced at Steph. 'How come you're here?'

'My mother died,' said Steph.

'Mine too.'

'She got TB. I had to come here, so that I wouldn't get it.'

'Mine got pneumonia, from the measles,' said Angel.

They stood up and walked further along the fence.

'Do you remember her?' asked Angel, softly.

'Not really.'

'Me neither. She drew pictures on my bedroom wall and told me stories about them. I can almost hear her voice, but I can't see her face,' said Angel softly.

'That's nice. My mum wrote me a letter telling me about her life.'

'I'm just learning about my mother's life …' Angel replied, almost to herself.

They walked further around the perimeter fence and

stopped at the driveway. Angel judged that the distance between the gateway and the house was a five-minute run with no cover. She had to find a better way.

'How long's he been here?' she asked.

'Who?'

'The Prime Minister.'

'Thirty years.'

'I reckon he must be eighty.'

'Older, your grandmother makes sure that he has all of the treatments. It was part of the deal.'

They walked on and stopped at the kitchen garden.

'I suppose treatments will be in short supply, now.'

'She's on her comms pad searching ... day and night, so my grandfather says. That's why she doesn't look so well.'

Angel thought about her grandmother's pallor and the wound on her forehead, it didn't seem to be healing.

'She's in our world now, no antibiotics, no drugs to stop transplant rejection. Her clock is ticking,' said Steph.

Angel was shocked to feel a wave of sadness. This woman, this awful woman was her only link to her mother.

'OK, I need some calendula ... marigold, you know? Do you have bees wax?'

Steph shrugged.

'Oil?'

'Nope.'

'Candle wax?'

'In our emergency supply. But why?'

'I thought I might try to make her a poultice ... or an antiseptic cream.'

Back in the kitchen Angel infused marigold and lavender flowers into alcohol. She stirred slowly, careful not to let the mixture get too hot. Tom and Jude sat at the table and watched her work.

'Good brandy, that,' he whispered. Jude nodded as she swept Hazelnut shells into the fire bucket. She spread the nuts on to a metal rack and stood it over the cool end of the hotplate.

'Do you have a herb garden?' Angel asked.

'That depends. What do you need?'

'Garlic and yarrow.'

'There's stinking nanny … wild garlic growing in the woods. Steph could get you some.'

Angel stopped; she could hardly believe what she had just heard. 'There's a safe way into the woods?'

'Yes, we cleared a path through, in the early days, in case we had to get away. But in the end, there was nowhere to run.'

She struggled to keep her voice level. 'You have nobody out there?'

'No, this is it. The Reapers, you know …' said Tom.

'At least you have Steph. Good job she got out, before she got TB,' said Angel.

'TB?'

'Her mother …'

'Oh yes, the TB,' said Jude flatly.

Angel wiped her hands on a cloth and moved her infusion from the heat. Her mind was buzzing. She should ask Steph where the path was. There was a sound. She jumped. It was bell from the library

Angel paused at the double doors and listened. She could hear the Prime Minister's voice and her grandmother answering. What they were saying wasn't clear, but at least they didn't seem angry. The hall clock chimed the quarter hour. She turned the handle softly and opened the door.

'Yes, but her stem cells–'

'Ah, Angel, do come in and join us,' interrupted the Prime Minister. Angel saw him raise an eyebrow to her grandmother. He got up, moved a dining chair to the space between the two armchairs and gestured elegantly for Angel to sit between them.

'Warmest spot in the house,' he added a little too graciously.

Katrin was dressed in a black suit and white top. Her hands rested together on her lap. She turned to Angel and nodded a formal smile.

'Good walk?'

Angel nodded, still shocked at what she had just heard her grandmother say.

'And you met the housekeeper's granddaughter? I wondered if she might be a little friend for you?'

Angel nodded again. The skin on her cheeks felt as if it was tightening in the heat from the fire and yet she felt cold inside. Katrin stared into the flames. After a pause, the Prime Minister coughed and Katrin turned to Angel.

'She can come with us when we leave.'

'Leave?'

'We've just got each other now. I need to see a doctor who

understands my particular requirements … and we need to start to pick up the threads.'

Angel's heart sank. She wasn't the only one in danger here. She wasn't about to let them use Steph if she could help it.

The next morning just before dawn, Steph and Angel stepped out of the kitchen door. It had been a cold night and there was heavy dew on the grass, it glistened in the early light. Threads of silver spiders' webs trailed down from the trees. Angel whispered to Steph, telling her what her grandmother had planned for them both.

'You're in real danger. You need to disappear for a while.' Angel pulled a cobweb filament from her face and then glanced at Steph; her face was pale in the early light.

'How long do you think that I should stay away?'

'Just until we've gone.'

They turned the corner of the gravel driveway and saw a soldier standing guard in the trees; unusually close to the house.

'Looks like they're keeping a close eye on you.'

'I know, I saw him from my window. I'm going to have to wait for the right moment, but you could slip away now. Just …' They stopped to pick some cobnuts from a bush.

'Just what?'

Angel took off her jacket and put it on the floor. 'Show me the path into the woods,' she whispered.

'Turn around and look at the trees.'

Angel put her hand up to shield her eyes from the rising sun and turned slowly, as if she was scanning for more nuts.

Steph peeled the leaves away from a cobnut and cracked the shell with her teeth. She spoke quietly as she threw away pieces of shell.

'See how the grass is shorter, running from here out towards eleven o'clock? Then it turns, level with the beech tree on the right and from there it runs at three o'clock towards that line of ash trees.'

Angel fixed the route in her mind then turned back to pick more nuts. 'That's the path that you need to take, head to the middle ash. The fourth tree in has a star on the trunk.'

Angel picked up her jacket carefully and tied the sleeves together to form a makeshift bag.

'The tree with the broken branch, right?'

Steph nodded; they began to walk back to the house. 'That's the one. The wood runs down to a river. There's a road bridge downstream on the right. You can cross there and head north. It has three spans, you could hide under there for a bit, but if you get really stuck … look up.'

'OK, thanks. And you?'

'I'll be fine.' said Steph.

As they walked towards the house, Angel looked at her bedroom window; it was too high to jump. The ivy growing up the wall looked old and brittle, its cover was too thick for her to see the state of the walls behind it. She didn't think that she would be able to reach the guttering, even if she could break her window and climb out on to the ledge.

'Legend has it …' said Steph smiling at her, 'that Lady Mary was imprisoned in your room for three years.'

'Nice.'

'She had two children during her imprisonment.'

'Friendly staff?'

'No, they looked just like her husband.'

'Bit of a puzzle then.' They smiled at each other.

'That old wardrobe could tell a tale. It's original.'

A flash of white caught Angel's eye. Jude was standing in the kitchen doorway, frantically waving a towel.

'What are you two doing outdoors?' she hissed. 'We're in lockdown!'

'We were going to get some herbs, but we saw soldiers, so we got cobnuts instead,' said Steph.

'Come in! Come in, I was scared to death.' Jude bustled them into the kitchen, tutting and urging them to walk faster. Angel emptied the nuts on to the table, then excused herself, leaving Steph to tell her grandparents that she would have to go away.

She paused to look at the writing on her bedroom door for a second and wondered how secure a prison it had been. Her trouser legs were soaked from the grass, so she draped them over the back of a chair, placed it in the sun and lay down on the bed to think. Her options were slim, and she didn't have long.

Her pillow was uncomfortable, so she pulled it higher up behind her head, but that didn't help. There seemed to be something hard and cold under her shoulder. She sat up, moved her pillow and found a beautiful red apple. Her heart missed a beat. It was cold and waxy with a tart fragrant smell. She touched it to her lips and felt a roughness. Looking closer she could see that it had been marked. In the light from the window, she could see a perfect letter R. 'Raph?' she whispered to herself, tracing the letter with her finger.

Heart beating fast, she searched the cupboard with the rattling panel; but found nothing. She tapped the walls; they were solid. She looked out of the window, and checked the perimeters of the woodland, the hedges and the line of the fence, but saw no one, just the silhouette of soldiers. She looked at the apple again as if it might tell her something, and it did; she smiled to herself, because this meant that he knew where she was.

Angel ate lunch in the kitchen with Tom and Jude. Steph had left straight after they got back, and they were worried. Jude whispered thanks to Angel and then returned to her cooking. As time passed it seemed more and more likely that Steph had made it through the lockdown. It was important to carry on as normal, but nobody's heart was in it.

Tom warned Angel that they had been told to cater for another military visitor in the morning. Things were moving fast.

Angel ate her cheese and bread, thoughtfully. 'You know what I fancy?' Jude looked up from her work. 'An apple.'

'We used to have an orchard. It drowned, the roots rotted,' said Tom.

'OK just a thought,' said Angel. They seemed to be telling the truth, no sign of teasing or a joke. They hadn't put the apple in her room and that meant that it really must have been Raph and he couldn't be far away.

'The key to my room … where is it?' Angel spoke softly.

'I have it,' said Tom. 'The only one.'

Jude was standing at the sink peeling vegetables; she put her knife down and listened.

'Can I have it?'

'Ah …' he said looking from Jude to Angel. 'Your grandmother wants you locked in your room tonight.'

'Why?'

'She thinks that you might run away.'

'I might, but why tonight?'

'The man who's coming tomorrow, well, he's coming for you.'

'Can I have the key please?' She tried to sound calm. She needed a backup in case she couldn't get out through the wardrobe. Jude put the potatoes in a pan and walked over to the table.

'If you escape and we haven't got the key, we're finished. We've nowhere else to go.'

'I know.' Angel's heart sank. She looked at their scared faces and drew a determined breath. 'Forget I asked, silly of me.'

'There's nothing silly about you,' said Tom.

'We were only saying the other night, you and Steph are a lot alike. And that we've got two of you to worry about now.'

'Don't. I'll be OK,' said Angel, with more confidence than she felt.

'We'll hold them up for as long as we can,' said Tom.

Angel ate a silent evening meal with her grandmother.

She wondered if she might tell her about the morning visitor, but the old woman ate her meal silently. When Angel got up to leave, saying that she was tired, her grandmother simply stared into the fire.

CHAPTER TWENTY-SEVEN

The clock in the hall chimed twice and Angel quietly got out of bed. Her room was full of shadows. During her stay she had managed to gather a few things together; a knife, some matches, some basic food and they were already in her bag. In the corner of her eye, a shadow deepened.

She heard a whispered voice, 'Are you leaving without me?' She turned toward the sound.

'Raph?'

'We're you expecting someone else?'

'Come here!' She reached out and grabbed hold of his collar, pulled him towards her and without thinking, kissed him full on the mouth. Then she stepped back, shocked at her own action. Her heart was pounding, but she needed to know, she searched his face … he was smiling. Then he pulled her gently towards him and kissed her back. He rested his forehead on hers and whispered that it was time to come home.

'How did you get in?' she whispered.

'Ah, the lady was resourceful; there's ladder on the wall behind the ivy. You get to it, behind a panel in the cupboard.'

'But, how did you find out about …'

'Mani. Quick we have to leave; the guards change over, in ten minutes.'

'OK but you need to know, someone's coming to collect me. Security is going to be really tight.'

'We'd better go then.' He took her hand and began to lead her towards the cupboard.

'Raph.' He paused. 'I have to make it obvious that I got out without a key … so no one gets blamed.' Together they moved a dresser to behind the bedroom door.

Then she slung her bag over her shoulder and followed him into the shadows in the corner of her room. She waited until he carefully slid the loose panel to one side revealing a blind space between the cupboard and the outside wall. When they were both inside, she slid the panel back. She felt a blast of cool night air as Raph opened the outer hatch. A barn owl screeched in a nearby tree.

The opening was completely covered by the ivy that grew on the wall beneath her window. Raph whispered that she should feel with her feet for the iron pegs below the hatch. They formed a rough and rusted ladder. Angel pushed her way into the twisted ivy and slowly climbed down. Above her, Raph closed the hatch and followed her.

Careful to keep to the shadows they moved around the corner of the building.

A sliver of a moon cast no light, the night was dark and still. She took Raph's hand and with her back to the hedge pointed out the path to the line of beech trees. Together they moved low and soft across the field.

Angel skimmed her hand across the top of the grass, and then stopped, took her bearings, and led him towards the distant line of trees. They reached the middle tree and froze.

The roar of a truck powering up the drive fractured the silence, its full-beamed headlights swept across the grass and cast their shadows on to the woodland floor. They hardly dared to breathe. Surely, someone would have seen them.

As soon as it had gone, they fled downhill towards the river. The floor was covered in leaf litter, slippery and treacherous. In the dark a fox screamed like a child. To their right, they heard a shout and the crack of gunfire. Raph pulled Angel to him and they sheltered behind a tree. They could hear the thud of approaching boots. They ran again. There was another shot. Raph gasped. They ran on. His stride was uneven. Angel linked arms and pulled him down the hill.

She could smell the river before they found it. It curved in front of them, dark and slow. She could just see that it ran under the central span of the bridge; the earth under the side arches looked deep in pocked mud and water-filled puddles.

'You OK?'

'Leg hurts. You go!'

She shook her head, took his hand and led him through the muddy shallows into the water.

'God that stings!' hissed Raph as it touched his wound. She pulled him out of the river and under the first arch. They could feel the thud of soldiers' feet pounding through the woods towards them.

It became clear to them both that now Raph had stopped running he wouldn't be able to move far. His trouser leg was torn. Blood was seeping into one of their footprints. She searched the bank for a stick that would help him to move, there was nothing. Then she remembered Steph's words and looked up; there in the shadows she could see a long dark shape hidden under the curved roof. She threw a handful of mud. It was hollow and it rocked.

'Help me! I think there's something up there,' she whispered. Raph braced his back against the wall, linked his hands and took her weight. She tugged at the old rope, then pulled her knife out of her bag and tore at it.

Footsteps were getting closer; they could hear hushed voices. She slashed at the rope again and one end fell to the ground, she jumped down and pulled it free. An old canoe slapped down into the mud.

The sound of running stopped, and someone called for silence; the soldiers were close. Together they lifted the canoe and moved into the water; Raph fell in smothering a gasp of pain. Angel helped to lift his leg over the side, pulled an oar from under the front canopy and climbed in. She gave two cautious pulls on the oar and they slid silently into the night.

Behind them, they could see torchlight searching the darkness, there was a burst of rifle fire and a barked order to hold fire. Angel used the oar to steer, until the river caught and pulled them downstream.

• • •

Dawn found them sitting on the wooded riverbank inspecting Raph's leg. The entrance wound was clean; the exit was a ragged torn hole. The bullet had missed the bone and major arteries, but it could already be infected by the river mud, so they washed and bound it with a strip from his shirt. It was the best that they could do, until they were far enough away to light a fire. For now, the primary need was to keep moving.

'I'll mend,' he said softly wrapping his arm around her shoulder. 'But tell me, how did you know the canoe was there?'

'Steph said something about looking up under the bridge. It must have been their emergency escape plan. The rope was pretty rotten, I think it must have been there for years.'

'I hope that they don't need it.'

'With me gone, and my grandmother off looking for emergency tissue matches, things might get back to normal.'

'Tissue what?'

'I'll tell you later. What worries me is that they saw the two of us. I hope that they don't think that you were Steph helping me.'

'Let's hope she stays well hidden.'

They slipped back into the canoe and keeping close to the cover of the bank, re-joined the river current. They took it in turns to paddle. Angel finally fell asleep, curled forwards over her knees. And a grim-faced, Raph paddled into the night.

By the second day the river had widened out and was beginning to gather speed. They took great care near roads and derelict areas. They couldn't afford to be seen. There had been distant signs of habitation; houses and farms but none of them looked lived in, and there were no signs of the army.

They agreed to rest under a road bridge and stepped stiff legged out on to the concrete ledge. Rats had used the dry concrete as a nesting area. Raph found a stick and flicked bundles of dead leaves and old rags into the water. They watched as tiny pink hairless bodies floated out of their disintegrating nests.

Angel gathered wood and dry scraps for fire making and stacked it in the centre of the bridge span, she then made a wider search and returned with a puffball mushroom, wild carrots and herbs. She watched Raph, checking that he didn't look feverish, his breathing was steady, and that he was moving about OK, then she touched his shoulder. 'I saw a clean-looking stream just over the hill to the south, and there's an old house up there. I'm going to look for something to clean up your leg. If there's any trouble, get into the canoe and go. You'll move faster and I can catch you up downstream.'

Raph kissed her gently and whispered, 'Let there be no trouble.'

CHAPTER TWENTY-EIGHT

The sound of a five-hundred-years-old door being broken down echoed through the corridors of Chequers. The doorframe screeched as it was split from the wall. Downstairs, Tom held Jude's shoulder and she held his waist as they stood in the open doorway and watched the sky lighten.

'Do you think she got away?' she whispered.

'Hope so. There was gunfire, but if they'd got her, they wouldn't be looking upstairs.'

'Blocking the door was a work of genius. They think she's hanging in the wardrobe and it was Steph they were chasing through the woods ...'

'God, I hope that's not true,' said Jude.

The sound of boots thundering down the stairs grew louder. Raised voices could be heard through the library door. Tom and Jude stepped back into the kitchen and waited for the call.

• • •

'Gone? Completely gone, not hiding anywhere?' asked the Prime Minister.

'Yes sir! She was confined to her room as per orders. The door was locked; I have the key.' He pulled the old iron key out of his pocket to prove it. 'It's the only one. I don't know how she did it, sir.'

Katrin sat in one of the leather chairs, waiting for the newly lit fire to give out some heat.

'And you're sure that was her running through the woods?' There was sarcasm in her voice.

'Yes madam, her and her accomplice.'

Katrin turned. 'Her what?'

'Accomplice ... male ... about her height, bit taller perhaps.'

'And the cook's granddaughter's still missing?' asked the Prime Minister.

'How did she get through the minefield? Fly?' Katrin interrupted.

'Not that lucky, ma'am, we shot one.'

'Which one?' barked Katrin. The soldier was shocked at her tone.

'Not sure, madam. There was blood in the footprints by the side of the river.'

Katrin drew a deep breath and looked out of the window. The fire back clicked as it drew in heat. She turned and spoke with ice-cold venom.

'Let's hope, for your sake, that you didn't kill her. I need her back, she's a tissue match ... and of course, family.'

The Prime Minister kept his gaze level, but slightly raised an eyebrow at the soldier who looked from him to Katrin, undecided for a moment about saying more. He spoke quickly. 'One more thing. We think that they had a boat. There are old ropes under the bridge; something was tied up there, out of sight. And there are marks in the mud where something slid into the water.'

The two men waited for Katrin to speak.

'Perfect! ... Are you tracking her?'

'We're having to do it by road, we don't have a boat and the riverbanks are too overgrown to follow on foot.'

'And, exactly, where does this river go?'

'It joins the Thames and then goes on to London.'

'Strangely enough, that's where I am heading. Maybe I can find her myself!' Katrin strode out of the room.

The two men waited until they had heard Katrin stop barking orders at Tom, and her bedroom door slam shut. They breathed out.

'Come and sit down.'

'Thank you, sir.'

The Prime Minister poured two glasses of whisky and handed one over; they sat down.

'You can stop that now, William.'

They watched the new fire blaze and then collapse for lack of new wood.

'Bit of a bugger, don't you think?' said the Prime Minister sipping his whisky, 'We've got a missing guest, missing mines, missing servant and a missing boat we didn't even know we had.' He paused for a moment. 'Still, look on the bright side, she'll be gone by supper.'

The two men sipped their whiskey and watched the fire die.

• • •

Just before dusk, Angel returned to the river carrying kindling, sticks, a pan, some strips of fabric and a rusty salt pot. She also had some wild garlic leaves and herbs in her pocket.

'Got the makings of a meal here,' she whispered as she ducked under the bridge.

Raph stirred, he had curled up into a tight ball against the damp and fallen asleep. He smiled and stretched.

'I think that we can get away with a proper fire under here, the smoke should spread out under the bridge and the concrete will absorb the heat.'

'Heat seekers might not pick it up, but we should keep an eye open for drones.' Raph nodded. 'I was thinking that we should get amongst people, or at least leave the river.'

'Depends how well you can walk. Let's check your leg.'

Angel carefully unwrapped the makeshift bandage and saw mottled layers of dried and fresh blood. Careful not to tear the scabs away Angel whispered quietly to herself, 'The entry wound is clean and dry.' She lifted his calf. 'The exit wound isn't hot, it's raggy and it's opened again at least twice.' She looked up. 'I would like to have stitched it, but I think if we let the air get to it a bit and then put clean bandages back on, it should be OK.'

Raph nodded, relief written across his face. He knew that if it had got infected, he might have lost his leg, or worse.

They boiled his bandages and dried them near the fire. Angel bathed his wound with saltwater and wrapped it in the clean dry strips. She could see that he was moving around more easily, but worried that he might open the wound if he did too much.

Raph cooked the mushroom stew. Angel sat with her back against the stained concrete wall and watched him work.

'You're a good cook.'

'I'm like my father. He loved food.'

She reached out and gently nudged his thigh with her foot. 'Do tell.'

'Ah, big, red hair and hands like …' He held his hand out palm up. '… like mine.'

'Who does your sister take after?'

'Oh, she's all my mother. Attitude included. She herds people with sheer force of will. I like to stand back and think. But it's difficult not to do what Mani wants.' He reached back and touched her foot. 'What about you? Tell me about your parents.'

Angel looked up at the rust-stained roof and thought. Raph moved back next to her and softly kissed her neck. She shivered and smiled.

'Well, I never knew my biological father, in fact I don't know who he is, or even if he knows that I exist. My mother ran away from home. I don't know what from, but I have my suspicions.' She arched her neck so that Raph could kiss her again. 'My mother died when I was two. I don't have any strong memories of her, but sometimes, I smell something and think it's her. I can remember us looking out of my bedroom window; I think that I can feel her just behind me.'

'Your dad?' whispered Raph.

'My *real* father is a bear of a man, a giant. He used to carry me everywhere on his shoulders. He smells of woods and fresh bread … and has a lovely smile.'

They fell silent and watched the river flowing past.

'Will you promise me something?'

Raph nodded. 'Anything.'

'If anything happens to me, will you go and tell him yourself. No messages …'

'Promise.'

CHAPTER TWENTY-NINE

Two days later, Angel and Raph, set out across a rolling scrub-covered chalky plain. They had loosely tied the canoe under a long canal bridge and weighed it down with rocks. It lay waiting for them, just under the surface of the water.

Raph's leg wound slowed them down, so Angel carried the bag and scouted forwards to find the easiest path. She caught rabbits and they ate well. On the fourth night, they slept hard and deep under the blunt remains of a dying oak tree.

Angel woke early and watched a pale and watery sun rise through the branches. Fine dew settled like a mist. She shivered and curled into Raph's side.

'You OK?' He turned to face her.

'Just restless.' She smoothed herself against his body. 'When things settle, shall we live like this?'

'What, under a tree?'

'No, just live and roam?'

'Let's roam a little now, shall we?' he said slipping his hand into the small of her back and pulling her close.

• • •

Noon of the sixth day, Raph and Angel climbed down from the plains and followed the elongated point of a star into a narrow ravine. They could smell the smoke before they saw any sign of a building. Logs had been arranged in a wide curve and covered with soil. A patchwork of moss and lichen had grown up over the sides and on to the roof. The front of the shelter was a rock wall, hidden behind bracken. A door opened on to a small clearing in front of the hut.

By the side of a fast-running stream they could see a woman, leaning on a stick, and bending down to sweep up a bucketful of water.

'Hello, can I help?' asked Raph.

'What? Oh, there you two are! We were beginning to worry,' said the woman slowly straightening up. 'You must be Angel and Raph. We heard someone got shot; there was a trail of blood by the river. We just didn't know which one.'

'That would be me,' said Raph, pointing at his leg.

'Well come inside and let me have a look.' She glanced at Angel and smiled. 'You look well …'

'Fresh air I expect. It's heaven up there.'

'Well come in. I'm Kamala by the way. Pleased to meet you both.'

Inside, she checked Raph's leg and approved of Angel's care. She left them eating salted fish and nuts, while she slipped away to send a message. When she returned, she brought instructions from Mani; they were to be collected in the morning.

Relieved and anxious, Angel and Raph slept on the floor in front of the fire. The damp wood hissed and bled sap. She pressed her ear to his chest.

'What are you doing?' he whispered.

'Memorising your heartbeat.' He kissed the top of her head and asked why? 'Because tomorrow will be different,' she replied.

Raph held her tight, long after she had fallen asleep. He watched the shadows behind the flames and wished with all his heart that he could stop the world from turning.

• • •

A black MPV with an Alpha insignia on the roof collected them at dawn. They sat in the back, securely strapped in with a broad armrest between them. There was a dark privacy screen between them and the driver. She told them that the journey would take a couple of hours. They held hands for a while but eventually fell to looking out of their side windows. Angel reached out for Raph's hand; he stretched his seat belt and shifted towards her.

'We'll be safe now.' He spoke over the noise of the engine. 'Mani will fill us in on what's been happening.' Angel nodded sadly, then turned to look out of the window. He gazed at her for a while, then stared at the passing countryside.

At first Angel assumed that the line on the horizon was cloud. But as they got closer, she could see that it was smoke rising vertically from the ground for about a hundred feet before being swept horizontally when it reached colder air. Nearer still, she could see that the single column of smoke was made of three separate stacks.

The windows darkened and an intercom button on the arm rest flashed red. Raph touched it and the driver spoke.

'There's something going on ahead. A convoy is heading this way. It's army. I'm pulling off the road, brace yourselves, then get down and keep down.'

They checked their seat belts and braced their backs against the seats. The car bucked and bounced off the road, then skidded to a halt, nose down in a hollow.

They unfastened their seat belts, slipped into the foot well and listened to the drum of army vehicles pounding past them. Angel counted ten, fifteen, twenty. From the strobing shadows, she guessed that two were heavy machinery; earthmovers perhaps.

The intercom clicked and the driver said that they were free to continue. The driver dialled down the window shading to get a better view as she reversed. The tarmac had been grazed and scraped by caterpillar tracks. Large pieces of the road surface had broken and slipped into the ditch.

They drove on in silence. The sky turned heavy … a strange warm grey. Ash specked the surface of the car and smeared the windscreen. A thick crust built up at the limits of the wipers' sweep. They moved slowly into what seemed like fog underneath the horizontal band of smoke. The car tyres whispered … the road was white. It was snowing ash.

They emerged into a hellish sunshine. Light sparkled on a stream at the side of the road. Angel looked, then looked again; it was red. The stream was running red. Then the stench hit them; the air stank of burned flesh and fear. She glanced at Raph who was looking out of his window in horror. A long line of trees had been ripped from the earth.

Her eyes followed the deep black tracks gouged out of

the hillside. She groaned as a bolt of horror hit her. What had looked like charred branches was in fact one … no, four … house high piles of charred bodies. Circled by burning pyres of smashed trees.

She felt Raph's hand touch her own and unfastened her seat belt, lifted the armrest and slid across to him. They looked at each other incredulous and horrified.

The intercom flashed. 'We have to get through here fast.'

They both saw the movement on the far bank of a bloody ditch at the same moment and Raph shouted for the car to stop.

'Someone's alive,' called Angel, rapping on the partition. 'But!'

'Stop,' Raph shouted.

The vehicle slowed to an idle on the side of the road, the driver sat ready to move. Angel scrambled out of the door closely followed by Raph. The heat hit her like a wall a second before the smell. She retched then pulled her sleeve down and held it over her nose and mouth and ran.

The grass was long and crunchy. Green spikes pushed through the grey carpet. Swirls of ash lifted behind them.

Angel reached the body first. 'Keep watch,' she mouthed to Raph. He knelt on the roadside.

It was a woman. She reached up and clutched at Angel's arm. She was thin, sixteen perhaps, her long hair was streaked with ash and blood. Angel looked down and saw that her right leg was a pulp of bone-spikes and rags. Her lips were blue. Taking her hand, Angel moved forward and cradled her head. She spoke softly.

'Hi, I'm Angel, what's your name?' She stroked hair from the dying woman's face.

'P-p-earl.'

'Hi Pearl.' Angel spoke in a whisper. 'What happened?'

'They said to meet here … join the army … fight the Reapers.'

Angel searched Pearl's eyes. The girl was fading fast.

'Who did this?' Angel moved closer.

The woman's tongue clicked; her mouth was dry. 'Army … trick …'

Angel held her close, rocked her gently and whispered, 'Sleep softly, sweet Pearl.' When the tension in her limbs fell away, Raph moved down into the ditch and helped Angel to lie her in the shade of an ash-laden stump of a hedge. They covered her face with leaves.

They looked around; there were five separate funeral pyres. People had been gunned down and then bulldozed into towers of flesh and bone.

Cold with horror Angel turned towards the waiting car. There was a loud crack; one of the pyres had collapsed, sending out a blast of fiery red sparks. It seemed to come from the heart of the fire, twisting and hissing. It raced towards them. 'Run!' shouted Angel. The heat hit them like a fist.

The rest of the journey was silent. The smell of burning flesh permeated her whole body. When Angel closed her eyes, she saw Pearl's face.

And a sharp cold hatred blossomed in her heart.

CHAPTER THIRTY

Mani looked tired and distracted; her hair was tangled into a bun and pinned on top of her head. She seemed eager to find out about Chequers and the Prime Minister, but she struggled with the welcome pleasantries. She shook Angel's hand and gave her brother a cursory hug. They were both blood-stained and exhausted and they smelled of death. She took them straight into her room and stood with her hands behind her back while they answered her questions. Then she told them in a voice flat with despair that funeral pyres were burning across all of Europe. The storm had brought a fraction of the success that they had hoped for.

'Alpha is still functioning. Your grandmother is the only surviving Elite leader on this continent.'

'Where is she now?' Angel was almost too tired to speak.

'In a clinic in London. Getting repaired … busy knitting everything back together. Course, she's got the old state right behind her … they need her patronage, now more than they ever did. She's cleaning up!' Mani spoke with anger and, Angel suspected, a little admiration.

Angel saw Mani raise an eyebrow at Raph. He ran his fingers through his hair and then shifted a fraction away from her side.

'So, now we have three problems.'

'Three?'

Mani paced. 'One, when their systems collapsed it took out a lot of our surveillance capacity.'

Raph nodded to himself thoughtfully. 'Two?'

'Two … as she takes over the other Offshores' systems and assets, it all becomes one big unit, making it much harder for us to play one off against the other.'

'Three?' asked Angel.

'You. You're the third.'

'What?' Angel felt cold. She reached for Raph's hand. It wasn't there.

'For as long as your grandmother is alive, she is going to be looking for you. She is going to turn the world upside down. It's going to be carnage. We've seen what she can do. And then … this is the thing … when she eventually dies you, inherit everything.'

'But I …'

'You don't get the choice. It's who you are.' Mani's eyes were cold. 'And just who *are* you, Angel? Do we really know?'

Angel stood up and left the room.

It was a silent meal that night. Angel had finally realised that there really was no help, no system, no community. Just brutalized and scattered people, waking up to the realisation that it wasn't just the Offshores who were preying on them. If they hadn't known before, it would be obvious to them now that the tatters of the old system including the armed forces, had a vested interest in the survival of the Elites, and that they were prepared to do anything to keep it that way. They had been hiding in plain sight. She remembered the Prime Minister's sense of entitlement; and the army's ruthlessness. She had seen it with her own eyes, and she felt physically sick.

She looked at her flesh, her arms, her hands, listened to her breath as it entered her body and drew down into her lungs. She could hear the pulse in her ears. It sickened her. She felt filthy to her core that she shared the same flesh as these people. It was as if she left a trail of darkness wherever she walked. Her life's energy was death, and greed, and it was who she was. She couldn't bring herself to touch Raph, she was afraid that she would contaminate him.

Mani and Raph watched her push the food around on her plate, and gag when she tried to swallow something.

'It's the shock,' said Raph as he watched her clumsily push her chair back and leave the room.

'How does she deal with things?'

'I've seen her hide and I've seen her fight.'

'Let's see where she goes with this one then. They have got to die.'

Raph pushed his plate away and leaned forward, 'Now listen to me, Mani.' He looked at his sister, cold and hard. 'I will do anything to bring them down but let me make myself crystal clear. I will kill *anyone* who harms Angel. Anyone.'

• • •

The temperature dropped hard that night and the morning brought a slate-grey frost. This place had been a station house. The railway tracks steamed in the early sunlight.

Trees shed ice crystals as the warmth of the first light stirred movement in the morning air. Raph watched as Angel rubbed a squeaky circle in the window with her sleeve.

'You don't have to do this,' said Raph from the bed. Angel turned around to look at him. The sunlight caught the frost circle behind her.

'But I do.'

'You could do nothing, wait until she dies, and let the others take over.'

'And then we're back to square one and meanwhile the resistance will be crushed for another generation.'

'True, but there's still the Stars.'

'And they might take longer to find. Their CB radio might stay under the radar a bit longer. But they will be found, and they will die.'

Raph longed to hold her, to feel the warmth of her skin, to breathe in the fragrance of her hair, but Angel had told him no. She said that she couldn't bear to touch him. They had lain side by side. He had stared at the ceiling until his eyes stung. When she rolled over, he had rested his hand in the warm space left by her body.

She'd tried to explain, but he only half understood. She wanted to think, to plan, to focus; but he just needed to hold her close to his heart.

'Are you ready?' asked Mani opening the door without knocking. She was wearing her leather jacket and carrying a motorcycle helmet. She passed a helmet to Angel and without looking back, they both left the room.

Raph lay on the bed and watched the edges of the ice

circle on the window bleed. Then with a heavy heart, he moved to the doorway and listened until the sound of the motorbike faded to nothing.

• • •

Mani and Angel stopped on a hill and surveyed the city. The Thames dissected it east to west. London had been burned, demolished and bulldozed into a raised platform of rubble and soil. There were two city walls. A high wall of steel arced in a semicircle from riverbank to riverbank around the inner city. The outer city perimeter was a tree-high spiked and electrified metal fence.

A high bank of rubble had straightened the furious river on its northern side; the south of the city had been flattened and left to die.

'We're just about ready.' said Mani taking off her helmet. 'Steph is waiting for you about half a mile further on.' She unzipped her jacket and gave Angel a battered phone and a solar charger. 'Take this. I've put some numbers in as decoys. There are two hidden numbers. "*" means, get me out, and you press "@" to speak to me.' Angel nodded and took the phone. 'Once you get in there hide it. Keep it charging. Hide the SIM card somewhere else.'

Angel slipped the phone into the inside pocket of her jacket.

'You don't have to do it like this, there could be another way …'

Angel looked at her. 'I do.'

Mani shrugged. 'Only turn the phone on in an emergency, they can track it.'

Angel handed over her helmet, they looked at each other for a second, then she turned and walked away.

• • •

Thirty minutes later Angel and Steph were sheltering under the shade of a tree, looking at the distant ruins.

'Did you go back to Chequers?'

Steph shook her head. 'No, I think they're better off without me. Too many questions. I sent a message to say we were ok.'

'Are we ready to do this?' Steph nodded. Angel took out her phone and called her grandmother.

'Darling, this is nice surprise. Where are you?' purred Katrin.

'Listen to me carefully, grandmother.'

'But my dear …'

'You're not listening! I can hang up. You'll never find me and let's face it, I'm all you've got. We both know you need me. So, listen.'

She could hear her grandmother breathing.

'Good,' continued Angel. 'I've a lot to learn … that you can teach me, but I won't allow myself to be used.'

'OK,' said Katrin, cautiously, 'but what exactly do you want to learn?'

'I need to know about my mother … and my family … Who I–'

'We do seem to need each other, don't we?' Katrin interrupted.

'I will not be locked up, drugged, or used. And most of all, I am not your donor.'

'You sound so much like your mother,' Katrin growled.

'And I am bringing a friend. You will do her no harm.'

'Very well, we can talk about this later. Where shall I send a car?'

'You're not listening again!'

'What's in it for me?' Katrin's voice was harsh.

'An heir, continuity, family around you in the future … connection to my mother … a second chance …'

After a long pause Katrin agreed.

'We'll be at gate six in an hour.' Angel hung up and moaned softly. Steph whispered her support and together they set out for the outer perimeter fence.

Angel was scared … angry and scared. She was walking into a spider's web, but she knew that for this moment and for this moment only, it was broken and vulnerable. There would never be a better time. She thought of her stepfather with great sadness. Would he ever understand? Would he be able to forgive her for not going home?

He had always known who she was, and he had protected her by keeping it secret. He'd also taught her all that he knew about how to survive, but not in this world. The odds were against her now. She doubted she would ever see him again. She turned to Steph. 'You know you're doing the bravest thing imaginable? Likely as not, we're not going to get out of here alive.'

Steph nodded and touched her arm. They walked on.

Angel thought of her stepfather's mantra … guard, hide, run, fight, kill, die … then she took a deep breath and added one of her own … destroy.

CHAPTER THIRTY-ONE

From the top of the hill they could see the outer fence. It was tree-high and electrified. They paused shoulder to shoulder, aware of the finality of their next move. Angel suspected that anyone making this next step was probably trafficked. It was a one-way journey.

A camera on top of the wall followed them to the gate which slid open to reveal a truck high tunnel of steel. Lights flicked on as they walked; behind them the outer door slid shut. The air inside was damp and still. Angel walked up to a green flashing light and spoke into the intercom. Then they stepped into the silence of London.

The river widened to the east. Few roads remained. The bustling old city was long dead. Every last building had been levelled to the ground. They were looking at a desert of rubble. Ahead of them a single-track road of crushed bricks ran directly to the inner-city wall. It branched off left and right to a scattering of prefabricated workers' huts. Brooding factory blocks towered over them, casting long shadows across the demolished and flattened city. Heavy grey smoke ripped out of their tall chimneys and dissipated over the Thames. Smaller factories and offices were scattered further afield.

Scrub bushes had colonised the area around the office buildings. Twisted trees grew where their roots could reach through spoil heaps to the natural soil bed beneath. A frosted covering of broken glass and tile sparkled in the sunlight.

They watched a black limousine emerge from the inner wall and turn towards them.

'No turning back now Steph,' said Angel quietly.

'I'm ready.'

It whispered towards them and stopped at their feet. Angel tapped on the driver's window. They heard a click and the darkened window slid down. An unsmiling young man dressed in a black chauffeur's uniform, slowly turned towards them.

'Hello, I'm Angel and this is Steph.'

The driver nodded, obviously surprised that they wanted to talk to him.

'And you are?'

'John, madam.' he swallowed nervously.

'Just Angel, thank you. Now John, we want to sit in the front with you. Is there room?' She peered past the driver and saw a well-upholstered bench seat. 'Oh good.'

'But?'

'We want a nice view, you know, see the sights and you can tell us what we're looking at as we go along.'

Steph pulled open the front passenger door. Angel skipped round to join her on the front seat before he could protest. The car pulled away with a purr. A glass screen separated them from the rear passenger compartment. Angel tapped it with her knuckle.

'Airtight I suppose?' John nodded. 'A passenger could

find themselves nodding off quite quickly back there.' A thin sheen of sweat glistened on his top lip. She tapped a button on the dashboard. 'And this?'

'Central locking.'

Angel looked at Steph. 'Locked in and asleep. Wouldn't want that would we, Steph?' She turned back towards John and smiled. 'Just as well we decided to sit in the front, with you.'

His eyes flicked towards a switch on the dashboard and Angel guessed that it was the one that would release sedative gas. 'Now John, what we want is a guided tour. Why don't you tell us what we are looking at?'

He cleared his throat. 'Well we're on a kind of ring road; all the other roads were dug up except this one.'

Angel and Steph looked around.

'And those?' asked Steph pointing to the barrack-type buildings on their left.

'It's where the workers live; male that end, female this.'

They looked at the buildings as they passed. There was a long line of standing water underneath the gutterless corrugated iron roofs; rags were pinned up against the windows. Pools of stagnant mud were covered in a haze of flies. In the centre, a security camera stood watch. It tracked the car as they moved.

'The security walls, do they run all the way around?'

'The outer one is 117 miles long. Of course, some of it is underwater now. The inner one is a half-circle; it runs down to the river at both ends.'

They both fell silent. Angel wondered how on earth they were going to get out.

'What are those?' Angel pointed at a network of tall white buildings. The towering smokestacks that they had seen from the first gate were connected to them by a single-storey brick building. Two trucks were loading or unloading their cargo at the rear. John seemed reluctant to answer.

'What do we have here?'

'Medic block.'

'Those over there?'

'Metal works, steel, mainly.' Angel opened the window. The air was sulphurous; a fine orange dust covered the tops of bricks and stones on the side of the road.

She closed the window and thought for a moment. 'The medic block, is that a hospital?'

'No, it's where they process parts ... and stuff ... you know, for transplants.'

'Looks busy,' said Steph glancing up at the smoke pouring out of the incinerator chimneys.'

'Yes, lots of people need treatment, especially now, after the great storm.'

'Really ... what sort of treatment?'

'Well apparently the old style is bad luck.' He looked at their uncomprehending eyes. 'It was the theme for the grand ball.'

Angel felt bile rise in her throat.

They drove on in silence. The inner wall drew closer. It stretched out to the sides as far as they could see. Angel slipped a knife from her jacket and moved it up against John's side.

He looked down and gasped.

She leaned closer and whispered, 'Steph and I are going to slip into the foot well. Tell the guards that we're asleep in the back.'

They drew up to the entrance. He pressed the comms button on his steering wheel and spoke. 'Hi, two sleepy packages for delivery.'

'OK John, health bay 4 is waiting. I'll radio on.'

'Will do.' The gate slid open and the car pulled into a tunnel as wide as two trucks.

'Is there any other way out of this tunnel, besides the gate at the end?'

'Service door on the left, about halfway.' He glanced down; Angel could see sweat glistening on his forehead. 'You know they're going to kill me, right?'

She thought for a moment and then told him to release the gas into the passenger compartment.

'When we get close to the service door, slow down. We'll slip out and open the passenger door a bit, it'll make it look like we came round early and got out. Tell them we kicked up a fuss when you pressed the button, but then we went quiet. You assumed we were asleep.' He looked at the knife pressing against his thigh, then at her and nodded.

The thrum of their tyres on tarmac echoed off the sides of the tunnel. John slowed and gave a quick nod. They slipped out of the slow-moving car, crouched low and ran alongside. Angel opened the passenger car door and left it ajar, a faint trail of yellow gas seeped through the gap.

'Stay down behind the car,' whispered Angel. Steph

nodded. They moved low and close behind the car and passed the service door where John was expecting them to stop. He paused at the second gate and the large doors slid open. Angel saw John wave to a guard and indicate with his thumb that they were in the back.

'Follow me,' said Angel slipping along the other side of the car into an arch of trees around the entrance.

The inner-city side of the wall had been painted to look like scenery around a stately home to give the impression of rolling parkland. The compacted bricks close to the entrance had been sprayed grass green. Trees had been planted in bands. They moved into the cover nearest to the wall, hoping to avoid cameras.

Angel stroked the mosaic bark of a large tree. All that was left of this part of London was a mass of brick and stone, tile and slate, sculpted into undulating rises and falls. Because it was less exposed, nature was moving back in where it could, buddleia and bramble had tapped into the subsoil. Moving along they found a massive pile of twisted metal reinforcement rods, sheets of metal and piles of asbestos roofing stacked against the wall. They pulled a sheet of corrugated iron, under the tree and sat down.

'What are we going to do now?' asked Steph.

'Make my grandmother realise that I mean what I say …'

'Do you think she'll have the driver punished?'

'Yes, I do …' Angel thought for a moment. 'OK, what I want to do is explore a bit, find somewhere to sleep, and then call her first thing in the morning.'

• • •

At dusk Steph and Angel climbed on to the high brick bank and watched the slate-coloured river race out to sea. On the far bank, the south of London had been demolished and then flooded. There was water as far as they could see, except for a single ridge that stood eroded but proud of the grey water. At their feet, waves slipped and sucked against the porous rubble; an emerald green line of slime marked the high tide line.

Behind, there were five large domes that appeared to be connected. Angel watched the sun slip behind them. It looked as if they were on fire.

'Better find somewhere to sleep,' suggested Steph.

They moved along the bank, careful to avoid being silhouetted against the evening sky. A sudden high-pitched chattering erupted just in front of them. They threw themselves to the ground and watched as one, then ten, then hundreds of black specks pour out of the riverbank.

'Water bats!' whispered Steph. They waited for the colony to fly into the darkening sky, then had a closer look at the entrance to their roost. Shadows made the wall look jagged and sharp. But there was something strange about the wall. Angel touched the surface thoughtfully.

'Am I imagining it, or do these bricks look organised, as if they've been laid here?'

'What?' Steph took a closer look. 'Now you come to mention it they do ... sort of.'

The hole in the bank side was deep, the smell of ammonia

overpowering. Angel picked up a loose lump of brick and threw it into the hole. It bounced, regularly ten or more times until it splashed into water. They looked at each other,

'Steps?'

'Flooded though,' added Angel

They sat down to think. 'There used to be underground railway tunnels, do you suppose they still exist?'

'Don't know, but we need to find out, as soon as it gets light.'

Steph and Angel caught what sleep they could in a hollow in the bank side; the rising river came close to their feet. At dawn they watched the bats return chattering to their roost and moved back to the opening to have another look.

'Seems deep,' said Steph.

They caught a glimmer of metal, possibly a handrail.

'We'll come back with a torch or something,' said Angel taking her phone out of her pocket.

After a moment of calm looking out across the river they climbed over the bank and started walking toward the domes.

CHAPTER THIRTY-TWO

'Morning. Are you all right? There are a lot of rats out there!' said her grandmother's voice.

'We're about three miles from the domes, to the southeast. Send John.'

'But …'

'Only John!' said Angel firmly, then she hung up and took the Sim card out of her phone. They placed it under a piece of a metal, a rectangle showing a battered large red circle with a blue bar across. Some of the paint had flaked away, but the shape was still clear. They tried to read it but couldn't, it was too mangled. Next, they buried the phone, and connected it to the solar charger, wedged into a shallow gap. It trilled into charge mode.

Angel looked at Steph and smiled nervously. She wasn't looking forward to seeing her grandmother again. Her intention was to finish the job started by the resistance, but now she realised that she was hoping for more. Meeting her grandmother had started an ache in her to know more about her mother. Destroying her grandmother meant killing that link. She hoped that she could see it through.

They walked along the bank and hid behind a small rise. A distant car moved out from between the domes. They watched it cruise past, checked that John was driving then moved on to the road and waved. He looked tired. He got out of his car and walked stiffly round to the front passenger door and opened it for them.

'Did you get into much bother?'

'Yep.' He tentatively touched his ribs.

'Much?'

'Reckon it would have got worse, if you hadn't come in.'

'What did you tell them?'

'That you went quiet, so I thought the gas had worked. Maybe the door hadn't shut properly. And that you must have got out and gone walkabout.'

Angel nodded in approval. 'How do you fancy being our driver?'

'How do you mean?'

'I can ask for you. I am going to ask for one or two things.'

'Reckon I could redeem myself …' said John thoughtfully.

'But you need to know, she doesn't control me.'

'I think I got that already.' He touched the bruise on his cheek and smiled.

'Right, we want to know if there is anywhere we can live outside those domes?'

'Is there anywhere left standing and safe? added Steph. 'Are there people living out here?'

John thought for a moment and then shook his head.

'The only people that I know about, live inside the domes. The city was just about dead before they levelled it. After the floods, typhoid did for a lot. In the end, people generally moved to where the food grew. And that left the Alphas … and the rats.' He shrugged. 'They did a bit of cleaning up, then they built the walls and the domes.

'See that hill over there? That's where they burnt the last of the bodies.'

'Ah, that kind of cleaning up.' Angel felt a shiver, she had seen piles of burning bodies and the horror was still with her. She wondered if the stench in her throat would ever go away.

'Do they ship stuff in?' asked Angel.

John nodded. 'Everything but air, and they clean that.

• • •

What had at first appeared to be a cluster of squat domes, ballooned out into a structure that covered about thirty acres. Each one was made up of different sized domes, like bubbles in soapy water held together by surface tension; thin and yet immensely strong. From a distance, they were opaque, but closer, they revealed city streets and trees, marble-faced mansion houses and blocks of elegant town houses.

Angel turned to John. 'It's massive. How many people live there?'

'Well, nobody really lives here permanently, although after that last storm we have more than usual. Workers live on the other side of the wall. You won't see them; they're underground.' Angel and Steph exchanged glances; a plan was beginning to form. 'This whole thing is just one of many places where your grandmother lives. She has that state building that you can see there ... on the hill in the biggest dome,' John added.

'But why have they made bubbles to live in?' asked Steph.

'Well they can control the weather in there. I think it's meant to be what the South of France was like before the desert …' He waited until they took it all in and then continued. 'It's surprisingly secure. They filter toxins out of the air in that small one at the back; water in the one at the other side.'

'What about food?'

He looked at Steph. 'See that dome nearest to the river? They ship food from the plantations into there.'

'And that smoke?' asked Angel indicating a pall of smoke rising into the morning sky.

'Incinerators, power generators … they ship oil and coal in by sea.'

'Where?'

'Ships berth upstream; it's more sheltered behind the third barrier. There's a helipad too.'

Angel looked at Steph. Was there any point in destroying this place, if it was just one of her grandmother's many homes?

'Let's go in, shall we?' Steph said softly.

• • •

'The phone's dead, we think they're in.'

Raph stood behind his sister watching her screen over her shoulder. He rubbed his beard and leaned forward. 'Yes, but does that mean that they're OK, or not?'

'Neither, it just means their phone's dead.'

Raph sighed and stood back. He was powerless to help; he hated it, but he had to accept that Angel had chosen Mani's way and not his.

'When will we know?'

'Patience, little brother, Brad's working on it.'

'Of course he is!' Raph turned away in frustration, then turned back. 'How come he's here with us?'

'He saw the light.' Mani smiled proudly.

'Do you think that she's really going to be able to do it? Kill her own family, I mean?'

'Well that's what she went for! Anyway, if she caves, Steph will step in, that's why she's there.'

Raph looked at his sister and realised just how little he knew her. She had run a spy in Alpha, and she had sent Steph to destroy what was left of them if Angel failed. A shiver ran down his spine. He realised that Steph would kill Angel if she got in the way. And he wondered if Angel knew. He had to warn her.

CHAPTER THIRTY-THREE

The air lock door closed behind them and the car moved into a wheel-wash station. John explained that it was there to keep out pests and diseases. Angel supposed that it made sense, considering the degradation outside; disease must be a real problem.

'Are there places like this in other countries?' asked Steph.

John shrugged his shoulders and drove them on into the first dome. Angel asked him to stop the car. He pulled to one side; his wipers made an auto-sweep to clear condensation from the cold windscreen.

Angel and Steph stepped out of the car and the heat hit them like a solid wall. Humidity pressed down on them; it felt like they were breathing water. Angel had never experienced heat like it, she began to feel dizzy. There was not a breath of wind. They looked around, tall palm trees reached skyward. Cascades of long green finger-shaped fruit curled down towards them. Low trees laden with blossom and orange coloured fruit lined the road.

'It's too hot to walk, at least, not until you get used to it,' called John from inside the car. He flicked the air conditioning up to maximum; Angel and Steph climbed back into their seats. They watched city streets, shops and pavement restaurants slide by in silence. In the next zone, there was a sea and beach area illuminated by electric blue lights. People lay on the sand safe in the knowledge that the waves that frothed inches away from their toes would never touch them. Hotels and bars faced on to the water.

Angel felt uneasy, she was a stranger to the trees and plants that surrounded her. She looked up; the dome hid the detail of the sky and she realised that she had lost her bearings. The ground was flat, there was no wind and the sun was just a diffused orange glow. Her heart pounded. Her senses told her to run, she was in a place that she couldn't understand, but she was already in too deep. She leaned forward, closed her eyes and let the cool air blow on to her face.

'This is it,' said John, as he pulled into a wide, sweeping driveway and stopped in front of a flight of steps.

A balustrade of white marble lined the stairs and tall ionic pillars supported a first-floor balcony. The mansion was pristine white; its tall elegant windows were shut tight. A man dressed in black stood waiting at the roadside. He stepped forward and opened the rear passenger door. Angel opened the front door and she and Steph got out.

Turning to John she whispered for him to stay safe. Then she turned back to the man, 'Hello, I'm Angel and this is Steph. Is my grandmother in?'

• • •

Katrin was reclining on a day bed. She was wearing a long white silk gown; her hair was long and blonde. She looked groomed but frail.

'Come in. Come in.' She smiled with her mouth and added softly, 'At last.'

'Grandmother, how are you?' said Angel, stepping forward.

She took a long look at the wound on her forehead. She could see that it was still not healing well. Katrin touched her forehead self-consciously and then frowned.

'I'm well thank you. Ah, and here's your friend?' She appraised Steph disapprovingly. 'You're going to have to tell me where you went? We know that you didn't help my dear Angel. We found blood by the river and we tested it. It was male. Imagine!' She smoothed her hair. 'We're looking forward to meeting him!'

Angel's blood ran cold. She stepped toward her grandmother and forced herself to smile. She leaned forward and touched her cold birdlike shoulder.

'I'm hungry grandma. Do you have any proper food?'

• • •

Angel and Steph were shown to their rooms. They were across a wide airy corridor from each other. Steph's room looked out on to a flat roof at the rear of the house, Angel's on to the sweeping road leading up to the front door.

Angel had a look around while Steph had a shower. The windows were closed and locked. A fan, high in the ceiling, lazily moved the air. The furniture was ornate and white; the bed was as wide as it was long. There was a painting of a small boy drinking out of a river; his horse, harnessed to a cart laden with hay, stood patiently waiting. Angel hoped that he was drinking upstream of the horse.

She moved around the room, picking things up to inspect them, and caught sight of herself in the mirror. Her skin was pale; blue shadows rimmed under her eyes. Her hair had grown since it had been cut so long ago in the quarry. Now, it was long enough to get in her eyes and was rough and spiky. Her clothes were crumpled and dirty from sleeping outdoors.

• • •

The next morning, after a restless night's sleep, Angel stepped into the breakfast room, closely followed by Steph.

'You look … better,' said Katrin brightly.

'Our clothes are being washed. I hope you don't mind us coming down in these?' Steph gestured towards the long towelling dressing gowns that they were both wearing. Angel tightened her belt and shrugged her hands up into her sleeves.

'No, of course not, and I promise that your clothes will be returned to you. I don't want a misunderstanding like last time.'

Angel smiled and nodded an acknowledgement. There was a buffet of cold and hot food by the table.

'I didn't know what you liked, so I asked for some of everything.'

Steph walked along the table, clearly amazed at the range of food. Angel picked up some bread and cheese; she stopped for a second, gently touched an apple, and moved on.

'Are you going to eat?' Angel asked her grandmother.

'Oh, my dear I don't eat.' She watched them sit down at the table. 'When you finish, I've arranged for you to meet some people.'

'Oh, who?' asked Steph popping a piece of salmon into her mouth.

Angel raised an eyebrow. Her grandmother looked at her and spoke softly. 'All I ask is that you see them. Please.'

• • •

'You're not taking blood … so don't even think about coming near me with that needle.' Angel's voice was flat and hard. Steph put the enhancement price list down and moved closer.

'I need your blood group. And your grandmother wants me to confirm that you are related. I can do that with a swab if you want.'

'I can do that myself. Give me the swab.' Angel took it and rolled it against the inside of her mouth.

'Blood?'

'No!'

Steph stepped forward. 'Do you need anything from me?'

'No thank you.' The doctor wrinkled her nose, picked up her bag and left the room.

They perched on the edge of the desk and waited for the next visitor. After a moment, Angel relaxed and flashed a smile at Steph.

'Don't want her to think that I'm too compliant … and besides after blood, who knows what she might want … organs?'

There was a gentle tapping on the door.

'Let's see who this is, shall we?' Angel opened the door a crack; a man was standing hand raised ready to knock again. He was small and skinny; his hair fell in tight curls over his eyes.

'Hi I'm Jay. I'm here to help with your …' He gazed at Angel's hair through the gap. 'My god, did you *actually* choose grey?'

Angel frowned. 'No it chose me.'

'And who did this to you?' he asked pointing at spikes of hair.

'Friends … good friends!'

'OK, can I come in?' Angel stepped back to let him into the room, checked the corridor was empty then turned to face him. Jay pulled a brochure out of his folder. 'Are we talking transplant, implant, extension or maybe …'

'Just cut it.'

'You want it shorter?'

'Yes, I want it too short to blow into my face, or to get in the way when I swim. I want it too short to need brushing. But I like to feel it blow in the wind.'

Jay visibly paled. 'Really? You're joking, please, tell me you are joking.'

'Or just let me have the scissors.'

'No. Let me, I'll do it.' He turned to Steph who was still smiling. 'And what about you?'

Her face suddenly stern, Steph asked what exactly was wrong with her hair. He looked at it nervously. Steph's hair was long and dark; it fell in curls below her shoulders. He cleared his throat.

'It's just that we don't do curly.' His voice weakened. 'I could straighten it?'

'No thanks,' said Steph moving away.

He implored them with a look. His hands trembled.

'It's just … it's just that you're both beginners here. I'm sorry, but you don't realise what we have to do. I can have you thinner in a matter of days … a weekend even.'

'Why?' asked Angel.

'It's the … you look better in your clothes. Why spend a fortune on clothes if they don't hang right?'

Angel watched the man squirm. 'I would like you to cut my hair. I don't want to be thinner. I like my shape. This is who I am. Do you understand?'

He wilted in front of her. 'OK, but what about clothes? I could make your hair match your colour palette.'

'My what?'

'OK, but your grandmother said …'

'Leave her to me.'

An hour later they had chosen some new clothes and Angel's hair was trimmed into shape. They were walking back towards Katrin's rooms.

Angel whispered, 'This heat and humidity crushes me. It makes me dizzy. Stars, sun, wind, clouds – they're my map and compass. I'm lost inside this dome. I'm going to have to get outside somehow.'

'You want me to come?'

'No, thanks. Maybe you could try and talk to some of the staff, get a sense of what's going on?'

• • •

Angel watched as John turned around and reluctantly drove away. She had refused his offer to park up further along the riverbank in case she needed him. She needed solitude and the mental focus to get to know this strange landscape.

She took a deep breath ... held it ... then slowly let it go. The breeze moved against her skin, like a gentle shower of rain. It lifted her hair and cooled her scalp. She smiled and felt alive again.

A hawk circled lazily in the thermals over the domes. Angel watched the car disappear then she turned and began to walk, then stride, then she broke into a run along the road. The sheer joy and freedom of unrestricted movement, of being alone, lifted her heart. She ran until her spirit was light, her heart beat loud in her ears, and her lungs were full of cool natural air.

She ran on until she reached the area where they had buried her phone and sat down. Ever since she had learned that they had found Raph's blood in the mud by the river, she had been on edge. She couldn't raise it with her grandmother for fear of showing that he mattered. She was scared that they might have got a DNA sample and if they did, she wondered, could they trace him? Her chest tightened at the thought.

Mani had warned her that using the phone could be dangerous, but she needed to know that he was safe. And yet she knew that if her call was intercepted her grandmother would know that Raph mattered and it would put him in even more danger.

She needed to act before she was in too deep to escape, but she also needed to be careful not to set hares running, or to give herself away too soon. It was a difficult balance. Things were so much harder than she had expected.

They had done one thing right at least; it had been a good idea of Mani's to send Steph. She was less important to Katrin and less threatening to the staff. Perhaps she could find a weak spot for them to work on? And what's more, it was good to have a friend.

Angel could see the marker, but simply didn't dare to use the phone.

She picked up a rock and threw it hard at another rectangle of metal half buried in the ground. She missed. Her aim was out! She was softening up! Two shots later her rock hit the target and bounced off at a tangent.

'Good shot!' said a soft voice behind her. Angel spun around to find herself looking into the deep brown eyes of a boy, perhaps thirteen years old. He was angular and awkward. His oversized clothes were dirty, the tab end of his broad leather belt hung down to his knees. Around his waist hung a torch, a short-handled shovel and a leather pouch.

'Thanks.' She stood up and checked for others as she backed carefully away.

'If you're from in there ...' He shrugged towards the domes about two miles back. 'You should go back. It's dangerous, 'specially after dark.'

She could feel him appraising her hair, her clothes, and her face. She clearly didn't fit. He frowned. 'If you're from somewhere else, you need to know they shoot to kill.'

'Well, I'm kind of both ... and neither,' she said. 'But thanks for the warning.' She waited; he continued to look at her as if he was trying to place her. Finally, he spoke. 'You're her, aren't you? The one they sent to finish this all off.'

'I'm Angel,' she said holding her hand out. He stepped back.

'Talib,' he mumbled.

'Talib, where do you live?' He glanced away. 'Do you live underground? Are there still tunnels?' He shrugged, clearly unhappy about the direction of the conversation. 'Will I find you here again, Talib?' she added softly.

'I'll find you ...'

He turned, ran down the bank of bricks and disappeared behind a tangle of metal. Angel expected him to reappear. But there was just silence. A large grey rat scuttled out of a hole. She picked up a brick and threw it. She hit it first time.

CHAPTER THIRTY-FOUR

Angel and Steph sat on the polished floor in the hallway outside their rooms, talking quietly. They assumed that their rooms would be bugged. The hallways might be wired too, but it was less likely.

'Your grandmother sent these,' said Steph holding out two envelopes. Angel took the one that was addressed to her, the embossed and textured surface of the paper felt like animal skin. Inside was an invitation to an event that evening to introduce them to her grandmother's friends … the Alpha community.

'I'm not sure we're in a position to refuse,' said Steph.

'No, you're right. We need to get her onside.'

'And avoid being locked down.'

Angel's nodded her head grimly. She would do anything to avoid that.

• • •

At eight, Angel and Steph stepped from their air-conditioned car into the heat. John had dropped them out of sight of the party; they wanted to walk the last few hundred yards. Through the surface of the dome the sky was black. Arc lights created a bubble of light around the beachside party and cast a crisscross of tree shadows on the ground around the circle. They could see over a hundred people on the floodlit marbled square in front of a palatial beachfront hotel. Behind them waves broke, azure, on silver sand.

Barefoot, Angel wore a floor length, slender, silver jersey dress. Steph wore a similar white dress; her dark hair had been pinned up. Katrina had sent them a selection of jewellery to choose from. Angel wore a turquoise bracelet; Steph a long necklace made of jet. She had quizzed Steph about functions that she had seen at Chequers; this was not going to be easy.

They linked arms and walked slowly towards the party. She knew that the chance of a listening device being able to pick up what she was about to say next was as low as it was going to get. Keeping her eyes on their destination, Angel inclined her head towards Steph.

'I saw someone outside this afternoon ...'

'What? Really?' Steph kept her eyes forward and smiled as she spoke.

'Yes, I think they live underground.' Angel paused for a moment to let the information sink in. 'They know about us ... and why we're here,' she added softly.

'God! How? Could you find them again?'

'No, but apparently they can find us. How did you get on?'

'Your grandmother didn't like you going outside. Be really careful.' They slowly walked on. 'The staff are very suspicious ... or scared.'

'Or both?'

Steph nodded. 'I did find out there's a lot of service work goes on in the basements. They all connect up.'

Angel heard her name being called. Katrin slipped from a group of guests in the centre of the gathering and gestured for them to join her.

'Here we go,' Angel whispered.

Steph slipped back a pace and followed her into a sea of suspicious faces. Angel could see at once that the mass theme had moved on from Bangladeshi to Chinese. The women had rosebud lips, their faces white circles. Tanned necks and hands were almost hidden by mandarin collars and long sleeves. Long black sleek hair shone in the arc light.

The level of noise faded to a whisper as people turned to watch. She could feel the heat of their stares as they silently parted to let her through.

'Why she's quite grey, poor thing,' whispered one woman.

'And she's got so much flesh … imagine!' said another in a high childlike voice.

Angel turned and smiled. 'Thank you.'

The crowd gasped, her voice was low, she sounded like a servant. They moved their attention to Steph. Were they mistaken? Was this the one?

'Ladies and gentlemen,' called Katrin from the side of the pool. 'Let me introduce my granddaughter … Angel.' Angel nodded and smiled. 'And her companion Stephanie.'

Steph raised her hand.

'After our recent … losses, it is of considerable consolation to me to find my dear daughter Lilith's only child. I *know* that you will make her welcome.'

Applause stuttered and then caught. When Katrin judged that it was loud enough she raised a hand for silence.

'Angel, Steph, do come and get a drink.'

They moved to meet her.

'Not the best entrance in the world! What on earth possessed you to walk? And where are your shoes? Still, I don't suppose they'll forget you in a hurry ...' She clicked her fingers and a waiter appeared. Katrin took a cocktail, Steph a glass of wine and Angel a glass of cool water. The sides of the glass sweated; she ran the cool surface across her forehead.

'I suppose that I should be grateful that you're wearing a dress.' Katrin caught sight of the turquoise bracelet on Angel's wrist. 'And your mother's jewellery.'

Angel's heart missed a beat, and she pressed the silver bracelet to her lips.

'Now I need you to mingle, talk to the men ... or at least don't scare them off. They're very keen to talk to you.'

Katrin stepped back and clapped her hands. Servants streamed out from the beachfront hotel, carrying trays laden with food. Angel was dismayed to see that although the choice was amazing the portions were minute.

Angel looked up, a sandwich halfway to her mouth, into the wide-eyed stare of a young woman. She took a bite, turned away and collided with a small slight man.

'Ah, so you're Angel?' His voice was liquid, his gaze slid over her body. 'I'm Felix.' He reached for her elbow to steer her. Angel stepped back, grasped his hand and shook it.

'Hello Felix, nice to meet you.' Then she dropped his hand and moved into the crowd.

The humidity in the dome coupled with the mass of perfume-laden bodies made Angel's head spin.

'Are you OK?' asked Steph as she positioned herself with her back to Angel, a fixed grin on her face, talking over her shoulder.

'Too hot … bit queasy. You?'

'OK … That one over there wants to meet you.' Steph indicated with a nod to Angel's right. 'And that one on the other side gave me his card to give to you later. Now … the tall thin woman in black wants to know why you have so much flesh. I said that it was normal. And … the one nodding at you now, near the tree, wants to know who did your hair!'

She glanced at Angel and they both began to laugh.

'That's nice. You both seem to be having fun.' Katrin's tone was icy, even though she appeared to be smiling at their joke.

'Bit of a strain, I'm not used to this kind of company, and there are so many people.'

Katrin thought for a moment and then nodded. She glanced around. People were in groups, apparently talking, but watching them closely.

'Very well, you may go. I don't suppose that it would hurt them to think that you're mysterious.' She raised her hand and snapped her fingers. A car slipped silently from behind the beachfront buildings and parked. John got out and opened the passenger door.

'Just this once, please, sit in the back.' Katrin smiled thinly and walked away.

They gratefully climbed into the back of the air-conditioned car.

'Thanks, John. Back to the house please,' said Steph closing the door. Angel turned to watch as a circle of people closed around her grandmother.

'John, do you have maps?'

'Of where?'

'Of this part of London. I feel so lost inside and outside.'

'I've got a navigation system in the car, so there's not much call for map books anymore, besides the city was flattened, everything is gone.'

'I know but I don't like feeling lost, and I'm curious about what used to be here.'

'OK, let me see what I can find.'

Angel smiled at him brightly and then gently ran her finger over the silver bracelet.

• • •

They met Katrin after breakfast. They could tell from her composure that the party had not been the success that she had hoped.

'I don't mind them thinking that you're aloof, Angel, but you were rude! I mean, why don't you watch Steph, see how she chats to people.'

Angel glanced at Steph. 'I'll get better …'

'You've got to realise,' interrupted Katrin, 'that even if you are talking nonsense, when you're rich, they hear powerful and influential nonsense.'

Angel turned to leave but her grandmother raised her voice. 'How am I going to find you a husband?'

'A what?'

'Life isn't one long holiday … ah, maybe you thought that it was? You need to justify your place here, just like everybody else.'

'I'll work.'

'You are the last surviving member of my family and your priority is to breed … a lot.'

'But I …'

'You don't need to carry them; we have women to do that. Though Lord knows, it wouldn't spoil your figure.'

Angel stepped forward. 'You mean–?'

'I mean,' interrupted her grandmother, her eyes cold, unblinking. 'Most of the families lost people in the storm. You will remember that I lost a son …'

Unbidden, the memory surged back; the jolting impact as she'd swiped him with the knife-edge of the rock. Had her grandmother seen it?

'Now is the perfect time for me to find you the right kind of man. Surely you can see that everyone is trying to patch things up?'

'And what grandma, is the right kind of man?' Angel matched her glare.

'Rich, powerful, hungry to profit from an alliance with me … weak, biddable. Oh, you know … the usual. There were three there last night. One had flown in especially.

And before you turn your nose up at them, remember there are other women looking for replacements. Women with everything going for them. There's only so much that I can compensate for your … for your … for you being you!' Katrin gestured with disdain at Angel's body.

'Well then it's lucky that I have no intention of getting married!'

Katrin stood up and glared. 'So … explain to me … exactly why you are here?'

Angel was struck by her grandmother's venom … her strength.

'We're related. I hoped that you would tell me about my mother.' She drew herself up to her full height and stepped back. 'But I can go.'

'You will do no such thing! You're the reason she left. I forbid you to leave me alone again,' shouted Katrin.

Angel turned and walked out of the room. She was in the hallway when Steph caught up with her, reaching out to touch her shoulder.

'That was something! Are you OK?'

'No!' Angel shrugged the hand from her shoulder.

'We need to stop and think. She is a pretty uncompromising woman. But I guess that's no surprise. You are related.'

Angel laughed softly and then threw herself on to her bed. Steph sat next to her. 'Oh Steph. I need to know about my mother.'

'And she wants you to be like her …'

Briefly, Angel caught Steph's eye. It was important not to forget that every word was being overheard.

'And I can't stand this heat, this humidity. It makes me feel crushed, it takes my energy away.'

'And we have no friends,' said Steph a little louder.

'Neither of us are used to being so idle! That's why I go out running.'

'Do you think that she might let us be outdoors more?'

'Or cook for ourselves? I might sleep better and get less angry ...'

Steph nodded her head in encouragement. 'Yes, but what does she want from you?'

Angel thought for a moment and then said, 'I guess ... she might find it difficult to look at me and see my mother. Perhaps that's what's making her so afraid I'll go. If she got me married, I would be bound to stay.'

They nodded to each other and continued to talk for their audience.

'Let's go out for a walk and cool down.'

• • •

An hour later they were sitting on the brick banks of the Thames watching it seethe towards them. Their faces burned in the cold wind.

Holding the SIM card between her lips, Angel clicked the back of her phone into place. Steph could see her hands shaking. Angel took the card from her mouth and slotted it into place. A message was waiting. She looked up at Steph, her voice was husky; just a whisper.

'It's Raph ... he's missing.'

'What?'

'Part of my deal with Mani was that she would keep him safe.'

'What do you want to do?' Steph watched Angel struggle with the bad news. 'I mean we can't leave and look for him … can we?'

'I need to know that my grandmother hasn't got him. I mean, Steph, they found his blood by the riverbank.' She shivered at the thought. 'Time to dig deeper, and quickly.' Angel hid the phone and after a cursory look around for signs of habitation, they started to walk back.

A small bundle of photographs was waiting on Angel's bed. They were tied together with an elaborate white ribbon. She pulled one end and the bow unravelled. The top photograph was of a tall silver haired young woman, pale blue eyes, turning angrily to look at the camera. Angel was entranced.

'Got to be your mother,' Steph whispered. 'You're just like her. Same eyes, same hair, same ears. Same angry look! Everything.'

Angel had no words; hungry to see her mother's face, she picked up another photo then another. Her heart was pounding. There were images of her mother as a baby, a young girl, on a horse, swimming, carrying books, lying on her bed reading.

'One thing we know. This is too much of a coincidence. She was definitely listening!' whispered Steph.

'Indeed, she was,' said Katrin from the bedroom doorway. 'Angel, we need to talk.'

Angel clutched the photos to her chest and turned to face her grandmother. For the first time, she saw the woman behind the kaleidoscope of surgery and saw herself. Her eyes ... her strength ... her independence. And then she looked deeper and saw the wreckage of a life of dreams achieved. The damage that unchecked power had done; and in that moment, she saw the self that she might become.

• • •

Katrin and Angel sat outside on the balcony looking over the formal gardens. Long low arcs of water irrigated the grass. Behind them condensation ran down the windows and puddled on the marble floor.

'I can't do this.'

'What this?'

'I grew up free ... outside ... doing things, working.' Angel paused. 'I need to live outside the dome. I can't bear the idleness; it makes me feel ill.' She glanced across at her grandmother to see if she was angry but saw that she was listening.

'But there's nothing there. It's not safe out there for the likes of us. We live in these places for good reason, Angel.'

'I could live close to you and the dome in a tent, or something, grandma.' Angel had to be careful, she didn't want to be moved away from London. 'Do you have temporary cabins?'

Katrin nodded her head thoughtfully. 'And you'd work?'

'I can't be idle ...'

'What can you do?'

'I'll have a go at anything. I just don't know how to be an ornament.'

'And the Steph girl …?' Katrin left the question in the air.

Angel knew that Katrin was making comparisons between her and Steph's more practiced social ease. And yet she had also caught her grandmother looking at her face, as though wanting to impress every detail on her mind.

She glanced again at the pile of photographs; her beautiful, angry, laughing mother. She wondered if Katrin missed her, and it occurred to her that other than her and Steph, she'd heard no one laugh since they'd arrived.

'And what do I get in return for letting you live in some shack?'

'I'll stay and try to get to know your people. And I'll get to know the business and then I can work.' She watched Katrin's eyes lost in thought and hoped that she hadn't overplayed her hand.

CHAPTER THIRTY-FIVE

Three days later Steph and Angel were sitting on the steps of a temporary shelter watching swallows loop through the warm evening air.

They had cooked potato and beans and their empty plates were on the step behind them. The building was a rectangular unit which had been used for storage in the docking area and still smelled of coffee. It had an electricity supply, and there was a small tank of water on the roof. They had checked it for bugs and found nothing, but just to be sure they had agreed to talk outdoors.

'This is better,' said Steph taking in a deep breath. She took the phone that she had been issued with by security out of her pocket, turned it off and placed it on the step.

'Much,' said Angel putting her phone next to Steph's. They stood up and walked into the deepening twilight.

The river sparkled as it splashed against the rough bank side. Lower down, black mussels tangled amongst the weed and ever present plastic. They sat and watched the moon rise over the marshland on the distant south bank.

A rock slipped down the slope to their left.

Angel saw a movement along the bank and nudged Steph. 'That's Talib, the boy I told you about.'

He beckoned for them to follow him, then turned and worked his way down to the water's edge He paused for a moment then disappeared.

Warily, they followed, high stepping over stacks of bricks and tangled weed. Hands skidded on mud coated tiles. Angel strained to hear changes in the sound of the river behind and the echoes from an open hall ahead. Steph stumbled and caught herself on the remains of a handrail.

'Are you OK?'

'Yeah, my shoes are caked in mud.'

They paused to kick their shoes against the wall, then moved on into a what sounded like an open chamber.

'Better hurry, it's only clear for a couple of hours,' a voice echoed from the darkness.

'Where are we?' asked Angel.

'Old underground. We're openin' it up, least the top levels.'

Arms reaching out in front, Angel and Steph followed the youth's muffled footsteps along the dark, mud-covered passageway.

'How high does the water get?'

'Fills this one.' His voice faded as he walked around a bend. 'Keep up.'

Angel and Steph strode into the darkness, focussing so hard on the sound of Talib's footsteps that they hardly dared to breathe. The sudden sharp smell of soot and diesel caught in Angel's throat.

'Where are you taking us?' called Steph.

'Next station; you'll see.' He seemed to be further away; they pushed on into the darkness. Angel realised that Steph was getting breathless. Their strides had shortened; they were walking uphill.

She was beginning to wonder if the whole thing had been a trap when they emerged into a larger space. A flickering candle had been placed on a shoulder high platform to their left. The youth leaned down and held out a hand to help them up. They paused to catch their breath before taking it and clambering up on to the platform.

'My name's …'

'Talib, we met once before,' said Angel picking a long cobweb from her shoulder.

He nodded his head in approval, and then he looked at Steph. 'You stay here.'

He gestured for Angel to follow him. She looked at Steph and raised an eyebrow. Steph nodded and sat down near the candle, her back against the wall. Talib lit another candle and led Angel along the platform. She glanced back and saw Steph watching her from inside a flickering bubble of light.

They walked through an echoing side tunnel into a wider area. Angel could feel the sour air moving gently around her.

'You got this one completely open then?'

'Mm … river at one end, more tunnels branching off at the other. The maps are weird … not to scale.'

He stepped into another side tunnel and gestured for her to follow him on to what appeared to be another platform. Talib held his candle high, Angel could see that the ceiling was festooned with cables, the green tiled walls were covered in heavy, dust-laden cobwebs. Something caught her eye. She peered into the gloom. There was a shadow, it moved. Then it became a familiar shape. She ran.

'Raph! You're here!' He strode towards her. 'You're meant to be somewhere safe.'

In his arms, she felt grounded. Her breathing was easy. He leaned forward and kissed her forehead.

'It's not good here. I hate it.' She lifted her face to his.

'I couldn't stay away,' he replied softly.

'They watch us all of the time.'

'I just needed to know that you're OK.'

'She's given me photos of my mother. They're …'

'Shhh. You need to know something …'

'When she …'

He placed his finger on her lips and spoke slowly. 'They're reaping old people for their silver hair.'

'What?'

'They want hair like yours.'

Angel's knees gave way, he held her to him. The horror took her breath away as images of people that she had met … of Star People, fierce and kind, ran through her mind. She could hardly say the words.

'I've … made … things … worse?'

'Get her to let you go to the factory … go see for yourself.' He touched her hair.

Angel rested her cheek in his open palm and whispered, 'You've got to go somewhere safe. I am going to sort this out, but I can't if I don't know that you're OK.'

'An attack's planned for three days from now. Three days Angel. OK?'

She nodded. He kissed her softly on the lips. 'And watch your back … around Steph … promise me?'

• • •

At dawn the next morning Angel stepped into the car. John took her out of the inner city into the outer area, populated by workers and factories.

'You're sure about this?'

'No. But it's got to be done.'

'What does she get in return?'

'I agreed to look for a husband,' said Angel. John nodded his head thoughtfully. 'And breed,' she added.

'High stakes then?'

'The highest.'

Ten minutes later they had passed through the tunnel. Angel memorised the drive, imagining it at the pace of a fast run. Looking at the top of the inner-city wall she could see razor wire sparkling in the early morning sun.

A truck laden with ash pulled away from the Medic block and took a track that led down towards the distant river. Its tyre walls coated in ash, left fresh ghostly imprints on the ground.

The Medic block looked like a two-storey factory. Tall incinerator chimneys stood to the right; black smoke poured into the clean blue sky. The entrance was a dark glass and steel office complex. A dead grey sky reflected in the smoked glass in the upper windows. The office administrator was waiting for her at the door. Thin and tall, she was almost identical to so many of the women that Angel had seen in her grandmother's entourage. Angel wondered if they had already met.

Now that she knew what to look for, the signs of 'evolvement' were easy to spot. Lack of expression, shiny forehead, perfect symmetry, flawless complexion; the woman gave an ear-to-ear welcoming smile.

'I'm Angel. I've come to look around.'

The woman appraised the trousers, running shoes and loose shirt that Angel had put on that morning.

'Ah, yes! You've come to select …' She turned and led Angel into the office.

'No. To learn … Take me to the factory. I know what an office looks like.'

'The factory? We don't normally do that.'

Angel took her arm and smiled. 'Ah, but I am family.'

• • •

Angel threw a rock into the river and shivered. 'You see that long grey stain in the water, coming upstream with the tide?'

Steph shielded her eyes against the sun and nodded.

'That's ash. They dump the ash into the sea by the lorry load.' Angel looked at her hands; they were still shaking. 'Most people … die … right after the *transplant materials* are harvested. Bad ones don't even get that far.' Her voice was just a whisper.

Steph watched a pack of wild dogs foraging on the far riverbank. Angel's horror was palpable.

'Some *materials* don't store well, so they keep the donors alive as organ incubators. Take bits away … to order.' She looked down and tried to calm herself, then forced herself to go on. 'That room was silent, Steph.' Her hand went to her throat. 'They take their larynxes out; it saves on painkillers.' She scraped her palm against the edge of a rock. 'They write on your hand with their finger.'

Angel's throat ached terribly, but she would not allow herself to cry. She didn't know how she would ever be able to bear the weight of what she had witnessed. She'd been trying to find a way to understand, or maybe, if she was honest with herself, to like her grandmother. She took a deep shuddering breath; but now that she truly knew her legacy, she knew she must destroy them all, every last one.

Mani was right, if she succeeds in killing her grandmother ... she inherits the Alpha empire. If she fails, she will be responsible for their destructive consumption continuing for another generation.

She knew with absolute certainty, that it would go on until there was absolutely nothing left. The talking times were over, now. There was no running away from this. Her mother had, but she would not.

There were no words to describe the horror in her head. Angel bit her lip and pushed it away; Steph need never know that some of the people in the silent room were just children.

CHAPTER THIRTY-SIX

'Ah, so you're Angel?' said Pup, the old man sitting next to Angel at the dinner table. He was lazily looking her up and down.

Mind still reeling from the horror of the factory, she'd been forced to attend a hastily arranged dinner for this unexpected guest. And she had to fight the urge to leave the table.

'Have we met before?'

'Almost,' he drawled. 'Twice.'

She took a sip of water and looked at Katrin who was trying to hold a conversation with the man next to her. She glanced up at Angel; there was a nervous flicker to her smile.

'You have your mother's eyes.'

Angel turned her attention back to him. She didn't recognise his accent. The sun damage to his skin was extreme. She had never seen such deep folds of neck skin. His lips were just two tight white lines of scar tissue. He had a lizard smile. She shuddered. Dark blotches bloomed through his thin white hair. He was the first person of any age that she had met since she came here, who had not augmented themselves.

'Don't you dare look at me like that, girl! I don't need approval. It's me that makes the rules, you know!' He swiped a trickle of deep red wine from his chin with a flick of his finger, and then tapped it dry on the white linen tablecloth. A blue-bruise stain blossomed where his finger had touched.

'Now tell me, Angel, how is your mother?'

'Dead.' She forced away the memory of the ash-coloured face of a small boy.

'Oh, shame … Let me show you something.' He pulled a slim wallet out of his jacket pocket, flipped it open, pulled out a photograph and held it next to her face for a second; his face twitched a brief smile before he handed it to her.

'This is my son.'

The picture was of a man of indeterminate age, dark hair, heavily tanned.

'Must be hard to recognise family when they can change so …'

She returned the photo. He smiled, a thin lip smile.

'Your mother and my son were really quite friendly once.'

'That's nice,' said Angel pushing food across her plate.

Scene after scene from her visit to the Medic block were playing over and over in her head. If she closed her eyes, she saw the silent room, one buzzing electric strip light over each bed, drug delivery conduits plugged into the wall behind. The rusty smell of old blood stuck in her throat. They had sighed and turned their heads to watch her as she walked past. The memory of the sound made her want to vomit. She wondered if she would ever be able to close her eyes again.

'Not very talkative tonight, Angel?' Katrin's voice cut through her thoughts.

'What? Oh, sorry.' She pulled her attention back to the room and smiled. Pup had arrived with his entourage at very short notice, sending Katrin into a spin of anxiety. Apparently, he hadn't gone into Offshores, but he was still a powerful player. She assumed that he was looking for her weaknesses, for opportunities to scavenge or for a hostile take-over. Angel's job was to take his mind off business, whilst her grandmother tried to make sure her operation looked strong and undamaged.

'They tell me that you've sent out instructions that no one is to have grey hair but you?' His scarred lips stretched to a thin white line. 'Most people think that imitation is flattery.'

'I think people should be themselves.'

'Good luck with that one.' He popped a piece of fish into his mouth and chewed slowly. 'Anyway, I am sorry to hear about your mother. I once had high hopes for her and Edward, my son.'

'Did they know each other very well?'

'I used to have a little necklace of a play-island in the Caribbean. Sunk now of course,' he added absent-mindedly. 'Actually, I think he would rather like to meet you. My people will arrange it.'

Angel got the uncomfortable feeling that this wasn't an invitation so much as a fact. She looked around the table for someone else to talk to, but no one would look up from their plate.

'Did you like her ... my mother?'

'Let's see ... she was beautiful in a stray sort of way. Active. Wilful. Outspoken.' He wrinkled his nose at a long-past memory. 'I'm told your grandmother has ambitious plans for you.'

'Does she?'

'She says that you're showing some interest in the family business. Perhaps I can show you mine. My farm perhaps?'

'What do you farm?'

'People.'

'You farm *people*?'

'Mm …' He popped a baby tomato into his mouth. 'For our own consumption.'

The room was quiet. Pup dabbed his chin with his napkin.

'Reaping is so hit and miss, don't you think? The general population is in such a sorry state. No pride, no dignity. Well … so we breed 'em. We specialise. There's the hi-beauty line … mature-quick-die-young. It's early days but it's looking promising.'

'What other things do you breed?' Angel hoped that she was hiding the disgust in her voice.

'Oh, you know, small and sturdy for heavy work, biddable for service work … I require a certain shape for my women.' His voice trailed off. Angel looked up and realised that people were listening. They looked excited and curious.

'So, will the demand for reaping stop?'

'Lord no!' he barked. 'Least not until we get the full baseline breed programme going. Besides people in this hemisphere are so behind the times.'

Angel looked at her grandmother, she wasn't sure how much longer she could keep this appalling conversation going. Her palms were sweating; the effort of smiling was making her face twitch. Her grandmother touched her scarlet smiling lips as if to shush her. Angel took a deep breath, forced a smile and turned back towards Pup.

'What did you do before all this?' She wondered too late, if he might be offended by the implication that he might be very old; but he was flattered by her interest. His chest expanded with pride.

'Oh, I made and broke governments, I wrote public opinion, told people what to think, made people into puppets and then strangled them with their very own strings.'

'Why?' asked Angel, her voice came from deep in her throat.

'Because I could, and nobody dared to stop me.' He sighed with pleasure. 'To be honest, I miss it. I could buy anybody, kings and queens, whole countries. Now I own them all.' He made a small circular wave with his hand. 'And the whole Pacific Rim, Asia and Australia … so far.' He took a sip of water and dabbed his reptilian lips with his napkin. 'Do tell me, what does your grandmother *really* plan to do with you?'

'Are you really called Pup?' Angel wanted to divert him from that particular line of conversation.

'Well it was a joke at first; you see, I called myself the puppeteer once and it stuck.' He raised his glass at Katrin, and she raised hers back. His eyes flickered as he looked around the room, pausing here and there just long enough to disturb. His gaze returned to Angel and he smiled.

'Course your grandma made her money on the markets, back when people believed in them. Now *there's* an illusion. Sleight of hand … keep it moving … distract … palm it … then move on. Money's just a number-promise. Always was.'

'And now?'

'People got it eventually, when the numbers got so much bigger and the promises so much smaller. By then, though, we had all the wealth and they had all the promises.' He leaned towards Angel; his breath was fetid. 'But believe me, the debts don't go away, people still owe me, big time.' A laugh rattled in his throat. 'Long may it continue,' he whispered to Angel, and then he raised his glass to the room and toasted himself. 'The puppeteer!'

CHAPTER THIRTY-SEVEN

Angel reached up and took the letter from Steph. Unable to close her eyes without seeing death mask faces, she had slipped out of the unusually quiet dome just before dawn and walked down to the cabin to watch the morning stars fade.

She opened the envelope reluctantly; it was unlikely to be good news. The writing had exaggerated loops and underlining. It said that Katrin had urgent business to attend to and had left shortly after the dinner the previous night.

'The visit's over?' Angel looked up in surprise.

'I got one telling me to go back to my grandparents,' nodded Steph.

'But we're …' something further down the page caught her eye. 'Pup says he's my grandfather! And I'm …' The words blurred, she held it out to Steph who took the letter and scanned it.

'You're to go with him?'

Angel looked at the river, and then turned to the domes and shook her head in disbelief, she had been so close. Another day or two and she would have been ready.

Steph sighed. 'Are you going to go with him?'

Angel shook her head.

'We had better get a move on, then. There are two people

waiting for you at the dome. I said I needed to say goodbye and that I would bring you back.'

They ran down to the slimy water's edge. The entrance to the underground was dark and ankle deep in muddy water.

'Where are we heading?' asked Steph.

'Maybe we can get Talib to guide us out through to an open tunnel so we can get out. If not, we'll just have to keep searching.'

'But where does he live?'

'No idea. I figure that if he hears us, he might come and find us,' said Angel as they plunged into the darkness.

The water around their ankles seemed to be getting lower. Either they were travelling uphill, or the river was receding. Angel paused to make a star in the mud on the wall, then they moved on.

They managed to find the first platform that Talib had taken them to, but there was no sound of him. So, they stepped down on to the next line; into hip high cold water and waded along the tunnel. Entrails of old wires looped between hooks on the tunnel walls, so they ran their fingers loosely along the top to guide them. Thirty stumbling minutes later, the echoes in the darkness changed; they had emerged into what sounded like another station. The walls were closer, and they could feel a platform on their right. They pulled themselves up out of the cold water and listened for any sound of movement, other than curious rats.

'Soon as those people realise we're not coming back, and they start searching, there's going to be …'

'One fell in the river and the other slipped on a brick and

broke his neck,' interrupted a voice in the dark. Angel spun toward the voice. There was a click and spark of a flint and a candle illuminated Talib's grim face. 'We've closed the old flood gates along the river's edge, should keep them out for a bit.'

'When's high tide?' asked Steph.

Somewhere overhead there was the muffled crump of an explosion. Tiles fell from the roof and shattered on the platform. Steph and Angel moved closer to the walls.

'Seven hours. That's them levelling the area around your place.'

'Pup's won't like not getting his own way,' said Angel, almost to herself. 'Can you help us get out of London?'

'Well, we can get you out faster if you can swim the tunnels. If not, we have to wait until dark and use a boat.'

Angel thought for a moment. 'There's something I need to do.' Steph started to speak, but Angel spoke firmly 'Alone ... family business.' She turned to Talib, 'I need a few things.'

They spoke in hushed tones while they waited for the boy to return. Steph wanted to go with her, but Angel insisted that she leave the city immediately, in the end they agreed that she would wait until nightfall. Talib returned with a backpack, a precious wind up torch and a roughly drawn map. She and Steph hugged, then Angel dropped back into the water and waded into the tunnel.

Steph watched until the torchlight had faded.

'I came to help her kill Katrin and finish Alpha. Not in our worst nightmares could we have guessed that Pup would come and claim her. She didn't stand a chance.'

'What do you think she's going to do?' Talib asked.

'No idea. Although the medic block really shocked her. I don't think she's slept since.'

'Well let's go and see somebody about giving her some cover, shall we?'

Talib led Steph through an archway and up an iron staircase to meet his people.

• • •

Angel felt afraid, but at the same time strangely free. She could still feel the stroke of the message that one of the 'silent donors' had written in her palm with his finger. At first, she had tried to tell herself that she had misunderstood, but no, his message was clear, and she would not fail him.

In this at least, she must succeed.

The only sound that she could hear was her breathing and the water lapping against the side walls. She stopped at every fork in the track, platform and doorway to check her map. Pairs of red pinpoint eyes were caught in the torchlight; too many rats to count. Something seemed to stroke against her hip. She stepped aside and saw what she hoped was a long brown eel. Talib had warned that some of the conduits, containing the rivers that ran under the old city, had broken and were discharging into the tunnels, so she must be prepared for anything.

At Moorgate, she climbed up on to the platform moved down to a lower line, then headed northwest. For the first mile, the still cold water was chest high. She wondered if closing the floodgates to keep Pup's men out was going to back up the whole system and drown her.

Angel balanced the backpack on her head and slipped the map and torch inside. Then holding it as high as she could she moved on into the darkness. She tried counting steps up to a hundred then going back to zero and started again. The cold leached the energy out of her body. She whispered numbers through chattering teeth. When she was too cold to shiver, she hummed the rhythm of her footsteps.

By twelve hundred, the water was up to her shoulders. Her arms ached from the weight of the bag. Her foot caught in some trailing cables and she plunged under the water. It tasted of decay and old oil. She kicked and came up gasping for air; her bag still dry.

She was exhausted, but she didn't dare to stop in case the water levels rose any higher. Cautiously, she sidestepped into the centre of the tunnel; away from the safety of the guiding walls but also away from the treacherous cables. On and on she moved, each step harder than the last. She tried to focus on the sound of the black water lapping against the walls. But each ice-cold splash that fell from the fractured ceiling was a hammer blow to her head. Pushing her frozen body through ice cold water made her gasp with pain.

The water rose up to her chin. She was tired, so tired. Her mind was closing down … it told her that it might be so much … easier … just … to allow herself to go to sleep … to drift off … let the water take her … after all she loved water … it was her element …

She was back in the time when she had allowed herself to drift in the lake and just float, to watch the stars, to listen to the hum of insects and the occasional splash when a fish jumped up to catch a fly.

Her pace was slowing; her body no longer her own. She stumbled and plunged under the surface into another kind of darkness.

Her mind was still. She didn't kick, just held the bag up out of the water… A buckle scraped against her skin. Angel saw hands, moving, a trembling finger forming letters in the palm of her right hand. A finger that was signing… *for god's sake kill us…* She pushed herself up out of the water and bellowed in rage. If there was one thing that she had to finish, it was this.

CHAPTER THIRTY-EIGHT

Drenched in centuries old mud and oil, Angel dragged herself out of the tunnel entrance and threw herself to the ground. She'd been close to giving up down there. But that was the easy part. The horror of what was ahead made her want to curl up and cry. But she knew that it had to be done, so she hauled herself up to standing and tried to scrape the worst of the slime from her body. She spat to clear her throat and wiped her face with her sleeve. Her hands stank of filth. Moaning with exhaustion and dread she heaved the backpack over her shoulders, then she checked for security patrols and movement around the factory. Nothing. She took a deep shuddering breath then pushed herself to run before her cold, wet body became visible to heat detectors.

She was close to the Medic block when a light flared from over the inner-city wall. Instinctively she crouched low and covered her eyes. A deep rumble shook the ground, rising to the crescendo of an enormous explosion.

Smoke from the factory chimneys ripped north.

Were the underground tunnels being bombed? Or was it the resistance attacking the dome? Either way she didn't have a moment to lose.

The sky lost its bloom. Dust and dry leaves lifted and skittered around her as the super-heated air pushed up by the wall, caused an updraft. There was movement ahead, she threw herself flat on the ground. The sound of shouting and car doors slamming seemed to echo all around her. With horns blaring and lights flashing, the vehicles accelerated towards the tunnel. When all was quiet, Angel started to move again towards the Medic Block.

One truck remained, its engine idling at the side of the building. It was parked under a rubberized chute. The driver looked like he was asleep, feet up on the dashboard, his hat over his eyes, waiting for the next load of ash. She moved closer and saw that his side window had been smashed and that a shard of metal had pinned him to his seat.

Angel walked toward the office, scooped up a handful of mud, stepped into the reception area and waited; the building seemed asleep. There was a click, the lights went on. She spun around and threw the mud at the sensor. It stuck; the lights went off. Picking up a heavy chair, she heaved it through the glass partition into the locked office.

Thousands of sparkling shards of glass fell at her feet. She shook glass fragments from her hair, flicked it from her shoulders, and stepped through into the office.

Holding her torch between her teeth she ripped open the desk drawer and scrabbled through the contents for an entry code. But all that she could find were stacks of brochures and business cards. She ripped the drawer out of the desk, used it to push the glass from the desk, then set it down and forced herself to search more carefully. She was just about to start on a filing cabinet when she saw what she was searching for. Tucked into the band around a stack of brochures was a card with four numbers on it.

Then at the back of the drawer under some loose papers she caught sight of a watch. It had a broken strap but was just like the one that she remembered her guide wearing.

Angel snatched up the roll of sticky tape and strapped the watch to her wrist. Then scissors, a screwdriver and a cigarette lighter went into her pocket.

Another loud explosion pounded against the front window. She flattened herself into a corner of the office. A ball of flames rose from the far side of the inner-city wall. Her ears fluttered with the change of air pressure. That was closer!

She ran to the door into the main building. As far as she could remember the watch face would have been opposite a small black sensor on the door as the woman punched in the numbers. Angel cupped her hand around her torch and read as she punched in the numbers, then careful that the watch face was opposite the sensor she waited to see if it would work. There was a soft click, she pushed the door open a little and peered through into the corridor. No light … no sound of people moving … she scooped a pile of glass into the doorway with her foot, settled the door carefully ajar and ran.

One floor down, the organ storage unit was working just as she remembered. Low lighting revealed rows of metal shelving, stacked three high, with industrial-sized freezers. A large scissor lift was recharging in the bay by the door. In the centre of the room raised on a platform was a metal and glass observation area. A flight of metal steps led to a walkway that circled the office in the centre. Angel ran over to the stairs; her footsteps echoed across the building. She paused and listened, nothing but the hum of the freezer units. She peered through the glass in the doorway, and then tried the door handle. Locked … tried the watch on the sensor … nothing … punched the numbers in … it didn't work.

Another explosion rumbled through the metal walls. In the office, she could see the back of a chair that had been pushed away from the control panel. Someone's coat had fallen to the ground, and a broken mug lay on the floor in a brown puddle; they must have left in a hurry.

She ran downstairs looking for something to help her to get into the office. It was dark under the platform. Using her torch, she saw boxes stacked in haphazard piles. She ripped them open only to find paper, organ transport packaging, and two stacks of cleaning fluid. She reached in and scattered them, pushing them out of the way, reached deeper into a pile and unearthed a red fire extinguisher. Yes! She heaved it on to her shoulder, ran upstairs and punched it through the cheap wooden office door, then she reached in and unlocked it. She worked along, systematically pounding the base of the extinguisher into the control panel, smashing the screens and keyboards.

Just in time, the word *Utilities* caught her eye. She put down the extinguisher. Breathless and exhilarated, she became aware of alarm bells ringing. She flicked off the alarm and fire sprinkler system, then sprinted downstairs, paused to set light to the boxes under the office and left the storage warehouse to burn.

• • •

They had taken down the sluice gates that held the river back and blown openings along the brick riverbanks. Steph stood and watched the hungry river reclaim the inner city. It eased its monstrous blue and silver tongue between short lived islands. It roared when it found a way into an old underground tunnel only to reappear spouting high into the air where it forced a way back to the surface.

A rag tag circle of armed men surrounded the main dome. It wasn't easy to protect. The complex had been built for pleasure not defence; no one had expected resistance. But now they were faced with an unknown assailant, a flat panorama of levelled ground and a fast-approaching river.

She watched a tight circle of black suited men emerge. They walked; weapons pointing in every direction, scanning for signs of movement. A hawk rising to take advantage of the rush of rats leaping out of a tunnel fell dead, dismembered in a hail of bullets.

Pup was at the centre, his hands on the shoulders of the man in front, a man behind held him by the belt. He stumbled along between his men, spitting fury and bile into the night. A helicopter roared around a bend in the river and hovered tree-high above a clearing. It spun full circle casting its beamed lights on to the ground. Then at a given signal it dropped lower, and a ladder uncoiled from its side door.

With his sparse hair flaring in the downdraught, Pup raised his fist and gestured angrily toward the riverbanks, then he grabbed hold of the ladder. Three times he tried to climb; three times he failed. His guards shouted to each other over the beat of the rotor blades.

Talib tapped Steph on the shoulder and indicated that she should take cover. She nodded and followed him to the mouth of a tunnel and dropped down on the bank to watch as two people dressed in black, carrying rocket launchers, ran along the riverbank toward the helicopter.

She saw that the guards had removed their belts and used them to strap Pup to a tall man's back like a baby. He was attempting to carry him, still struggling and shouting up the ladder. Pup looked like an obscenely angry long-legged child. In his fury, he wrapped his arm around the man's neck and pressed it on his windpipe. The man tried to tuck his chin down and fight the stranglehold. Each step was a fight against gravity, the downdraught from the rotating blades and Pup's death grip. Almost at the top of the ladder, the man missed a tread and stumbled. Pup punched the side of his rescuer's head, and then turned to shake his fist and roar at the elements. A hand reached out from the helicopter, caught hold of his waving arm, another caught hold of the belt and hauled the two men aboard.

There was a flash of white and the helicopter lifted and tilted to avoid rockets. One man fell from the ladder and landed hard; a cloud of dust circled his splayed body. The ladder was pulled up. Pup was flown north, away from the river to safety. His remaining bodyguards turned and ran.

Steph and the other fighters watched them disappear and then turned their attentions to the dome.

• • •

Angel heard the rockets explode. A flare of light illuminated the fire escape that she was using to get to the 'silent ward.' A helicopter roared low and loud over the building. As she ran she wondered if it was escaping or attacking.

She leaned her forehead against the door and waited until she had caught her breath. This was the place that haunted her nights and her days. She took a deep breath then punched in the numbers, waited for the click, pushed the door open and stepped inside.

There it was again; the high-note smell of bleach and a low-note of blood ... and rot ... that she had found impossible to forget. Just as hard to blank out was the cold, the rows of beds, the harsh strip lights, but most of all, the silence. She moved to the first bed. A young woman without a scalp was tethered by chest, arm and hip straps. She was ashen with pain. A drug line snaked from her neck to a control panel on the wall behind the bed head. Four lines of beds stretched the full length of the warehouse, each one occupied. The theatre door was at the far end, next to the body disposal chute, there in case anyone succumbed before their due decommitment date.

Angel cleared her throat and stepped inside. The door locked behind her. Curious heads lifted and turned towards the unscheduled noise.

Tissue removal usually happens in the morning. Angel remembered the voice of the woman, proudly showing her around. *The people near the end of their donor journey are positioned closer to the chute.*

She could see, as she walked along the row reaching out and touching toes or shoulders, that some people were pale, bathed in sweat, their eyes distant and lost.

No larynx, no screaming, no painkillers ... She began to feel the nausea rising. Angel stopped in the centre of the room, cleared her throat, forced herself to smile and began to speak.

'Hello, it's me. Angel.' Her voice faltered, 'I came ... I came to visit you before. Do you remember me?' A woman raised her head and nodded.

'I've come to tell you ...' A man cupped his hand to his ear, Angel forced herself to speak louder. '... that to my eternal ... my eternal shame ... I am related to the people who've done this to you.' She wiped black-stained tears from her chin. 'I am going to fight this ... put a stop to it. Bring them down ... I promise this butchery will stop!'

There was silence. She forced herself to continue.

'When I was here, one of you asked me ... to ... to kill you.' Tears were now freely running down her cheeks, streaks of white on her oil-and-soot stained skin. Impatiently, she wiped them away. 'I want to try to help you to get home.' She walked along the rows, willing people, imploring them to nod, or to catch her attention. But no one moved. 'Or ... if you want ... I will do as I was asked. I will end this for you ... right here ... right now.'

Angel watched and waited. There was a silence, and then a hiss, a sigh, a smile, a nod. Some of them waved, a man fought to sit up; it was the one who had written on her hand. He mouthed the word ... Yes.

She knew that they weren't in a state to escape and in the outside world there were no hospitals, no drugs. They were choosing a quick death over a slow one.

And she knew what she must do. She bowed her head and wept.

It started with a finger click, a hand slap on a hard metal frame, a clap, it built until the whole room echoed applause … with assent. She took a shuddering breath of resignation and moved towards the nurses' station. Her legs, heavy and weak, trembled as she stood at the console. All eyes were on her. She looked up and spoke.

'Please know that this is done with love … May you all find peace.'

The console panel had lines of red flashing dots; each represented the heartbeat of an occupant of a bed. She pushed the button for anaesthetic and morphine and sent it along the lines. She watched and waited; hardly breathing, until every single light had stopped, and the applause had fallen silent.

Then she turned off the lights and quietly left the room.

CHAPTER THIRTY-NINE

Angel was thundering down the stairs, the fire in the basement was spreading fast. She stopped and peered over the stair rail and saw a rolling pool of darkness waiting for her at the bottom. She was struggling to think clearly, her face was tear-streaked, her throat ached. She couldn't stop thinking about what had just happened ... what she had done. She could still hear the sound of their clapping, but their silence felt louder.

And then she realised that she could still hear them, they weren't in her mind, and they weren't fading. She gasped in horror. Had the drugs not worked? Were they going to be burned alive? Had she failed them too?

Smoke curled down over the stair treads above her. The voices she could hear were getting desperate. She turned, ready to run back upstairs and kill them all over again. But then she remembered ... they had no voices. Were there more donor units? Her heart in her mouth she ran down a flight and the sound got louder, down another and it got quieter. Now she knew which level it was coming from. She looked over the rail into the pit of the stairwell and estimated that it would be impassable in fifteen minutes. She just had time to investigate if she went now.

Angel punched in the code and stepped into the corridor. Black smoke curled along the roof just above her head. It was like being underwater looking up at the surface. She ducked down and ran toward the sound of shouting. It led her to the back of the building, to a door marked, fire exit.

The corridor floor was beginning to feel warm underneath her feet. Angel kicked the horizontal bars and the doors flew open. The shouting stopped. She found herself looking at a group of grey-haired, blue-eyed women, clamouring around an exit door. They turned around shocked by the sound of the doors crashing against the wall.

It smelled like a slaughterhouse. The floor was rough concrete; drainage channels ran towards large grates to the left and right. Black hosepipes were coiled at each side. Brooms and shovels rested against the wall. A bale of clothes, shoes and a small pile of jewellery sat waiting for collection.

Angel wiped her hand across her forehead. The women were silent.

'Is that the way out?'

'Yes, but it's locked,' spoke a small voice on her right.

An explosion shook through the building. The doors behind Angel blew wide open and acrid black smoke tumbled into the room. She spun around and fought to close the doors. Some of the women rushed over. But the wood was hot to touch and the hinges damaged. They managed to prop the doors together, but the poisonous smoke was already ankle high.

The women began to shout, 'Please help us get out.'

'It's locked.'

'We're going to …'

'I've got the code.' Angel said, leading the way to the exit. She hoped that her pass code and watch worked in the all areas of the building. She held the watch to the sensor and punched in the numbers, but nothing happened. She could feel the women move closer. She tried again … nothing.

'Once more for luck,' said a calm voice by her side. Angel looked down at her small kind face. Someone else held out a scrap of cloth. She breathed on the watch face and polished it free of dirt, then held it up to the sensor and punched in the numbers.

They held their breath. Angel pushed the door, nothing … then she kicked it in frustration, and it swung open.

'Hey what's this!' shouted a man from the loading bay outside.

There was an angry roar from the women, Angel watched them surge down a flight of metal steps armed with brooms and shovels. She waited until his screams had subsided into yelps, then she stepped outside to find the truck driver hiding under his own cab, in danger of being swept out and beaten to death.

'Can any of you drive a truck?' she called. They stopped and looked at her. 'Can you drive?' The women shook their heads. 'Then I suggest that you let him live until he's got you home.'

'Are you Angel?' asked the quiet voice by her side. Angel turned and nodded. 'We've heard of you. But we hardly dared to believe it.'

'Believe what?'

'That you really exist.'

Angel looked at the grey-haired woman, who was standing by her side. Her hair was long and sleek, but her eyes had milked over, damaged by the sun. She must have been the easiest reaping ever. The woman reached out and stroked her shoulder. Her touch was as soft as a feather.

'There's a star around you, it's beautiful. But it's made of tears.' She smiled sadly. 'You left a piece of your heart with them, didn't you?'

Angel knew at once that she was talking about the Beguinage and nodded.

'Do it right, Angel, do right ...'

Before the woman could finish her sentence one of the others gently took her arm and led her to the truck. The driver sat in his cab, nervously waiting for his, for once, living load to settle down. Three sat next to him, armed with tools, the rest were in the back, sitting on tarpaulin.

Angel was exhausted. The pure anger ... the horror ... the disgust that had driven her for so long evaporated. In its place was something else, something worse.

She was deaf to the indignant howl of the driver when the women poked him into action. She didn't feel the spattering of grit that hit her as he pulled away. She just took a deep breath and ran.

• • •

Steph felt the rumbling before she saw the light. A spout of flames burst over the wall. A second explosion rolled over her head, so like thunder she half expected rain. And then she smiled and whispered to Talib that the factory had just blown up. And Angel would be coming back for her very soon.

• • •

Angel ran in a dream, she leapt over piles of rubble; numb to the branches slapping and whipping across her face and arms. She ran so fast she felt weightless, like she might leap from a rock and just fly.

As she ran … her mind stilled … and she knew … with ice-cold certainty … just as her mother had been hunted, so had she been hunted. She hadn't thought of it before, but now she knew that anyone she ever loved, any child that she might ever have, would be forever prey.

She stopped running because she had to … there was nowhere to go.

CHAPTER FORTY

Morning found her in a hollow by the wall. She didn't remember stopping or lying down, but she must have. She was curled up on her side. Her face and neck felt warm. She touched her cheek and found that it was covered in a silky layer of ash. She was in a world of grey. In the distance, she could see that the factory was just a blackened skeleton, the incinerator smokestack was gone. Its absence like a missing tooth.

Trees and undergrowth had been burnt back to reveal the ghost footprint of the roads of the old city. Here and there she could see the stumps of walls where there used to be buildings. It looked like a map.

Angel stood up; she was thirsty and stiff. She looked around and saw that she was standing in the remains of a building, it was the shape of a circle. She could see the shapes of floor tiles and the occasional imprint of bigger blocks. With her toe she swept ash from one that was close. There was writing. She squatted down, blew the ash away and began to read.

Here lies Gill … 69 … a much missed friend … loving wife … mother … grandmother …

Angel moved over and swept the ash from another stone and then another … *Ann 84 … Geoffrey 71 … Jean 68 …* Did people live this long? *Mother, grandfather …* She sat back on her heels. Yes, they really had lived that long, and they had children and grandchildren who remembered them.

Her mind flooded with memories of funeral pyres, factory ships, of living organ banks, and of an eternally unfinished tapestry for dead children and she lay down in despair. She gently rested her hand on the words and tried to imagine what it was like to live in a world so benign. But she could not.

She felt the downdraught before she heard the noise. Then the shadow of the helicopter rose over the wall. It was flying slow and low. Angel scuttled back until she was against the steel city wall, alarm pounding in her chest. Ash was being lifted by the wind. It began to swirl and billow around her. She curled down and put her hands over her face. The roar of the engines was deafening; she couldn't see, and she couldn't breathe. She was being buried in ash. The helicopter seemed to hover there for an age, right above her, but just when she couldn't bear the noise or hold her breath a minute longer, it moved further along the wall.

Something brushed her shoulder, she froze.

'Come here. They're bombers.'

Angel lifted her head; a tall, angular man with waist-long dreadlocks extended his hand out to her, his face anxious but kind. 'They've done for the tunnels on the other side, now they've moved over here.'

'Let's go!' beckoned a woman behind him. She was armed with a homemade crossbow.

Angel dragged herself up to standing.

'They know we're here somewhere. We let the people out of the sheds not long after you blew up the Medic block,' said the man.

'Nice job, by the way.' The woman reached out and grabbed Angel's shoulder. 'Follow me.'

They guided Angel, one in front, and one behind as they ran along the edge of the wall, then stopped at what looked like a cluster of foxholes under a jutting piece of the concrete foundations. The man pulled a stump of charred wood away to reveal a larger hole. Silently, they slipped under the concrete ledge and into the hollow cavity in the centre of the wall.

The woman lit a lamp. Angel could see that the walls were ten paces wide at the ground but seemed to narrow as they got higher.

'Does this …?' Angel was shushed.

'Circles the inner city,' whispered the man. 'Made of steel, bedded on concrete, sinks into the river both ends.'

'They're patrolling the top, so we have to be quiet,' whispered the woman. 'I'm Ciss, by the way, this is Mathias.'

It was surprisingly warm within the metal walls. They must have absorbed heat from the fires on both flanks. The sides clicked and groaned. She felt sure that she heard footsteps behind them and glanced back into the darkness. Ciss caught her attention and pointed up, someone was patrolling the top of the wall. They stood in silence until the footsteps had gone, then moved on.

The heat was intolerable, Angel felt breathless and so thirsty. She touched her lips, they were cracked and dry.

A hand touched her shoulder. 'Just about ten minutes from the camp. Are you OK?'

She nodded, put her head down and tried to keep going. Her mind drifted, she wondered if Steph had got out OK? Or was she dead, lying somewhere in a collapsed tunnel? Angel shuddered and stumbled. Her two companions tucked their arms under hers and walked her the rest of the way.

• • •

Angel woke to the tang of seaweed. The air on her cheek felt moist and cool. She opened her eyes and saw a tin of water by her head. Raising herself up on her elbow she drank it so fast that she coughed. She realised that she was on a raised wooden platform. There were sparks of firelight dotted along the walls. People were clustered around them, talking and cooking. She looked up; smoke seemed to be gathering in the apex. The wall near to her, felt cold to the touch, perhaps it was night outside?

Looking the other direction, she saw moving water. It sparkled in the firelight and seemed to sigh. The ground near the water's edge looked like wet sand, small footprints showed that children had walked into the water, and then back again.

Ciss' face appeared over the side of the platform. Her dark skin shone in the lamplight. She gestured for Angel to come down and join a small group of people who were sitting around a nearby fire.

'We're close to where the wall dips down into the river,' she explained. 'The platform's for spring tides.'

'Do you all live here?'

She looked at her and smiled. 'No, we lived in the underground, this is our back up.'

Angel turned to a man on her right. 'Is it bad out there?' she asked.

'Hard to say until we've had a proper look, the dome's gone, we blew up the refinery and the docks. We're waiting to see what's left when they've finished retaliating.'

'What time is it?' She looked at their puzzled faces. 'I was meant to be meeting up with a friend … at nightfall. Steph …' Her voice trailed away.

'It's two whole days since the fighting started.'

Angel's heart sank. 'How can I find her?'

'These people you can see here …' The man gestured the length of the lit tunnel. '… are all the ones we know about. 'Course there could be others, hiding. But if your friend had any sense at all she'll have gone, even if she did wait till night.'

'Everything is flat, sweetheart, nothing's left.' Ciss touched Angel's shoulder. 'And now we need to work out how to get you somewhere safe.'

CHAPTER FORTY-ONE

Steph stood on a hillside, about thirty miles from London. They'd led her along surface tunnels, minutes before the levelling began with a vengeance. A Star lookout had picked her up and taken her to a safe house.

'No, I don't know where she is.' This was her first chance to call Mani. 'She didn't make it back to our meeting point. Mind you it was pretty wild out there.' She listened for a moment. 'I've no idea. Anything could have happened. The factory went up like a bomb. I think she was heading there, but I'm not sure.' She nodded her head. 'Not much left of the domes, we blew them up, used the gas lines … yep.' Steph checked a large black bruise on her arm. 'And we took out the river defences. Pup got away, and Katrin.' She grimaced. 'Mm, London's pretty much done.'

The phone clicked and she handed it back to the woman by her side.

'I'm going to have to get back; they need me. But we're missing a woman, about my height, short grey hair, sharp blue eyes, wild looking, name's Angel. Can you pass the message on? If anyone finds her, whatever state she's in, let us know immediately, please. We need her.'

Steph picked up a map.

'Now, where am I?'

• • •

Angel waded into the water until it was up to her thighs. She took one last look at the people standing on dry sand inside the wall, took a breath and ducked down, to find the hole under the wall.

Outside, the night was cold and starlit. She climbed out of the water on to the edge of the concrete foundations. The wall stretched uphill to her left and down to her right. It was rusted and battered by salt and storm. Ahead, the moon shone a ragged ladder across the shallow water.

They had told her to cross quickly, this inlet filled faster than a person could run. She fastened her bag tightly across her chest and stepped in. It was bone-chillingly cold. She ran with a high stepping stride. Mud oozed between her toes and stuck to the arches of her feet. Her legs quickly tired, each step heavy and slippery. She staggered, fell, got up and ran harder.

Approaching the far bank, she could see the shapes of what might once have been buildings. The moon slipped effortlessly behind the fan of a cedar tree. Spikes of marsh grass stabbed up from the slime. She must be getting closer.

Once on firmer ground, she sat to rinse mud from between her toes and pulled on her shoes. She took one last look at London, then she turned and ran.

By dawn, Angel estimated, that she must have run about fifteen miles. They had told her how to find an old drover's road. Centuries old, it had once had wide verges for grazing livestock being herded to London's meat markets. It was overgrown now, but the ancient hedgerows were easy to spot amongst the younger trees in the overgrown fields.

She found a large ash tree and sat down to rest in a fork between the roots. The rising sun washed the sky with pink and birdsong greeted the dawn. Angel tilted her face up to the sun, closed her eyes and smiled.

It sounded like a wasp at first. She surfaced from sleep, just enough to make sure that it moved on, but it didn't. Then she realised that the birds were quiet. Something wasn't right. The buzz became a throb and then a roar. She rolled into the deep grass and nettles at the side of the tree and covered her ears. Three … five … nine shadows moved over her … they were black helicopters, flying in formation. They weren't searching; they were moving too fast. She waited until they had crossed the horizon before she sat up. Perhaps there was another uprising somewhere or maybe some other place was paying the price for the destruction of London.

She snapped a large dock leaf, crushed it between her fingers, rubbed the green juices on to the nettle stings on her face and neck, then picked up her bag and moved on.

Two days later found her on the outskirts of Colchester. There were signs of fighting and looting, but they were old. There wasn't even any evidence of dogs or rats.

Five days and she was getting closer to the Midlands. The east-west armed sorties were becoming a regular occurrence. Each night, they lumbered overhead and each morning they returned, their missiles gone. One night she had seen a distant pall of smoke. She had no idea what place it was, but it was clear they were sitting ducks, they had nothing to match the destructive force of the helicopters.

Angel took to sleeping in trees, in case refugees from the fighting or soldiers trying to finish the job came too close. She wondered if anyone was looking for her, perhaps they assumed that she was dead? Yes, she thought to herself, everyone was safer if it stayed that way. She was on her own, now.

On the sixth night, she sat picking the last of the meat from a cooked rabbit carcass when she heard an unfamiliar sound. This was a different kind of helicopter. It was much bigger, slower; much closer to the ground and it was moving up from the south. She kicked soil over the embers of the fire and took cover under the trees.

The next morning, Angel set off northwest, out from under this new air traffic route. She'd decided to move inland before heading north again.

On the twelfth day, Angel chose to rest for a few days in a forest. The magnificent oak and ash of the ancient woodland had died. Their blonde-bleached branches shone out against the sky, stretching up over a lower canopy of smaller living willow and birch. The remnants of strings of wild hops and ivy that once stretched up into the top canopy, were just brown tattered garlands blowing in the breeze.

The forest floor was a deep carpet of leaf litter, it seemed to breathe with each step. She saw signs of fox, rabbit, pheasant and badger as well as plants that she could eat. Further in, the ground grew boggy, then it dropped down to a flooded basin. Drowned trees stood up to their branches in clear leaf-lined water. It was fresh and sweet to drink. Higher black rings showed her that the water sometimes rose much higher, but for now it was perfect.

She caught a fish, wrapped it in leaves and buried it in the ashes on the edge of her fire. Then she lay back on the forest floor and watched the Milky Way spiral over her head.

The next morning she woke to birdsong, after the sweetest sleep that she could remember, and knew that this was where she was going to stay.

• • •

Raph had ridden for three days and nights. It hadn't been easy with his motorbike headlights taped over. His back and shoulders ached from crashing along the deeply rutted tracks. He was covered in dust and his hand was bleeding. He was exhausted but couldn't stop. In his waking dreams, he saw her injured … starving … lost. He was racing to get to her before the Elites found her again. They would be looking for her and this time there wouldn't be the same kind of welcome. She wouldn't be family; she would be their bespoke body donor or a bargaining chip.

He shook his head to push the thoughts away. His motorbike shuddered over a line of deep fissures in the tarmac, he leaned forward to look for a more level surface and something caught his eye … bright lights on the horizon. He threw himself under a tree, covered the engine with his blanket and held his breath.

Heavily armed helicopters thundered overhead. He

supposed that they were travelling to Warwick or the outskirts of Coventry. He peered out and saw a light systematically searching nearby woodland. There was a burst of gunfire, then the helicopter moved on, leaving only the sound of screaming to break the heavy silence. It stopped … eventually.

• • •

The sun was hidden behind rain-laden clouds when he arrived at the outer perimeter of London. The river had widened since his last visit, just a few weeks before. Much of the inner city was now a grey mirror image of the sky. The outer city had completely burned out, only the factory shell remained, a black and twisted tangle of metal. There was silence, no wind, nothing.

He drove on, deep in thought. A lifetime ago, in what now felt like paradise, he had made a promise to Angel that he intended to keep. He had promised that if anything happened to her, he would tell her stepfather in person. He looked down and sighed; he would do it, but not before he had moved heaven and earth to find her.

Scorched and scoured clean by fire and rain, the roads stood out against the ash. He parked in front of the shell of the Medic centre. The final blast had curled the metal structure out, like a monstrous nest. Looking back, he saw a wide circle of shards of metal and glass embedded into the earth. It must have been one hell of an explosion. He tried to sense her … was Angel here? There was nothing.

He rode up to the soot-stained inner wall. Razor wire hung down in long vicious loops, ripped from its fixings along the top of the wall. The security doors had been blown away at both ends of the tunnel; it was empty and smelled of old smoke. High in the roof, smashed strip lights hung down from their cables.

It began to rain obliterating his tyre tracks and footprints, and he knew that it would be erasing Angel too. He slumped down in the shelter of the tunnel and slept.

• • •

At dawn, Raph rode into the city. The dome had burned and melted into circles of crisp, black plastic. The air was foul. There were small circles of ash where the trees had been. Fire and explosions had gutted the buildings inside the dome. There seemed to be a beach of ash and cloudy blue still water. He turned and looked out to the rest of the city. Nothing moved apart from the river and clouds, and they marked their own time.

Raph rode on, to look for the hut where Angel and Steph had lived. His search was impossible, but he had to carry on.

He heard a click and a hiss and spun round. There was a flash of light in the distance. Unaware of him, a figure was pointing a blue-tipped flame at the wall. He pulled up behind her, but she didn't hear. He leaned on his tank and watched the ice-blue flame melt a line in the wall.

'Hello.' Raph turned quickly to find himself being

scrutinised by a man dressed in black; a large hammer hanging from his belt.

'You taking it down?'

'No just cutting doors and windows, we're tired of being in the dark.'

'OK … I'm looking for …'

'Aren't we all, mate.' The man turned away. The woman stopped cutting, turned off the welder and stretched her back.

'I'm looking for a woman called Angel,' he asked, fearing the answer. 'She's missing … I need to know if she's alive.'

'Who's asking? Are you family?' The woman pulled off her goggles.

'God no! I'm a friend.' He held out his hands. 'I really need to know.'

'Better come this way.' The woman kicked the wall and a large rectangle of metal fell back and landed with a clang.

He left with his hopes raised. For the first time in days Raph felt that Angel might be alive. She had got out of London safely. He smiled to himself as he left the city of ash behind him. She's a survivor, my Angel, he whispered to himself.

CHAPTER FORTY-TWO

'He's destroying towns and cities across the length and breadth of the country.' Mani told the meeting. Twenty representatives sat around a rough wooden table; a sheet had been stretched taut over a pine-panelled wall to act as a screen. Images of burning villages and refugees hiding in ditches flashed in front of them. They watched in horror and sadness.

A dark-haired woman from mainland Europe nodded her head. 'He has done the same to us,' she shrugged. 'Nothing is out of his range.'

'Do we know what Katrin's up to?' Mani asked Brad. He stood up and cleared his throat.

'Looks like Pup intends a hostile takeover of what's left of Nova and Alpha.' He paused to let the information sink in. 'Interestingly he seems to have something on Katrin, she's standing back and letting him do it.'

'Oh, that will be Angel,' said Steph.

'How come?' asked a small dark-haired woman.

'Pup's son is her father. From what we can find out, there'd been an *arrangement* … an expectation between Pup and Katrin that their children would marry, and the family businesses would combine. But Lilith, Angel's mother, ran away after some incident at Pup's birthday party. There was a massive falling out between the families.'

Mani looked at the faces around the table and nodded at Steph. 'Steph tells us that he claimed Angel, and Katrin let her go without a fight.'

'But from what I can pick up from Alpha's comms, Katrin is trying to team up with Nova's people. They're letting Pup overstretch …' Brad spoke with authority. 'It isn't easy to get this kind of information, but …'

A door clicked. His audience looked at someone behind him. He turned to see Raph, standing with his back against the wall. He looked exhausted; his face and clothes were dirty. He held a cup of water in grimy hands.

'Ah, can I introduce my brother, Raph,' said Mani. 'Nice of you to join us, finally. Any news?'

Raph cleared his throat. 'She got out of London alive, but no one's seen her since. I've looked everywhere …' He looked at Steph and smiled sadly.

'Thank you Raph. So, friends, as far as we know she is still alive, at least she isn't definitely dead … I think we can use this.' The attention of the room moved back to Mani. Brad pursed his lips; his moment had passed.

'How?

'Well, between the fight for their business and a two-handed search for Angel, there's lots of room for confusion. Let's make the most of it, shall we?' She was thinking on her feet. 'Resistance, distraction, rumour … false sightings?'

People began to nod.

'We have images of Angel. If you send us ones of your towns, we can have her *travelling* across Europe. We can run them ragged,' added Steph over the rising noise.

'They won't be half so keen to bomb if they think she's there!'

'They'll have to come in on foot, and we'll be ready.'

'Now we stand a chance!' said one of the Stars.

'It won't last for long, but we can play them for a while … ' said Mani.

'Until?' asked the woman from France.

'Until we get a better idea!'

The meeting broke up with a plan. Mani was going to coordinate them; Brad was going to feed disinformation to Pup and Katrin. The resistance was going to prepare communities to ambush the search parties.

Steph was just leaving the room when Raph stepped in front of her. He looked deflated and lost.

'Not so fast, Steph, I need some answers. Why did you leave without her? How was she when you last saw her? How did she take learning that Pup was her grandfather? Anything … help me … please.' His voice cracked.

Steph led him to a corner of the room, and they sat down.

'Well she really struggled with her grandmother, and she had no time for the company.' She glanced away, wondering what to say. 'I tried to cover for her, you know, cover for her lapses … her inexperience.'

'Did she upset them?'

'No, on the contrary, she fascinated them. That exasperated her even more.'

'Was she fine in herself?'

'She hated it all, the domes, the food, the lack of purpose, the sitting around. In fact, it made her feel ill … it was all so pointless.'

Raph nodded, his next question was almost lost in a fog of exhaustion.

'So, there was nothing …'

'Well, she did see some photographs of her mother. That affected her a lot. They were so alike.'

'So … what was her plan?'

'She didn't say …'

'And her grandmother?'

'I honestly think I would have had to deal with her.'

'OK, so why didn't you two stick together at the end?'

Steph told him about Angel's visit to the Medic block, about how things had taken a sour twist when Pup arrived. She explained their rendezvous plans and that she'd waited long after the deadline, but Angel didn't come back.

'You looked?' He searched Steph's face; she nodded.

'How did she get out?' Steph asked softly.

'Some people rescued her and set her right.'

'How was she?'

'Filthy, caked in dirt and ash … thirsty … haunted …'

Steph sighed and touched Raph's arm. 'Maybe, if we can really play one off against the other, we can give her some space to find her own way back.'

• • •

That evening Steph watched the patterns that the wind made in the marsh grasses on the dunes. The shadow of a cloud raced across the beach and out to sea. She'd stepped out for some fresh air. Turning her face into the evening breeze she glanced back at the field centre that they were using as a base. It had been a nature reserve and was well hidden. In fact, it had taken some time to reclaim it. Brambles had taken over whole rooms. Alder and willow pressed tight against the windows. It was like living inside a hedge.

Steph had known that the longer they were in London, the less likely it was that Angel was going to be able destroy it. She'd watched her begin to see her grandmother's qualities and connect with them. Pup had tipped the balance, though, that and the Medic block. Steph was grateful to Pup in some ways. He'd brought things to a head.

Did she really hope that Angel was alive? She'd watched her fall to a crushing rock bottom. If she were to live would she be able to cope under the suffocating burden of reality … of power … of privilege … of being hunted, her whole life long?

Angel could never turn a blind eye to the consequences of her privilege. Only someone born to it could be that blind. To see the rest of the world as worthless vermin, to blank out their humanity, Steph knew in her heart that it was beyond Angel. Maybe it would be kinder if … She shook her head and turned her face away from the wind.

She wrapped her arms around her body and sighed. She knew that she'd been ready to kill Katrin. But was Angel? If she couldn't, would she have let Steph do it? And if it had come down to it … if Angel had tried to protect her grandmother, could Steph have killed them both? She was glad that she'd been spared having to find out.

Earlier there had been hard words between Raph and Mani and he had walked out; he had more than likely gone back to Leeds. Mani wasn't sure. It was difficult to say if Mani's concerns were about being able to control him or if she was afraid to lose him. Perhaps he'd gone to look for Angel again?

Over the next few weeks, Steph watched as Mani coordinated the misinformation with imagination and flair. She set up and led wild goose chases across Europe. Pup and Katrin locked into a personal war, were each determined to catch Angel before the other. They sent search parties out to follow up leads, and even more to follow the other's search parties. Their surveillance became more bad tempered and desperate. There'd been more than one pitched battle over the sighting of a girl who looked like Angel. Rewards had been offered and threats made.

Star people spread the word and led ambushes and attacks. Bombing stopped anywhere there was a rumour of Angel's presence. The resistance was building up, and there was a growing supply of stolen weapons.

Steph couldn't decide if it would be a kindness if Angel had died, but dead or alive she was turning out to be an excellent bait and Mani a skilled trapper.

CHAPTER FORTY-THREE

Sometimes, Angel woke with just the wisp of the sensation of her mother's long hair brushing against her face. Other times she could smell her sun-hot skin as she leaned forward to whisper something into her ear. Angel would try to pull back, to dream some more, to savour those elusive sensations; but the effort always woke her.

In her dreams, if she looked down, she could see her mother's suntanned arm around her waist. To feel her body heat … always against her back. Angel woke, longing to be able to turn around and …

And then sometimes in the darkness of the night, in her tree-top lair of woven vines and dried moss, Raph was breathing softly against her neck. She could feel his heartbeat, steady and strong against her back.

Asleep, she was haunted; awake she went through the motions of survival. Catching and storing food, foraging, exploring the forest, planning her survival, it was automatic. She could do it with her eyes closed … except then they would come to her … and she would long for them all over again.

At first, she had spent hours, sitting by the water, sifting and sorting through the events since her reaping.

It became harder to connect with the girl in her ivory tower of ignorance and secrets. The girl who had never

314

thought beyond the limits of the Old Lakes that surrounded her home. Or the girl who bathed in the morning mists.

It was easier to conjure up Raph; he was a more recent memory, and she could remember the taste of his kiss, the sound of his heart when she pressed her ear to his chest. Her mother... she was already so many lifetimes away.

She stopped counting the number of days since she had last spoken to anyone. Her voice, when she shouted at a bird trying to pick from her drying rack, was a shock to them both. It felt like someone else.

• • •

Eventually the season began to turn. The water level was beginning to rise. The sounds of the forest were changing. She fashioned a blanket out of rabbit skins. Her hammock up in the old forest had been hidden by the green living trees, but their leaves were beginning to change colour and fall.

• • •

Her mother's hair smelled of chamomile, it brushed against her cheek, she leaned forward to speak ...

A scream!

Was that a child?

A scream from the other direction had her reaching for her knife. It was dark, she could hear something on the forest floor ... breathing ... the sound of steps ... light steps and then a howl, ancient as time itself chilled her blood. It was a pack of hunting wolves.

She lay silent and still. Was her stash of food safe? Had she tied it high enough up the tree? There it was again in the distance, the haunted child-cry of a fox. The wolves paused, took their direction from the sound and moved into the deep forest.

Angel lay awake and drew herself back into her only memory of her mother. They were sitting in her room, looking at her bedroom curtains, almost transparent and torn in places. She remembered that there were fairy story characters printed on the fabric and smiled. She'd reached forward to touch the curtain … and her mother had … taken her small hand and guided it back against her tummy … and covered it with her own. She whispered something; her hair had brushed against Angel's cheek as she spoke. Then there was that familiar feeling … safety and …

Angel sat up; eyes wide open. They weren't looking at the curtain at all; they were hiding!

'Keep quite still, mummy's little angel. Wait until the nasty men have gone.'

Her mother's words were clear. Angel had been in danger since the day that she was born. She turned her head to look at the morning star, hovering low over the far horizon, took a deep breath, and told the forest, '*I can't do it anymore, this has got to end.*'

• • •

She rolled her blanket up into a tight pack and tied it to her backpack. Her air-dried fish and meat were wrapped in papery leaves and tucked into the side pockets. She expected to be able to find fruit and berries along the way. Angel looked around her camp one last time. She didn't feel sad. In another world, she could imagine returning with a boat or the tools to build a winter-proof shelter. In this world it was time to go.

Angel walked down to the water's edge and knelt to take one last drink of its clean sweet water. She caught a glimpse of her reflection, and quickly ruffled the water. Then she tied a scarf into a turban around her head to cover her hair, picked up her bag and headed north. Her time in the forest had made her quieter, more watchful. She'd grown used to the stillness and could move into the grey; it was as if she was wrapped in her own shadow.

• • •

She had been walking for about fifteen days; listening and sensing the air, when she realised that a plan had been gradually forming in her head. Without being aware that a decision was being made, she found that she was walking north ... to York. In her dreams, the starburst threads of the patchwork tapestry seemed to reach out and draw her to it.

Each night, wrapped in her rabbit-skin blanket, she fell asleep to the memory of the sound of children playing outside the window of the isolation room. In the morning, she resumed her journey, hardly emerging from her dream state. Soft forest floors gave way to hard-baked clay; gently rolling hills became ridged and rugged outcrops of limestone.

• • •

It was time to settle down for the night. She had left the rocky limestone and was walking along a path that followed a stream running through woodland. She found a large lattice barked chestnut tree with a hollow at its base. There was space to sleep sitting up and she would be warmer out of the wind.

It had been a misty day. A thickening haze hung over the stream. And it was beginning to creep across the track. She expected that by dawn it would have cast its cloak around her.

She eased herself into the hollow, settled down cross-legged and arranged her blanket up around her shoulders. Pulling the tail of her scarf up over her face, she rested her bag on her legs, lowered her head and slept.

In the early hours something cold touched her hand … and then her ear.

She opened her eyes to check if it was raining, only to find herself, looking into the eyes of a large dog. It was standing an arm's length away and seemed friendly. She checked but couldn't see anybody around, then clicked her tongue and invited the dog closer. Its weight leaning against her leg was a comfort. Angel moved to allow it to ease itself into the tree trunk by her side. Grateful for the warmth, they slept.

'Here girl!' a man's voice called from the depths of the morning fog. Angel thought that she must be dreaming. The dog grunted. There was the voice again. Angel tried to push it out into the open, but it leaned into her.

'Where are you?'

The dog barked into the fog.

'There you are!' A figure emerged. 'Leila? Here girl.' The man leaned forward and pulled on the dog's collar. He froze. 'You! It's you, isn't it? Just look at you!'

Angel pulled her scarf away from her mouth.

'Mac?'

He pulled her up to standing and hugged her. Angel couldn't believe that she had travelled this far, or that she had, without realising it, found her way back here. Mac was stronger than when she had last seen him, and he didn't need his stick. With him leading and Leila by her side, Angel wrapped her blanket around her shoulders and followed them to the quarry. She felt the pull from York grow in her heart.

At first the quarry seemed the same, but as she got closer, she saw fruit tree saplings growing in containers in carefully cleared spaces. The pond looked clean and managed.

'Oh Angel. Is that you?' Jen shouted from the shed over the entrance to the cave. 'Come here.' She wrapped Angel in her arms and held her. Then she stepped back and looked at her. She touched the blanket and then the scarf.

'Well if this isn't the best disguise ever!'

'When I found her, she had Leila and a tree protecting her,' said Mac.

319

'Disguise?' Her voice was low from lack of use.

'We have women popping up all over the place, dressed to look like you.'

'Why?' Angel asked softly.

'To stop the bombing … your family want you alive. We're using you to stop the raids. They're both blundering around, trying to catch you first!' Mac laughed.

'And you look nothing like you!'

'I swear you could walk through a crowd of people searching for you and no one would give you a second glance.' Mac touched her arm. 'I'll pass the good news on to …'

'No!' shouted Angel. They both looked at her, shocked by her outburst.

'OK, better come inside, I guess you've got a lot to tell us.'

Leila led them into the quarry cave. It had changed too; it was lighter and there was enough food stacked and racked to last them through the hardest of winters. Aris had gone soon after Angel left, determined to settle scores and to make sure that her children were safe, but Jen had decided to stay.

Without speaking, they took Angel's bag and blanket and led her to a chair. Mac brought hot water and then Jen helped her to strip and wash. Clean and dry, she was wrapped in a soft cotton sheet and led to her bed. Leila followed and lay down by her side. She slept as if she was quenching a thirst …

She dreamed of heartbeat monitors blinking out, of fire and black acrid smoke, of ash streams in dark waters, of search helicopters and wolves. And then she settled, Raph was breathing on the back of her neck; she felt his arm resting on her belly. His smell of fresh air and apples woke her. She smiled and turned; the bed was empty.

She pulled herself up and sat with her head in her hands until the need to cry became an ache in her throat and then a sigh. Then she stroked Leila's ear, and walked outside to look for Mac and Jen.

Over a meal of eggs and fresh hazelnut milk, Angel told them about the sea storm, how she had met her grandmother, about Steph and Raph, and how London had finally died.

'So that's who you were calling last night … Raph. Is he important?'

Angel waited until she could trust herself to speak. 'I need to get to York. To the …'

'You'd be safer here. They have been on the receiving end of some pretty ruthless attention.'

'Where's Raph, Angel? Did he die?' Jen asked softly.

'I don't know.' She had never allowed herself to consider that possibility, but now it was there, she was terrified.

'I need to get to York, but secretly. Can you get me there without Mani or the Stars knowing, please?'

'Course we can … can't we Mac?'

In the evening, Jen showed Angel around the quarry. They'd hidden crops in between cover plants, and they had a beehive. Angel could see how good they were for each other. Jen seemed more confident; she radiated satisfaction and Mac looked happy. They paused to look at the pond.

Jen spoke softly. 'Can you tell us why don't want us to tell the resistance, or even the Stars? If you can't, that's OK.'

Angel thought for a moment. 'I don't know how secure their comms channels are.'

'OK, but Mani?'

'I don't trust Mani. If she could use me, she would … without a second thought.'

'And Raph?'

'If he had to choose between me and his sister …' Her throat dried up. 'I'm afraid he might choose her.'

Jen nodded and arms linked, the two women walked back inside.

CHAPTER FORTY-FOUR

Mac found Angel sitting on a rock, with Leila leaning against her leg. Both were enjoying the warmth of the early morning sun; their shadows blue against the limestone walls. He told her that he'd sent a radio message to York through a trusted friend. It said that he had a surplus of forest fruit and a rare medicinal herb, good for yellow dye. To be collected in person.

'Medicinal herb … rare?'

'Angelica. They're always on the lookout for it to dye their wool.'

'You think they'll come?'

'I do.' He nodded, and then he too leaned against the wall and together they watched the day begin.

Two days later a message arrived to say that the trade was agreed, they would bring wool in return.

Cheryl met them on a low point on the banks of the Trent. She passed the wool over to Jen and packed the fruit and herbs into the front of the canoe. They were going to use a longer route back this time. She had brought a bigger canoe and Angel could rest when she needed to.

'Take good care of her.' whispered Mac as he helped Cheryl to prepare to leave.

'She's …'

'Changed …' sighed Mac.

• • •

Long after curfew, a boat laden with herbs and fruit, slipped into York. The woman rowing the boat, pulled with a timeless rhythm. Anyone watching, might have thought that they had caught sight of her for a fraction of a second. But then perhaps the moon had gone behind a cloud and when they looked again, she was gone. In time they might have put it down to birds or a branch floating along the river.

The boat with its precious cargo slipped between houses, under a low bridge and moored against a secret jetty. Two people moved silently toward a nearby building holding baskets high and low.

In the safety of the office in the quiet Beguinage, Angel sat down and wept. Miriam picked up her candle and joined Olayah and Cheryl as they moved back into the shadows, to wait until Angel was ready for them.

They knew that there was no weakness in her crying.

They were astonished by her appearance, she was pale … ashen, her hair almost white, but more than that, her previous aura of self-reliance and strength had coalesced into a calm, mature and focused power. This wasn't the young girl they'd met before, lost and unsure of who she was. This Angel was a tempered knife-blade of a woman, who had had the courage to face herself and not to look away.

They waited patiently for her to pull back into the room and look up.

'Thank you,' she spoke quietly, 'I need your help. But I'm putting you so much more at risk. If it's too much, say, and I'll go.' She looked at them; they dare not look away.

'Angel, my dear, you've woken up the world. At last we're fighting, resisting, organising,' said Miriam.

'We have risen, my dear!' whispered Olayah.

'And there's no turning the clock back.' Cheryl added.

Miriam leaned forward. 'Now, I don't know if we can keep you safe, or for how long, but we will do our very best.'

Angel looked at the kind, brave women who were standing in front of her and nodded. She knew what she had to do to save them from her family's monstrous greed. And stood up and hugged them one by one.

The following morning Angel woke to the sound of breakfast being served on the other side of the tapestry. She lay in the darkness behind the shelter of the star. It had grown since her last visit. Women had added more patches to mark their losses, but there were also some new shapes around the edges. When she looked closer, she saw that each patch was a baby's footprint. The tapestry was beginning to include celebration as well as grief.

She lay on her makeshift bed and listened to the singsong laughter of cheerful mothers and children eating their first meal of the day. She'd slept fitfully, working on her plan by candlelight.

By the time the dining room had gone quiet and people moved on to start their daily routines, Angel was ready to talk. Miriam tapped on the door and Angel slipped from behind the patchwork tapestry and stretched. There was food and a drink waiting on the table. They sat down and Angel ate.

'We got more candles and a bowl of lavender. Do you want books?' asked Fenna.

'We'll stock you up with food and drink. Were you warm enough?' asked Cheryl.

'I was fine, thanks. Now I need to contact someone. Can you do it under the radar … everybody's radar?' She paused to make her point. 'I need to speak to Steph; she was in London with me.'

Miriam nodded thoughtfully. 'Is she with Mani?'

'I expect she is; she won't have been able to go back to Chequers and they seemed to be working together.'

'OK, then yes we can do that.'

Angel handed them a note that she had written in the early hours of the morning. Things were finally moving.

'Now tell me again how you used my name to fight?'

The women smiled and spoke about her decoy journey across the country and into Europe. They told her about the young women who were volunteering to dress like her and to appear and disappear along her fantasy route. And of the ambushes and traps lying in wait when Pup or Katrin's forces took the bait. Their weapons were being captured and a new fighting force was growing.

The conversation came to a lull and Cheryl asked Angel why she didn't want Mani to be involved. She waited until her feelings had settled into a single thread.

'Because she sent Raph to reap and then rescue me … and for her to do that, she must have known who I was.' She paused and bit her lip. 'And so, I have to consider the possibility that it was her who found me and set me up in the first place.'

The women sat back in amazement.

'Do you think she planned it all?'

Angel shrugged.

'And what about Raph?'

'My gut feeling is that she used him. And she would do it again. If it came to the crunch, I don't know how strong a hold she has over him.'

The women nodded, Raph would not be allowed to know that Angel was here.

CHAPTER FORTY-FIVE

A cold dark dread had descended on Steph. Each dawn made it less likely that Angel was alive. She had given up reliving their time in London, trying to spot the moment that she could have done or said something different and changed the outcome. She simply couldn't find that pivot point … all roads led here.

She watched Raph plan searches and disappear for days, weeks even. He returned ashen, exhausted, less himself. They had given up talking about Angel. But sometimes they would seek each other out and just stand shoulder to shoulder and look out at the rain, or by the gate and search the road … no words … just waiting.

Mani was busy coordinating the decoy rebellion. Steph would hear her victory cheers through the thin walls. Brad was always close by, ever watchful, basking in Mani's joy. But they were beginning to pick up a change in Pup's raids on 'Angel sightings', they were getting less random. And Katrin, significantly weakened by the loss of her London base was struggling to defend herself from his attacks as well as search for Angel. Undamaged by the storm, Pup was at full strength and making gains. Things were coming to a head.

So many dawns, thought Steph as she pulled on her shoes and coat. It was her turn to walk into the village to pick up provisions. She checked her pocket for messages that Mani had given her to pass on to the storekeeper for the Star People.

It was good to get away from the house, but she wondered how long before the decoy game went sour. Then what were they going to do?

Elsie was usually in her kitchen. Steph opened the door and called. There was no reply. She moved into the house and called upstairs, no sound. She went back outside and called. A small noise, a knocking came from the shed.

'Elsie is that you?'

'Steph, come here!'

'What's happened?' Steph tried to open the door. It moved a fraction.

'Hang on.' There was the sound of movement, then Elsie peered around the door. 'Come in.' Steph squeezed in around the door 'Got something to show you.' She pulled Steph towards her and gestured with pride at an old bicycle. 'Do you want it? My hips … you know.'

'Well if …'

'I've been saving it for …' She shrugged. 'No good to me.'

An hour later, Steph was pushing an old bicycle with a bag of apples hanging from one handlebar and messages for Mani under the vegetables on the other. The bike was in need of some repair, but Elsie wasn't easy to refuse.

Later that evening, getting ready for bed, Steph shrugged off her jacket and felt something in her pocket. It was a small scrap of paper. She took it to the light. On it was written '*Beguinage, Thursday night. Tell no one. A.*'

Her first impulse was to shout with joy, to run and find Raph, and then she read it again. Tell no one? Surely, she could tell Raph? She patted her pockets to see if there was anything else. But they were empty. Elsie must have slipped it in there in the shed! She picked up her jacket ready to rush back to talk to her. But Thursday night … that's two days away. How could she get to York by then? She smiled, of course, the bike!

Through the night she and Raph worked on it, straightening spokes, cleaning rust from the gears.

'That's about as good as it gets,' said Raph straightening up and stretching his back. Steph thanked him and gave it a little test along the drive.

'I've got this urge to get away. I've been here since …' They looked at each other sadly. 'Will you cover for me? Tell Mani I'll be back in a few days.'

'Just go,' said Raph, he understood the urge to keep moving.

● ● ●

Steph walked through York's main gates, handed her papers to the guard, who checked them against the list or permitted visitors, noted the time and let her pass into the busy city.

York had taken many hits in the early days of resistance. The air smelled of sewers and old smoke. Soot-stained debris lined the streets behind the gate. She smiled as she watched a child poked a stick into a crevice in the ruins of a building and encourage a grubby lop-eared terrier to dig.

After dark, Steph made her way to the Beguinage. Miriam and Cheryl led her to the office and left her to wait. After what seemed like an age the door handle gave a soft click. She turned to see Miriam and Angel walk into the room. The candlelight on the table flared and then dimmed as Miriam left them to talk.

Standing in the corner, Angel seemed transient; a shadow image projected on to the wall. And then she smiled and stepped forward into the light. They looked at each like old friends long parted, neither of them sure they still knew the other, but hoping all the same.

'I waited for you,' Steph blurted out.

'I couldn't get back.' Angel held out her hand, Steph took it and they wrapped their arms around each other. 'The Medic block … was hell … I only just got out in time. I couldn't get back into the tunnels.'

'We fired at Pup's helicopter. Damn near got him … they flattened the underground. I only just made it out.'

'People hid in the deep sewers and inside the walls, they're going to rebuild.' Angel smiled at people's resilience. Steph stood back and looked at Angel's face.

'Where did you go, Angel? We looked and looked for you.'

'Hid in the wall, and then I crossed the river and found a forest to live in. I needed space to think.'

'Raph has …' Angel put her hand up to stop her talking, but Steph carried on; '… has combed London … everywhere … searching for you.'

'Is he well?' Angel said, 'and Mani?'

'What?' Steph was surprised that Angel showed so little concern for Raph. 'Oh Mani, she's getting ready for the big push. We've totally closed the shipping down, so they can't reap. And we've got them on a wild goose chase …'

'With me as the goose.' Angel smiled.

'Well yes, you're the ultimate prize, and meanwhile we've nearly got enough weapons to knock them out of the sky. It never occurred to them that we might fight back. I guess we stopped believing that too. Turns out we were both wrong.'

Steph looked at Angel in the sepia light and couldn't look away. There was a sense of peace around her. Not a peace brought from an absence of fear, but rather a peace born of facing it. She saw Angel's lips moving and brought her focus back to the room.

'This is what I need you to do,' said Angel.

• • •

Steph left York at dawn. She could see that the city had taken more than its fair share of pounding. The ancient walls were largely undamaged, and wooden walkways had been built to bridge the gaps. Stone from what was left of the west end of the minster was being used to rebuild and fortify the city.

Clifford's Tower stood high above the rubble an unlikely watchtower and beacon of hope and defiance. It stood on the high mound, and its four bastions topped by a walkway had become the city's lookout site. No-one could arrive at York's gates without being seen.

• • •

Next, Angel met the city's leaders. Miriam and Cheryl sat by her side. A relationship of sorts had been built between the Beguinage and the city after Angel had gone. She spoke clearly, telling them what she wanted. There was silence after she finished. Was she asking too much? She watched their weary and earnest faces and waited. Finally, they nodded and swore themselves to secrecy; the plan would only work if it were a surprise.

'You want us to move people out of their homes?' asked a woman.

'And outside the city walls,' asked another incredulously. 'But we've been repairing the walls to keep the army out, why should we ask them to leave their safe places?'

'Because,' said Angel calmly, 'I'm going to draw them here, where they will fight for me. This wild goose chase will end in York.'

'How can we help you?' asked a woman's clear voice. Angel turned to look at her and smiled.

'I need you to help me bring them down, and then mop up any stragglers. And I need four special volunteers …'

The conversation continued into the night.

• • •

Katrin was shaken awake; it was eleven o'clock. She ripped her eye pads and earplugs away and screamed to be left alone. She had been living at Chequers since her flight from

London. A makeshift control room had been created in the library, but she spent most of her time in her bedroom. The Prime Minister looked around her room in distaste, she'd brought very little with her and from the evidence, it seemed that he now had the answer to the problem of his missing wine.

Katrin pulled on a dressing gown, tartan wool with large pockets. They'd found it in the attic. It smelled of camphor. Lord knows what it would smell like if she got close to the fire, he thought, as he watched her hunt for her shoes. It would have been funny to watch her fall from grace, if his own fate weren't so inextricably linked with hers. He took a note from his pocket and held it out for her. It was written on a page that had been torn out of a gardening book.

'What? What is this?' She snatched it from him. Someone had pushed it through the letterbox last night. She unfolded the paper and inspected it.

'Have they no paper?'

'No …'

'Oh … OK. What does it say? Where are my glasses?' She grabbed her spectacles from the desk by the window, fumbled with them and scanned the letter. 'It says … It's a message about Angel!' She looked up in surprise, then she read aloud: 'Angel says that she wants to talk to you. Only you. Not Pup. If she sees that you've brought anyone else, she'll leave for good. Meet her at Clifford's Tower in York, tonight at seven o'clock.'

She threw her glasses down on the bed. 'What? How dare–!' Then she paused to think. 'When? I can't possibly.'

'I believe the army has one helicopter left, if that is any use.'

'Very well then, tell them I shall be borrowing it, will you? We should be back by morning.'

• • •

'You did what?' Mani slammed her tablet down on the table. Steph waited a second to check that Mani had stopped talking; it wouldn't do to interrupt.

'I sent a message, from here, about an hour ago … to Pup. Telling him that Angel wants to see him at Clifford's Tower at seven o'clock tonight. That's in three hours. If he hurries, he can just make it.'

'But you got back yesterday. You should have told me?' Mani was red faced and spitting. 'I could have done something.'

'She has a plan.'

'She has? Let's hope it's better than the one she had for London! It was our best chance ever and she let them both get away!'

It was clear from her face that there was no point in telling Mani again that what happened to Angel in London was beyond anyone's worst nightmares.

'Tell her from me, that she had better not blow this!' Mani bellowed, then she turned and strode out of the room. The door slammed behind her. A map of Europe slipped from the wall and curled up on the floor. Steph could hear her bellowing orders as she walked away.

Now, thought Steph, time for the part that Angel didn't ask for. She picked up her coat and went to look for Raph. He'd got back from another search two days ago; exhausted from trying to second-guess her state of mind. His searching was becoming increasingly erratic.

She found him standing on the riverbank, hopeless, hands in pockets. She walked up to him and softly touched his shoulder. He sighed and turned, smiling gently; she was his last link with Angel.

They walked slowly along the bridle path deep in conversation; Steph told him of Angel's plan and what he must do.

Neither noticed that Mani was watching from the window, a deep scowl on her face, her knuckles white with rage.

CHAPTER FORTY-SIX

The people of York were accustomed to air raid practices, and so in the end it wasn't difficult to convince them to participate in a full evacuation drill. And in the cover of night, they had slipped through the city walls out into Hambleton forest; a dense cover of native trees that stretched from York north to the Scottish borders. Only punctuated by rivers and a giant white horse, etched into a hillside.

The Beguinage was empty. Angel was alone, sitting in the refectory, thinking. She had gone over the plan in her mind so many times, it felt like slow motion. And time was getting close. The setting sun caught her locket in the centre of the tapestry and sparkled.

She walked over to the tapestry and touched it softly with her fingertips. It never failed to move her. She cleared her throat and through trembling lips, whispered to the children woven into its fabric, of life and love, of hope and freedom, of a life worth living and in the end a death worth dying.

She knew that she could trust Steph to do her part. The people of York had vowed to do theirs. She hadn't told them about her own piece of the plan; she hoped that when it was all over, they would remember her with kindness.

There was food and drink on the table. She sat down and

tried to eat, but it tasted of ashes. She just looked at the tapestry of life and death. After a while she stirred, took her knife and cut a heart from the hem of the white, felt cloak around her shoulders and carefully tucked it behind one of the lines of thread that radiated out from the centre.

• • •

Clifford's Tower stood high above the city, the last remaining part of its ancient castle. It was shaped like a four-leaf clover with a central ring of stone. Angel stood at the foot of the high defensive earth mound where stairs led up to a portcullis entrance on the south-east side.

Inside, it was an empty shell, but from outside, the tower looked strong, defiant and proud. The deep limestone walls had stood for hundreds of years. Angel looked up and smiled, she had chosen well.

She climbed the steep stone steps and walked into the centre of the tower. It had once had two floors; she could see a ring of gaps where thick beams had rested. Worn spiral stairs led up inside the walls to a parapet walkway that ringed the top of the tower. She stepped into a doorway, rested one hand on the stone, worn smooth over the centuries, held her cloak out of the way with the other and climbed the dark twisting stairs.

The wind at the top was sharp and blustery, gusting from the south. She stood, cloak flapping, holding on to an iron rail. From high up, the city revealed its ugly battle scars. Buildings had been bombed and there were signs that runaway fires had gutted whole rows of tightly packed houses. The river shone silver as it snaked its way through the city and beyond. Behind her, loomed the deep, dark heart of the tower.

Someone called from below; she leaned carefully over the parapet and saw a small gathering of people. She waved and went down to greet them.

Three women, about her height and build, nervously stepped forward to meet her. They were her special volunteers. Each wore a white felt cloak just like Angel's except for the missing heart. She tied a blue scarf around each of their heads and then one around her own. It hid her silver-grey hair. She nodded, satisfied that it would be hard to tell them apart.

'OK, it's a bit windy so take care up there.'

They nodded and glanced up at the parapet.

'Are they really coming?' one asked through chattering teeth.

Angel shrugged. 'I think so, it's a battle of wills, they won't be able to resist. Now who wants south … north … or east?' They each chose a point of the compass and with it a lobe of the tower. 'Right, when you have done your bit, get down so that they can't see you and make your way down the stairs. Hide there, the walls are really solid and should protect you.'

The women nodded.

'OK, I'm just going to check with the others, I suggest you find somewhere to keep warm.'

Angel left the women huddling nervously in an archway

and walked over to the others. A dozen people were working together to set their weapons up in the arrow slits in the walls. Positioned around the whole tower they could have had full cover, but they didn't have enough weapons for that, so the plan was for 'the angels' to draw the action to them on the west side from whichever direction that they arrived.

Above the tower the sky was darkening fast. A line of swans passed overhead; the wind hissed in their wings. The silent city made the fighters nervous. Angel went over the plan once more to focus them.

It was dark when she climbed the stairs for the last time. The women were in position, sitting with their backs against the wall, talking across the void. Angel sat on the west side of the circle looking across at the eastern sky. Venus was rising. When it was too dark to make a silhouette, she stood, wrapped her cloak around her body and waited.

A distant church clocked was chiming the half hour when she spotted lights in the distance, one in the south and one in the east. She smiled to herself; she knew they would be early to try to catch her off guard. She called out a warning and her group of fighters settled down ready for battle.

• • •

The noise was deafening, they could feel the pulse of the blades, slicing through the night air. Angel signalled to the woman in the east, who nodded and pulled the hood of her cloak down low over her face, then stood and waved.

A searchlight fixed on her from the army helicopter, she

shone white against the night sky. Pup had arrived from the north, Katrin from the south and they both moved around towards the standing woman. The clatter and the downdraught from the both helicopters, appeared to catch her by surprise; she reached out to grab hold of the railing, stumbled and then hid behind the parapet wall.

Out of the corner of her eye, Angel caught sight of movement in the darkness below. But she was too busy signalling to the woman to move towards the stairs and for the next one to stand up, to take more notice of what was happening below. A loudspeaker from the army helicopter bellowed over the wall.

'Give it to me!' screeched Katrin. 'Is this thing switched on? Angel darling, it's me, I came as soon as I could.'

Pup's voice bellowed from the black private craft further around the tower: 'What the fuck is she doing here? Angel get here at once!'

The second woman stood and waved, the helicopters inched nose-in, around the tower.

'Listen to me.' Pup had decided to use a more conciliatory tone. 'Sweetheart, she is finished, your future is with me and your father.'

The woman walked around the parapet, Angel could see her meet the next crouching woman and then pretend to fall below the sightline of the two helicopters now vying for position. She slipped into the entrance to the stairs and hid. The third woman stood up and looked into the glare of the searchlights.

'No, she's mine, you bastard! Angel, I lost your mother

because of him. Please I beg you … Get closer you idiot, I need to see her.'

Both helicopters pulled closer. They were as near as they could get without catching their blades on the wall or touching each other. The roar was deafening. Blinded by the light the third woman struggled to move along the wall. Her heart in her mouth, Angel watched, but she couldn't help … she couldn't risk being seen until the woman was out of sight. Both of her grandparents were hovering just out of reach of the weapons.

Unable to wait any longer, Angel got ready to crawl around towards her, but the woman stumbled, her hand slipped from the rail. The force of the downdraught caught her and pushed her screaming into the void.

Horrified, Angel knew that she could do nothing for her, the momentum had to be kept. She stood up slowly as if she was pulling herself up from the floor. The lights were full in her face. The helicopters sidled around the tower. Angel walked until she was facing west.

'Stop messing about girl!' shouted Pup.

Slowly she climbed up on to the top of the rampart wall, her feet on the inside of the safety rail and waited for her grandparents to be in front of her. Her hood ripped back and revealed her face. She was calm. Concentrated. Going through the motions of her plan. She held her arms out, and her cloak flared out like wings flapping against the black night sky. She pulled at one end of her scarf; it unravelled and lifted, vertical, a blue line pointing at the sky. She let it go. It shot into the darkness above her.

Silver-haired and defiant; there was no doubt in Pup and Katrin's mind that this was Angel. They watched in horrified silence. Without looking down, she lifted one foot up and stepped over the safety rail on to the outer edge of the wall. Her cape billowed and flapped behind her. She stepped over with her other foot. The sound deafened her, the light blinded her, and she was fighting for breath against the force of the air from the rotors. Angel mouthed the word … *die!*

'God she's going to …'

'Angel: no, you're mine!'

'Get closer!'

The helicopters moved closer.

Angel stood up on tiptoes, ready to dive from the tower into the deep, deep night.

There was a flash from below, she felt of a line of heat as a rocket shot from one of the arrow slits. The angle wasn't right, it narrowly missed Pup's helicopter, but both pilots instinctively banked … their blades clipped and shattered, sending fragments out in a wide chaotic arc, clattering against the stone walls.

Angel watched them begin to fall. Everything was right. They were all going to die. She closed her eyes and found the stillness in her heart.

And time stopped …

She took a breath …

Braced herself for the dive …

Soft hair brushed against her cheek …

Warm hands took hold of hers and wrapped them around her waist …

A voice whispered in her ear...

'Trust me, Angel.'

They fell backwards into the void.

And time ...

... began again.

A blinding blood-red chrysanthemum of flames filled the sky. Sharp tongues of flame shot through the arrow slits in the walls.

Angel opened her eyes, waiting to hit the ground. But she felt herself slow ... and impossibly ... rise again ... then fall more slowly. She felt a heartbeat against her body, then everything went black.

• • •

The women of the Beguinage lowered the safety net that they had made from a mesh of bed sheets, on to bales of soft wool.

Raph picked up Angel's limp body, wrapped her cape around her and carried her out of the tower, and down the steps.

She was in limbo. Her memory of being held safe, on her mother's knee collided with one explosion and then another. Surely, she was dead?

Raph held her face close to his chest and ran. She didn't need to see her grandparent's wreckage, or the body of the woman who had fallen from the wall; curled into an impossible shape.

She let herself be carried; there was comfort in it.

• • •

The people from York, who had come to deal with any survivors stood around the burning wreckage, leaned on their sticks and scythes, and warmed their faces. They nodded and talked to each other without taking their eyes from the fire. It had happened … they had seen it, and when the wreckage cooled, they would find a souvenir to prove it. There would no doubt be reprisals, but York was ready now. Let them come!

The women of the Beguinage folded their sheets. Then used one to wrap the woman who fell, she was a hero. They had waited in the shadows with their makeshift safety net and tried to catch her, but she'd bounced off the wall and they couldn't get there quickly enough.

Grim faced, they'd watched Angel climb up on to the top of the wall, and spread her arms, ready to dive into the flames. Raph had been hiding in the stairwell; he couldn't make a move until Angel was facing the helicopters. He'd only just made it. She had been about to dive. There hadn't been a breath between them until they'd shuffled underneath their two falling bodies and taken their weight.

Miriam and Cheryl looked at each other and smiled, Steph had been right to guess that Angel hadn't planned to see the morning. It was something about the way she talked, the things that she didn't say. They picked up their wool and silently left the tower. And walked back to the Beguinage arms linked and smiling.

'Tomorrow, shall we begin a new tapestry?' asked Miriam.

'Yes, one with Angel and a tower?' nodded Cheryl.

'Two angels, I think. One called Angel and one called Raphael.'

CHAPTER FORTY-SEVEN

Mani arrived at eight, with a group of fighters. She walked up to the wreckage, still burning at the bottom of the tower. A troop carrier from Pup's base had circled the city once, hovered over the carnage and then banked fiercely and returned the way that it had come.

'What happened here?' She tapped the arm of a man who was leaning on a makeshift weapon, watching the fire.

'She pulled 'em so close, they crashed into each other.' He rubbed his scorched face with the heel of his palm.

'Where is she?'

'Reckon they took her back to the Beguinage … the women who caught her, and the man that stopped her jumping. My heart was in my mouth. It was …' He chuckled. 'Haven't been this warm since … ever.'

Mani squinted into the fire for a moment then she turned and strode away.

• • •

The refectory was empty but for two people. Angel sat on a chair, eyes unfocussed, staring into the distance. Raph knelt at her feet. He wiped her hand with a damp cloth. Her face was red, her hair singed at the front. She hadn't spoken a word or looked at anyone, she just stared into space and shivered. He dabbed her forehead with the cloth.

'Never had much use for eyebrows, myself,' he said softly.

Angel took a shuddering breath; her eyelids flickered. 'What?'

He dabbed her cheeks, her nose, her lips and whispered, 'Never … ever … ever … doubt me … I beg you.' He moved his face close to her and breathed her breath, soft and tender, he needed some part of her to be in him. A tear splashed on to his face.

'I couldn't be sure,' she whispered.

He touched her face with his shaking hand. 'I die without you, Angel.'

'And Mani?'

'She's my sister … you are my life.' He kissed her tears. Salt and smoke.

'You really wanted to die with them?'

'I couldn't see any other way.'

• • •

Mani could be heard shouting as she strode along the corridor. She opened the door and slammed it shut behind her. The star quilt shuddered.

'Why didn't you wait for me!' she bellowed at Angel.

Angel turned to look at her. 'My family; my business.'

'Anyway, it worked, didn't it?' said Raph, standing up.

'It needed to be secret,' Angel explained. 'I wasn't sure how secure your comms were.'

'Totally!' Mani was outraged.

'Anyway,' said Raph. 'You can still bring your people in to help with the fighting, there's bound to be reprisals. You can still help.'

Mani turned on him. 'Did Steph tell you what she was going to do?'

He nodded and pulled Angel towards him.

'You should have told me!' Mani tried to calm herself. 'You can't keep disappearing like this little brother. I need you near me.'

'Mani, I would have looked for Angel my whole life long.'

She frowned. 'But what use, Raph, what use?'

He paused, not sure how he could explain, then he looked at her and spoke gently. 'The use is ... I'm only truly alive when I am with her ... no one else ...'

Mani crumpled. Raph reached out to touch her shoulder; she shrugged it away.

'Thank you for the wild goose chase, though, you fixed the old me so firmly in people's minds, that I became invisible.'

Mani smiled weakly and acknowledged Angel's words.

'Suppose I'd better get back and spread the word that they're dead ... and Angel lives.' She held Raph's gaze, then turned and left.

EPILOGUE

At first, Angel was too exhausted to travel more than a few hours a day. She slipped into silence, a dream state that worried Raph. So, they just wandered, and ate and slept. He held her at night, afraid that she might leave. He had his own nightmares.

And gradually, as time passed, she smiled when he talked, or at her thoughts. She reached for him in the night and pulled him close.

• • •

They had crossed the mountains heading northwest. It was his turn to row. They'd reached the New Lakes and Angel leaned over his shoulder. Her hand brushed his hair, as she pointed to the distant hills that were home. He turned to look …

The boat moved and he heard a soft splash. He turned. She was gone. The water's surface was smooth. Frantic, he looked around, pushed the oar out of the way, then stood up and called her name. A flash of silver caught his eye; he kneeled and peered down into the water. There at the bottom of the lake, stretched out on a bed of stones was Angel, smiling. Her arms moved gently with the water. A silver fish darted across her face and her eyes followed.

Just when he could bear it no longer, her eyes fixed on his and she kicked and rose to the surface.

She rested her arms on the side of the boat and smiled, water dripping from her silver hair. Raph took her outstretched hand and pulled Angel out of her element and into his arms.

APPENDIX

The characters in Storm Girl are entirely imaginary. However, many of the locations exist. Some I don't know yet, but I am sure that one day I will find them. On a recent visit to York I found the perfect bridge for Angel to canoe under on her first visit to the Beguinage.

I was born and live in Lincolnshire, a beautiful sparse county situated in the East Midlands of the UK. It is bordered by the Humber to the North, the North Sea to the East and the Wash to the South. Rising sea levels (at 2 degrees warming) are predicted to take out a third of the land. We already have permanent evacuation routes signposting people to higher ground and disaster plans ready to roll. I have good friends and family who have already been affected by serious flooding. I mourn the certainty of the seasons and fear severe weather. My heart is with people living in the global south. The consequence of the climate crisis knows no political boundaries and sadly those who are least to blame are already paying the highest price.

Angel's world is one where rising sea levels and the failure of the global breadbasket have caused war, famine and societal collapse. Many natural and built features that we might know today have been lost. Coastlines have changed, rivers and floods have destroyed wide areas of land and most of the country has returned to the wild.

Here are some of the landmarks that I used for Angel's journey:

Angel's home is in the Old Lakes situated in an extended Lake District. It is an area of great natural beauty situated in the North West of the UK. When she escapes from the Reapers, she sets foot on the coastline inland from Humberstone on the North East coast of Lincolnshire. When she moves inland to the quarry, she is in Sherwood Forest. Her canoe journey takes her over a flooded vale of Ancholme, over the town where I was born (Brigg) and the Post Mill on the hill is at the nearby village of Wrawby.

Read's Island exists in the river Humber and has an interesting history of its own. The Humber is tidal with strong rip tides. I was always told that if you fell in and were caught in one of the underwater rip tides, you wouldn't surface until you were far out into the North Sea.

Clifford's Tower in York is one of the first things that Angel sees as she approaches the city and is the setting for her final showdown with her grandmother and grandfather. The tower has stood on a mound of earth close to the River Ouse since 1069.

A Beguinage movement existed in Europe in the middle ages and offered accommodation to emancipated lay women. One can be visited in Bruges. The Beguinage in York is imaginary.

Raph's home under the viaduct in Leeds exists and until recently was the base for the excellent Slunglow Theatre Company. They had fruit trees and vegetables growing in bathtubs and their toilets were built in garden sheds.

The town in Cornwall where Angel waits out the great storm is Fowey.

Most of the information about Chequers is imaginary, but Lady Mary Grey was held there in the 1560's, in what is still called the 'prison room'. The layout of the building and the existence of the escape ladder are my invention.

As I write, the world's eight richest people own more than fifty percent of the rest of the people on the planet. The word Kleptocracy comes to mind. The social context of 'Storm Girl' is one where super rich dynasties now own the planet, and everything on it is an asset to be exploited for profit.

Refugees and defenceless communities are easy picking for traffickers, who kill them, enslave them or harvest their organs.

Whilst Storm Girl is a work of fiction, world events in the early 21st century meant that I didn't have far to look for inspiration.

In 2016 conflict and violence caused by zero rainfall, crop failure, and inhospitable environments caused 6.9 million displacements. Disasters caused 24.2 million displacements, the majority of which were caused by weather related hazards.

http://www.internal-displacement.org/global-report/grid2017/

We build real and virtual walls to keep out refugees and people fleeing natural disasters. A 'journalist' in a daily tabloid paper in the UK has called refugees vermin. Some European countries call refugees a risk to security and a terror risk. Refugees are completely at the mercy of others. Murder, imprisonment, rape and trafficking is not unusual.

https://medium.com/trt-world/how-6-eastern-european-nations-have-hunted-down-refugees-in-policy-and-in-pr actice-2e6040ab9264

In 'Storm Girl' the Elites live on Offshore cities. They do this for two reasons; to be beyond the law and later because it wasn't safe for them to live on the land. Such Offshore cities exist. For example:

https://www.ibtimes.co.uk/freedom-ship-floating-city-super-rich-10-526754

Slavery did not disappear in the 19th century, it simply changed its name and continues in every country in the world. There are an estimated 40.3 million people in modern slavery around the world. They are being hidden in plain sight and undoubtedly slave labour is adding to your personal quality of life.

https://www.antislavery.org/slavery-today/modern-slavery/

Organ harvesting from Falun Gong practitioners (an ancient Chinese spiritual discipline in the Buddhist tradition) is reportedly taking place in China. People are executed on demand in order to provide organs for transplant.

https://en.wikipedia.org/wiki/Organ_harvesting_from_Fa lun_Gong_practitioners_in_China

I think I will leave humanity's inhumanity there, I don't want to labour the point.

The climate emergency is a scientific fact and we are ahead of target to hit many tipping points that will catapult us into unknown, irreversible and dangerous territory. In preparation for and to support Angel's story I did several courses from Future Learn. They are free short MOOCs – massive open online courses – and I heartily recommend them. Other MOOC providers are available.

https://www.futurelearn.com/courses/categories/nature-and-environment-courses

ABOUT THE AUTHOR

Linda Nicklin is a Lincolnshire based writer and environmental activist. She is doing everything that she can to leave a habitable planet for your children.

To find out more about her go to lindanicklin.com

If you have enjoyed this book, please consider leaving a review for Linda to let her know what you thought of her work. You can find out more about her on her author page on the Fantastic Books Store. While you're there, why not browse our delightful tales and wonderfully woven prose?

www.fantasticbooksstore.com

Printed in Great Britain
by Amazon

45722044R00206